BOOKS & SMITH

New York Editors

THE CATALYST

A novel

SELIN SENOL AKIN

The Catalyst

Published and printed
in The United States of America

This is a publication of Books&Smith

Cover design by Edgar Smith
Edited by Edgar Smith
Author Photograph by Ksenia Kolesova

ISBN: 978-1-7346563-0-5

I dedicate this novel first and foremost to my daughter, Dalya. I started writing it before you arrived, but you sure have been the catalyst in my completing it. I hope to be able to make you proud as you have made me already, just by being who you are.

I'd also like to thank my family, especially canim annecigim (with your tough love and all —why do you always have to be right, well, 90% of the time anyway?) and biricik daddycigim (you have been a blessing any daughter and granddaughter could ever ask for) for always being there for me through thick and thin… Dearest Kemal (Kaptanimiz) for supporting my dreams always, even amidst the unjust conditions life and politics unfortunately gave you… My late grandparents and dear uncle Aydin: I hope somewhere up there you can sense my happiness over this, and I hope you're proud. The truly loved are never forgotten, even after the end of physical life on earth.

To Edgar Smith, my extremely talented editor, publisher and fellow writer, for your belief in this story from the very start… I'm forever thankful.

And to you… yes, you, dear reader, for your interest in either supporting me or (those who do not know me at all) your genuine desire to get to know this story. I hope I'll leave some lingering questions in your mind (I've always loved philosophy, spirituality and psychology.) Thank you for being a part of this journey with me.

May you always be on the lookout for positive catalysis in your lives,

XOXO

Selin Senol-Akın

"A series of vibrations. What does it matter,
the source of the catalyst...?"

Wayne Shorter

Many are the Jinn and men
we have made for Hell:
They have hearts wherewith
they understand not,
eyes wherewith they see not,
and ears wherewith they hear not.
They are like cattle,
nay more misguided:
for they are heedless
(of warning).

(Surah Al-Araf, 179)

Chapter 1

The Last Supper
(December 11, 2010)

Do we get an explanation for life after death? He stood still in place, staring blankly at the awe-inducing sight before him—a scene devoid of motion, except for the motor running in his head. *Perhaps she is beginning to now find out*, he thought.

The girl's long dark hair, wavy and up to her curvy hips, looked beautiful as ever to him, albeit it was now covering her naked back as she lay face down on the cold kitchen floor… without life. *What is the purpose of everything experienced in life?* he wondered, *and are there repercussions in the afterlife if such a place indeed exists?*

It was hard to believe that just last week the two still couldn't get enough of each other while roaming around their local shopping mall— their Saturday ritual. This was his beloved long-term girlfriend, after all. Maybe it was all the dramatic breaks and time apart they'd faced throughout their relationship that always seemed to make their reunion sweeter. It must have been this lingering passion between them that had proved to be too much for him to handle as he lost his final nerve that cold white winter day.

He'd come to realize she was one of those women who depended on her charms to get herself out of any mess, including verbal ones she often got herself in with friends, classmates and coworkers. *Spoiled bitch. That's what you ultimately were*, he decided. Whatever he did for her never seemed good enough. She almost subsequently wanted something 'more' –bigger, newer, pricier– to satisfy her relentless greed. If she was given a gift (like the cashmere scarf he'd recently bought her for the winter holidays), she would decide she didn't like it, though it was the same one she had dropped hints about just two weeks or so earlier. She wouldn't exactly verbalize her dismay, though her half-hearted smile and the tone of her voice often told him all.

It wasn't always like this, he thought, still staring at her beautiful corpse. When they'd first met that fateful day in January at a local café, in fact, she'd seemed very shy and modest. She was even rather prudish in taking a long time to give herself to him, which had pleasantly betrayed the notions of Norwegian girls he'd been told about from his local beer-mates.

She had been fresh out of university and working as a waitress—which had been bothering her pride. He missed that down-to-earth girl who viewed their modest dates over coffee as the most romantic moments in the world. Ever since she got that job at that fancy office, she seemed to have raised her expectations in life. She began dressing like an heiress, causing him (being the only man in her lonely, raised-by-a-single-mother world) to overwork his butt off to keep this princess' whimsy requests satisfied. That job of hers had long become a thing of the past (much to his joy), yet he could tell its glimmer had still been lingering in her brain.

"Ungrateful, that girl," his mother back home would often tell him, though she'd only met her once in person on a visit she'd paid her son. "I got the chills about you two the minute I met her. Mother's intuition. She's a pretty face but there are plenty more like her out there for you to find, with much better character."

He should have listened to her. Yet his mom wasn't too different from his Linette, now, was she? He would always see that his father was miserable, coming home from a long day's work to her sourpuss face. He was glad this new version of himself didn't see them as often as before. Perhaps that's why he was so drawn to the live version of this beautiful corpse in front of him, and had put up with her for as long as he did—he found her type familiar. Whatever the reason, she was now in the other world, paying for her sins. He was sure of that.

Her words from their argument that morning still kept shrilling at the back of his mind. He'd realized she still appeared to have secrets to hide even after she'd quit the office, making him grow more and more possessive over her lately. Try as he might, he could not get the memory of those 'emergency meetings' Linette used to have with her rich boss. He had met the guy at a fundraiser everyone was invited to at one time, and he hadn't liked the guy straight off the bat. Not even one bit.

"You're just jealous since you'll never be as successful as John, no matter how hard you work!" Her words continuously replayed inside his brain.

John. Since when did she start to call her ex-boss by his first name? The boyfriend could feel his blood beginning to boil like unstirred soup, even just at the thought of the man's name. She hadn't worked with him in a while and the two of them were now in different cities, yet he was sure that they were keeping in touch. *He could still he be visiting her. The bastard is rich enough to afford frequent flights,* he thought. *His wife probably thinks he's attending meetings.*

The boyfriend started asking her about him again and Linette had gone off the deep end. *All I was trying to do, naturally, was protect our love,* he reasoned. He'd wanted to make sure her new world had been able to be secluded from predators, yet a glimpse at her phone the other day proved that she had still been keeping in touch with this man. *How dare she? And how dare she say those things about me just being jealous and insecure, knowing how much I've done for her?* The boyfriend decided then that this had been the last draw.

Pretending to invite her over for an apology session later that evening after their big fight, they'd had their final dinner together over good wine. *The last supper,* he chuckled to himself. He had led her softly into the bedroom, disrobing her easy black slip. She'd had no undergarments—she knew he liked to get straight to business. It was for the best anyway. He could admire her art (her beautiful body) one last time. Holding his breath, he kissed her full lips as intensely as he could, in an attempt to savor the taste of her tongue right before injecting the cyanide-filled needle into her neck.

A part of him hurt along with her pain, watching her collapse in his arms without a peep, yet the other part of him was happy to see the shock on her face. *That's right, Linette. Your man isn't as weak and desperate as you thought him to be. He won't always be a puppy, taking your mistreatment in return for just a little affection and attention from you.*

He realized he could have killed John a long time ago, rather than her, to vent his anger, but what would have been the point? It was women like her who were to blame, he was sure of it. Men would always be men, he believed, and when a woman responded to a little flirting, of course, men would keep pushing boundaries to feed their egos and see how much they could get. It was in their nature.

As far as he was concerned, it was a good woman's responsibility not to fall for illicit flirtation; to be loyal to their significant others, if they had one, or at least to their own morality and character before they flirted back with someone they knew they shouldn't have——like their married boss. *John will forget about her in a heartbeat,* he thought. *Poor Linette. She should have valued me, her loving boyfriend, much more.* He had after all moved heaven and hell forward and backward to be next to her.

The part of him that was feeling a tang of guilt for what he had done appeased itself by saying over and over in his mind that this had all been for the best.

"I did love you, Linette," the boyfriend spoke to her lifeless body, eyes still open as if she could hear him. "It's just your time to be with the beautiful angels now. I can't keep wasting all my money on you and your childish desire to possess more and more silly, worldly goods. I have to save up for my own future, and if you're alive, I can't fight off my addiction to you. I have to learn to be a little more selfish, perhaps like you. You will inspire me to be a stronger man, Linette. Your death will not be in vain. I *will* be 'successful', as you've put it. You'll see…"

Chapter 2

The Meeting
(December 11, 2012)

Kaitlin Maverick was lost. After yet another day of mostly window-shopping to fill her time, she was now running aimlessly through strange, monstrous green bushes she'd somehow stumbled upon after deviating from her usual path home. Her particular sense of boredom that day, mixed with her innate sense of adventure, had her mistake a curious looking alleyway just behind one of the city center's local banks –and behind one of its many statues– for a longer, potentially more interesting route.

Why haven't I noticed this path before? she wondered. Slowing down to catch her breath, Kaitlin crossed her arms extra tightly around her body to keep warm from the winter breeze —not that the winds during the summer blew much warmer most of the time in this part of the world. *After all, I have been consciously noting every other detail about the few lively streets this town does have for fun,* she thought with a smirk. Robert Frost's '…the road not taken' crossed her mind. She remembered at one time thinking that accepting a marriage proposal at the height of her wild-girl days would precisely *be* her 'road less traveled by' of choice.

Ever since her marriage to Paul Maverick, computer specialist, less than two years ago, Kaitlin had been attempting adaptation to the small-town life of Stavanger, Norway, where his job in Statoil Petroleum had taken him years before their union. The port city was adorable enough, with several modern shops and cafes servicing both an international crowd of professional families and locals. It was also near several famous natural wonders, including some of Norway's most famous fjords, which drew millions of tourists annually, many of whom arrived on large cruise ships to awe at the inlets between majestic cliffs.

Yet Kaitlin's relatively livelier life back in Toronto (which she had thought of as being spiritually-unfulfilling when she was a single woman) had somehow been gaining value in her eyes as of late. Visually and population-wise, the two cities were as different as could be. Yet each had their own lovely perks and similar cultural lifestyles. She sometimes wondered whether it was really the cities' relative sizes that were the cause of her current mini-crisis—her inner personal dilemmas dealing with her sudden descent into the role of being a housewife. Years of social activism, thanks to her mother's charity circle, alongside dedicated years as a ballerina and a well-earned university degree in Marketing, with honors, had ultimately thrown her into the exciting life of a prominent advertising agency back in Canada. She'd been working full-time before Paul swooped her up, albeit long-distance, and eventually married her.

Paul was handsome enough, according to her girlfriends' constant praises as well as her own taste in men. He was tall and lean with sandy brown hair, with a nearly constant smirk on his face that she'd first found smug but gradually endearing as she'd discovered he was a bigger softie than she initially thought. A decade her senior, although he'd made good money in oil in his recent years, he'd come from a humble background with three younger siblings to look after, and had never forgotten it. Immigrants from Budapest, his father had been a small-shop owner in Montreal and would take several work shifts in restaurants and gas stations to provide for his family. His wife and Paul himself would often help him out in dealing with customers and carrying supplies, respectively. Being the oldest and the only male offspring in his immediate family, he had worked his way through college and developed a self-righteous sense of duty to care for his younger sisters early on that could explain the traditional ways in which he often acted with Kaitlin—ways which in the long run she had to admit she appreciated, despite being overwhelmed at times.

Kaitlin's upbringing was as different from her husband's as day from night and as Stavanger from Toronto. Her mother was born into money and had taken on a prestigious role in an influential organization to help the city's poor in Toronto from her own mother before her. Kaitlin's grandfather had owned a chain of gas stations, and she had even thought of it as 'fate' when Paul told her that he'd also always been 'in the business of petroleum', winking while he said so to her on their very first date. They were originally being set up by her Aunt Mae, who resided in Montreal, near Paul's family. Kaitlin's mother, however, never fully approved of the union arranged by her older sister. In fact, after meeting Paul's family when she visited Montreal during Mae's big 50th birthday party, she never did quite take with Mrs. Maverick's 'lack of high-society mannerisms', as she'd coined them, and argued incessantly with her sister for introducing 'that woman's' son to her daughter. But Mae had always thought otherwise, having grown close to Mrs. Maverick upon their many conversations as neighbors, and was convinced Paul and Kaitlin would make an adorable couple. "Paul is such a good man, Linda," Mae would tell her sister. "And handsome, too. He's really worked himself high up. He's really going places professionally."

When they'd first been introduced, Kaitlin herself hadn't warmed up to Paul at all, finding him to be too serious and *plain as vanilla*, she'd thought, smiling to herself as she recalled the exact term she'd used when referring to him at the time.

"Ouch!" A sharp corner of a branch caught on the sleeve of her jacket and scratched her uncovered hand as she squeezed herself through two particularly close trees. She cursed herself for neglecting to actually put on one of her many brand-name gloves she'd bought on *salg[1]* and accumulated back in their apartment. Sometimes she had to admit that Paul was right about her head 'always being in the clouds', despite how annoying he could be.

With a completely different sense of fun and humor from her own, Kaitlin had never thought she and Paul would become good friends like they first did, let alone eventually husband and wife! In fact, Kaitlin hadn't ever swooned over wedding magazines and dreams of marriage like many girls around her seemed to have for years——often thinking something was wrong with her for being that way.

---

[1] Salg: sale in Norwegian

Yet here she was, 'newlywed' –she supposed, since it had only been a little over a year–, and bored. The couple would still experience moments of absolute cozy bliss from time to time, which Kaitlin felt thankful for, yet it was a complete one-hundred-and-eighty degrees from her previous life of trying to climb the professional ladder as fast as she could. She used to jump from one networking event to another, as well as from guy to guy, unfortunately. It had turned out to be hard finding a commitment-ready man when most she'd met were more ambitious to earn more money than to land a loving relationship. In Stavanger, life was more about either sitting home bored until getting drunk on weekends or getting yourself involved in climbing rocks (or any other sort of sporty leisure activities) for excitement.

Those days of frequent outings together were, for better or for worse, seemingly long gone—especially now as she was smack in the middle of late afternoon flies and lovely smelling flowers with only trees and more trees to keep her company.

The wooden path was like any other myriad green area in the city, yet there was something peculiar in the sudden way all outside sounds had seemingly stopped when she made a sharp left turn from a particularly lush area consisting of an almost purposefully-arranged pile of twigs, that managed to chill Kaitlin to the core of her entire set of bones.

"I can*not* possibly be lost in this place!" she exhaled out loud, having just been in the city center what seemed only like several footsteps ago.

She was beginning to get worried about the blackness soon to set in, although she began to thank her lucky stars just then that Stavanger – located in the southwestern corner of Norway– didn't experience the longer hours of winter darkness that the northern portions of the country did. The city's summers also experienced more darkness at night than the rest of Norway, though the famous Scandinavian phenomenon of the 'midnight sun' *did* affect it as well. Kaitlin smiled just then, recalling the beautiful lavender twilight-appearance that she and Paul were able to experience from their balconies during the past summer: a vision of purple instead of black, even close to 10:00 p.m.

Looking straight ahead, Kaitlin noticed there were pine trees so tall they seemed to blend into the pink-hued sky, mixed with leafless shorter trees. They reminded her of the designs on the special shutters they'd had to purchase for their bedroom to increase the darkness in the summertime —since Kaitlin had trouble sleeping without complete darkness. Gratefully no major bugs seemed to thrive in the Nordic cold; how she would surely have panicked just then if that had been the case. Kaitlin didn't want to make any more turns out of fear of getting lost even further, instead attempting to look in all directions for any signs of homes or buildings ahead that may have led her back to more familiar roads. *Why can't there be at least one or two really tall buildings in the sentrum[2] that I could spot for direction?* she thought. Her eyes sought the early-nineteenth century Valberg tower in the town center that adorned the profile of the city, but to no avail.

The leaves on the ground were all shades of brown, with several beautifully-bright red ones. The only noise she could hear was that of tiny chirping birds, and that of her own nervous, heavy breathing. "Oh God, this is just what I needed! Perfect!" she found herself exclaiming even louder than before.

As her eyes followed a couple of birds suddenly dashing to the left and she turned her body to look in the direction they were flying, she could swear she saw the figure of a man looming up ahead, watching her with piercing eyes. She blinked once, and now could only see a leafy bush in his place. "Ok, now I'm really getting paranoid... must... walk back...." As a big city girl, she was practically raised accustomed to cautiously eyeing each of her surroundings with every footstep, *but Norway enjoys relatively low crime rates*, she reminded herself. Suddenly afraid of the silence, she started to hum the soft tune of an annoying but catchy pop song that seemed to be playing every five minutes on Norwegian radio.

"Hey, I just met you... And this is crazy... But here's my number..."

A sudden increase in the noise of birds made her turn around and gasp as she saw what their commotion was about. There indeed stood a man. A young, blond, smiling man who began to reach out his hands with palms facing outward toward her in a defensive way, as if to appease her astonished state.

"I'm sorry if I've startled you, Miss..."

---

[2] Sentrum: inner city center

Staggered simultaneously both by her realization that she wasn't alone in this God-forsaken place and her lack of fear once setting her sight on the statuesque face of this man, Kaitlin managed to whimper something along the lines of "…Umm, no, no… it's okay… I just…"

"Are you alright? You look a little lost, yet I couldn't help but also notice the pleasant smile on your face, eyeing your surroundings with such *wonder*, Miss."

Wonder? Kaitlin thought to herself. *I doubt that. More like downright confusion is more like it.* The slick smile on this stranger's face would have been countered by her with an annoyed sigh if it had come from a typical slick passerby on the streets of Toronto. Yet for some unexplainable reason, any anxiety Kaitlin had been feeling was now replaced with intrigue.

"Well, yes, you're right… on both accounts… I mean… I am indeed lost. I was just walking around in the city when a wrong turn must have taken me to this… forest or wherever, you know…" Kaitlin mumbled with about five hand gestures per second. "But, yes, yes, I'm amazed as well, yes. I mean, it's absolutely gorgeous here…" Her nervous laughter caused a friendly chuckle from the stranger.

"Thank you," said the stranger with a smile, continuously gazing non-stop into her hazel eyes, with the greenest eyes she had ever seen. "Gorgeous, indeed."

"Thank you? Why, umm, am I missing something or are you just being cute?" The moment her brave, bordering-on-flirty final choice of adjective had left her mouth, Kaitlin wanted to slap herself on the head for talking so casually with a stranger. *Cute? The horror! My proper mother would have scolded me for days,* she thought.

"Well, allow me to explain then, Ms. Wonder… But, aha! First, let us do introductions, shall we? The name is Finn…" He reached out his hand and Kaitlin wanted to slap herself again, this time for becoming excited as if she were a single woman, admiring this man's firm and beautifully shaped hands alongside his eyes, which she had already observed a little too closely. *I have no idea what's going on here or what this is,* she thought.

"This is the part where you reach your hand out to shake mine and state *your* name, Miss. That is, if I haven't forgotten the pleasantries of the real world living out in the woods for so long." The electrical smile hadn't yet left Finn's face as he spoke.

"Oh, sorry, it's Kaitlin," she shook his extended hand feebly. "Kaitlin Maverick. It's nice to meet you. Did you say you've been living in the woods? Did I hear correctly?" Giving him a quick look up and down, his clean, loose, dark-grey trousers with his crisp white button-down shirt would not have given her that impression.

"Well, yes. You see, this is our little part of the woods actually. Logging for major paper companies is our profession, while some of us also help the locals with herding their sheep. We also hunt and sell to local markets… various things like that…" Finn reached into the back pocket of his form-fitting blue jeans. "Allow me to give you my card since I've had the pleasure of your company for these brief few minutes…"

"Us… like a family? A team?" Kaitlin interrupted, founding herself even more intrigued now. The tingle of electricity she'd felt from touching his hand was also still palpable in her palm. "Oh sorry, thank you, yes." Staring at the card, she was surprised to see that the only information had been a local telephone number and his name, Finn Dufeu. *French origin, is it?* she wondered. She didn't dare ask him out loud, however, deciding that would be overly friendly.

"Yes, my friends and I work the woods. Though we call ourselves *The Group, Inc.,* we're not exactly an organization or company as much as a group of friends *–close* friends who enjoy nature. We just run our little business to make ends meet and get by, you know."

His emphasis on the word 'close' had, for some unexplainable reason, instinctively bothered Kaitlin, but she was concentrating more on trying to understand what exactly the deal was with this new acquaintance. *What is a handsome and well-spoken man like him doing living in the woods, and moreover, how exactly did he manage to run into me?* Kaitlin couldn't make any sense of the question in her head whatsoever.

"That explains the lack of an organization name on the card, but, just your name? Mr. Dufeu? I mean, there is no profession listed," Kaitlin stated.

The stranger chuckled almost immediately, throwing his head full of blond curls back. "Logger? Sheepherder? Hunter? Master of any business one could ever hope to attain from these woods? What exactly would *fit* in the description, Ms. Kaitlin, that would be appropriate and explanatory, yet, also, charismatic enough so that people actually call me?" He said the last part with a wink and Kaitlin wanted to roll her eyes at his self-assuredness, feeling more at ease with herself now upon realizing that the magic of his looks had slowly begun to dissipate, enough for her to ridicule him inside her head.

"Well, why would anyone call you, then?" Kaitlin retorted. "I don't mean to be rude, but, in order to network best, shouldn't the person you give your card to remember who you are in order to remember what you do and how you could be of help to them?"

"I'd like to think that I have made an impression strong enough so that they won't forget, Ms. Kaitlin," Finn replied with a smile. "I mean, judge all anyone wants, just because people live in farms, or in cabins like we do, it doesn't mean we're incapable of worldliness or business. Technology does wonders."

"Of course, I see," Kaitlin responded. By now she was even more annoyed with his attitude. Who did this strange man think he was? His looks could have gotten him so far, but what was this cockiness about?

"It's *Mrs. Maverick*, by the way. You keep saying, 'Ms. Kaitlin.' I mean, I don't have a card, so, just wanted to remind you of my last name." She hoped that her sudden way of letting him know she was married hadn't come across as a bit arrogant and rude herself.

"No problem, Miss." Finn hadn't seemed fazed in the slightest, as if her marital status didn't matter one bit. "I'm sure I won't forget. Relax. Don't worry."

Don't worry? The nerve of him, turning the conversation around to favor his own self once more, Kaitlin thought, peeved even more so now upon remembering that she was still in the middle of nowhere. She was indeed lost! And she needed to get home, and away from this man, as soon as possible before it got too dark.

"Ok, then. Well, thank you for your card, and for your company, but, alas, I should get back home… If only I knew how…" Kaitlin began looking around her and all she could see was countless trees and wildflowers for miles. "Certainly, you must know this area better than I do, then, if you live around here?"

"Oh, yes, of course… We live just behind there…" Finn pointed at some indistinct location in what seemed to be a random and far-off direction among the trees. "You can't miss it. We're the only cabin in these parts. And, of course, allow me to help you find your way… Come with me, I'll take you to the city center…"

"Oh, thanks, but that's not necessary. I mean, if it's out of your way, just let me know the direction and I'll walk…" Kaitlin didn't want to be impolite despite her uneasiness—it wasn't like this guy had threatened her or anything.

"It's no trouble at all, Miss," Finn interrupted once again with a smile. "Just follow me, it won't take long. We just have to head left… don't want to head to the *right.*"

Was it just her imagination or had he just tried to imply something about not being 'right'? He couldn't have been that forward, could he? Or was she just being silly? *Certain words in the English language can be taken out of context at different times, after all,* Kaitlin thought. Maybe he was being subconsciously political, favoring the liberal left. Weren't a lot of young Europeans leftist? And this Finn *was* a bit younger than herself, it seemed, wasn't he? *Whatever,* she ultimately decided.

Finn led the way confidently through what appeared to be a smooth path between the trees, stooping lower only once to avoid some tangled branches—glancing toward Kaitlin and holding several branches up so that they didn't scratch her face. "Thank you," Kaitlin said with a smile.

"Here we are," Finn exclaimed after what seemed to be only several minutes later. "There is that little town-lake up ahead. You ever feed those swans? You're good to go!"

Kaitlin couldn't believe her eyes. Certainly they were now out of the greenery and behind the statue that she remembered first having made a left at, getting her lost. Why couldn't she just have passed it straight on for her usual fifteen-minute walk home? She also just then realized that she had walked what seemed like an eternity in the woods before running into Finn, yet he seemed to have brought them back to the city center in what must have been a matter of a couple of minutes. How could that have been?

"I *do* love those swans, yes. And I'm still… lost, no pun intended, as to how I could have physically gotten lost so far deep in that area," Kaitlin said with a nervous laugh, tucking a piece of her auburn hair behind her right ear. "I mean I didn't even know such a forest existed here. I thought it was mainly stores and houses. Maybe I was walking around in circles or something. But, I digress. Thank you, for leading me back."

"Sometimes some things happen for a reason, Miss," Finn said, gazing deeply into her eyes once more. "I, for one, am very glad that you got lost and ran into me. Don't forget my card, if you ever want to feel *wonder* again… perhaps working with us, or just spending time in nature, I mean…

"Yeah, I will," Kaitlin responded, feeling herself blush like a school girl this time. Any trace of being annoyed at his arrogance had faded now that she felt safer in the vicinity of the familiar city center once again. "Thank you, again," she emphasized, playing with the card in her hands.

"By the way, it *is* French. My name."

"I'm sorry?" Kaitlin asked, taken aback by his unexpected answer to the question she'd had in her head earlier.

"I heard a hint of a French or Canadian accent in the way you speak," Finn explained. "I could never differentiate between different accents quite accurately… I figured you may have hence found my name familiar as well…"

"Oh, well, I'm from Canada… Ontario… and I suppose you could say I'm bilingual: I do speak French, yes…."

"Bien. Nice… Well, take care, Miss." Finn smiled again, keeping it short and brief, letting her know their conversation had run its course for that moment.

"You too," Kaitlin replied. She turned to her right and began heading closer and closer to the lake, surrounded more by birds than people except for some local students drinking smoothies after school. Looking back, she was stunned to see that he had disappeared, just as fast as he had first appeared earlier.

As she headed home, Kaitlin tried to push the handsome image of Finn and the craziness of what had just happened back into her mind, and attempted to concentrate instead on how exactly a forest that huge had been in such proximity to the center of the city. The city was full of such areas, certainly, but they were all at least a ten-minute-drive away, and often surrounding bodies of water like lakes and inlets.

Part of her was feeling very, very bothered and strange. Yet the part of her that didn't mind this sudden rush of excitement and mystery into her life; oh, how was she going to deal with that part?

Chapter 3

Kaitlin woke up the next morning with what she felt must have been one of the most emotionless, dumbfounded, and dumbstruck face expressions ever in her life. She positioned her body a little closer to the edge of the bed to see her face in the mirror on top of her dresser. Yup. She had guessed it. A countenance which still stood almost-frozen in surprise, aside from her usual disheveled hair, greeted her that morning in the reflection.

It'd been three hours since Paul left for work and, like usual, kissed Kaitlin back to sleep for having woken her up with his alarm clock. She felt lucky they'd had a good deal of leftover food at home for dinner from the night before, as the state in which she had managed to walk herself back home in after the whole 'forest' incident was worse than her regular confused states over what to cook for her picky husband for dinner. Paul had apparently also had a very tiring day, and after catching the local news in Norwegian together –which *he* could now understand and *she* could only make out through imagery and the occasional subtitles (unless they'd agreed on watching the BBC news in English)– both had gone straight to bed.

Walking to the living room closet after splashing her face with the same pore-opening cleanser she'd been using since her days in North America (she was glad globalization had hit Norway just enough to sell some of her comfort items), Kaitlin instinctively reached into the right pocket of the sports-jacket she'd worn the day before. There it was: Finn's mysterious card. Placing it on the kitchen table before turning on the coffee machine, she found herself glancing at it all throughout breakfast.

She ate her breakfast of toast with extra cheese and sliced tomatoes at a quicker pace than usual that morning, and quickly put on her sweats and sneakers (followed by her 'Norway-weather-coat', as Paul had called her waterproof garb, over her pajama top) and headed out for a quick run around their neighborhood. She needed to get out of her head with a joyous activity… and fast! Aside from tuning into her favorite weekly Canadian soap opera online, these days in Norway her hobby had developed into going for a run with the I-Pod in her pocket blaring catchy tunes.

Their house was situated in a more beautiful location than she had ever lived in, that was for sure. Going outside always allowed Kaitlin to come back down to earth whenever she'd felt herself pondering various 'what-ifs'. She felt luckier than ever for the fates to have allowed her to be at this place at this particular time. The fjords by shapely cliffs up ahead were visible the minute she stepped out of their apartment building by the North Sea. The birds circling the low-lying bushes upon her usual running-path had a peculiar yet vibrantly-colored hue on their heads, unlike any bird she'd ever seen back home.

There were also particular black birds with long thin orange beaks playing near the water that morning, she noticed. Water was flowing over a myriad of rocks with a thunderous sound she swore she could compare with Niagara Falls, although obviously the creek she was now passing by at a rapid walking-pace was much smaller in size. Whatever was bigger than she was accustomed to –like the mountains– appeared celestial to her, and whatever was smaller –like the buildings– only seemed cozier. *This must be heaven,* she thought. *So all thoughts of strange forest men, leave my head! Now! Bad!* She chuckled.

Despite daylight, the rays of the sun hadn't fully shown themselves from behind the clouds in almost a week now, and the fog which had set in that morning was absolutely the most enchanting one she'd ever seen. Kaitlin paused to catch her breath right by a small inlet of water where several private boats were tied by the locals. Staring straight ahead, she could see that the green mountains were almost invisible beneath the layer of mother nature's smoky breath in the cool air. Even in the middle of the summer the temperature here was almost always autumn-like, with winds making it especially cool by the water. Despite the city's reputation as being warmer than more northern Norwegian cities due to the Gulf Stream, Paul had always told her to pack for her new life accordingly, as there were apparently really only 'two seasons' here: cold winter or warm winter.

If more people knew about this city, it would sure give London a run for its money, Kaitlin thought. A few drops of rain began to pour on her hair just then, almost immediately frizzing out her reddish-brown mane. That reminded her: wasn't she supposed to join Paul on some business trip out to the UK soon? She couldn't wait for a break from her daily routine.

They luckily hadn't begun to lack their sexual passion just yet, as her longer-term married friends back in Canada had always lamented; yet there was little to do together in this small town except go jogging or shopping together. She sometimes felt that perhaps there was even less for the two of them to do in particular, since spending her days mainly only with her husband showed Kaitlin how little they actually had in common. She'd often come across countless magazine articles saying one should marry their best friend (and this had in fact played a great role in her decision to marry Paul), yet living together seemed only to bring out the worst sides of each other. When she'd finally agreed to date him, Kaitlin was certainly surprised to discover this traditional man who'd made a rather dull first impression on her could actually be quite fun to be with once he got to open up. But sharing the same living space had somehow subdued the exciting nature of their romance –once her carefree attitude managed to clash with his strictly-principled and orderly one. It was as if they had become like their parents in such a short time – with daily conversation mostly revolving around grocery lists and weekly chores more than anything else. A comfortable friendship had indeed formed, yet a 'best-friendship' certainly had not.

It hadn't been this way when they were dating—when she was promised that things would only get better once they were no longer kept apart by distance and had each other's company on a daily basis. Despite the warnings she would hear from her friends –especially her best friend Sandy back in Toronto– the ten-year-age gap hadn't been an issue to her initially when Paul was wooing her with childlike carefree-runs through the city park in Toronto where he'd visit her, nor when he couldn't wait to get his hands on her. He had, in fact, given her the first orgasm of her life; she later convinced herself this had been a sign that she was meant to be with this man.

She knew that somewhere down the line the intensity of their connection would naturally decrease as the two became more familiar with one another around the house as man and wife. "Those first couple of years are the best, and then it all dwindles downward from there!" her mom's friends would tease. Years, they would say. Kaitlin sighed. With her and Paul, however, it had merely been months when they already seemed to have reached that road.

Kaitlin suddenly felt the urge to do a little shopping-therapy to get herself further away from the pool of thoughts she was drowning in. Apparently, running wasn't going to be enough on a day like today. She'd walked as far as one of the mini-malls in the city center. She checked the digital time placed on a wide screen across the street from it, along with the temperature. 13:15. 5 degrees Celsius. She had just enough time to buy some hand lotion or yet another scarf or pair of gloves, at a reduced price, and then pick up some vegetables before getting back home in time for Paul's early arrival. That was one of the perks of Paul's job here: Kaitlin would never have been able to even *dream* about getting out of work before 4 pm back in Canada. And now here they were, having more opportunity to hang out as a couple due to her husband's comfortable schedule. And although he preferred to spend half of his free time at home taking a nap when Kaitlin would have preferred to be going out for a nature-drive (blasting loud music in the car), she told herself she had to be more thankful.

She loved her husband, that was for sure. Regardless of their differences in age and sometimes vitality, at least he wasn't anything like the casual men with commitment issues she'd always happened to attract back in Toronto. Her last heartbreak before dating Paul—an unemployed momma's boy, in fact, had had the audacity to tell *her* that *she* was the one who hadn't been well-suited for marriage, besides several other underhand insults which she'd still managed to swallow during her state of crazy-in-love naiveté.

Two starred-scarves later, Kaitlin headed toward the escalator she knew would take her up to the local kitchenware store. Lord knew she wouldn't even give such stores a second look before she'd gotten married. She smirked as she headed in, and bumped into at least three other ladies. *A crowd? Here? That's odd*, she thought.

"Hei, hei!" a cheerful Barbie-blonde greeted her in Norwegian in front of a wooden table full of various appliances on sale. Mystery solved.

Paul could spend literally an hour in this place, but she knew she'd just look around.

"I'm just looking, *takk*[3]," she thanked the sky-eyed sales girl. She enjoyed how the locals couldn't always make out whether she was Norwegian or not—not as easily as they could with the various Asians and Africans that also crowded the city anyway. She wondered whether Finn was born in Norway or not, despite having hinted that he was of a French background.

"Well, I was just going to ask if you needed any help," the girl responded in English. "Just let me know!"

Kaitlin nodded with a smile and headed straight to the back of the store in an attempt to roam freely and indeed 'just look'. Twirling her hair in front of at least four different-colored small pots with boulder-sized price tags, she could hear the women she'd bumped into at the store entrance all laugh hard at something someone had just said, now in line and all holding at least two or three of the items from the *salg* table. Kaitlin wondered what they could possibly have found so amusing when they'd likely soon be going home to cook something for their families, with their new colorful kitchen toys.

She slipped out of the store behind them, and out of the mini-mall toward home—picking up a bag of baby-spinach leaves and onions on the way. She was beginning to think the loneliness inside she'd often feel, even in a room full of acquaintances, had precisely been the reason for her to get married as soon as the chance presented itself. After all, the idea had never even crossed her mind like it seemed to have with her female colleagues, or at least not yet. They'd often form a clique around during lunch breaks (sometimes even with women's magazines like teenagers) while Kaitlin would be chomping down on a salad, wrapping up an assignment alone at her cubicle. The one or two close guy friends she had would tell her they were just hating on her because she was 'gorgeous.' Apparently, with wavy chestnut hair and angular features, she had 'that striking, ambitious look' which was 'threatening to women.' These were in fact the words her gay friend Marcos had told her. She sure

---

[3] Takk: 'thank you' in Norwegian

missed her conversations with him the most, alongside Sandy and her mom, whom she counted as the three people she ever felt she could rely on.

"Hmmph," she smirked, remembering Marcos's flatteries. That was the old Kaitlin. Nowadays she didn't even want to get her hair blown out—back home, styled hair was something she wouldn't be caught dead without, alongside a manicure and pedicure. Well, that, and maybe also because in Stavanger it had cost over twice as much. Paul, bless his heart, would constantly reassure her he found her beautiful no matter what. Regardless, Kaitlin's mood would drop at the thought of those days, since they reminded her how being a housewife in Stavanger had over time dampened her usual desire to dress up.

In the beginning, Kaitlin would go all out primping herself for various dinner-invitations they would have to Paul's circle of friends from work. However, Paul's slightly macho side had come out when he'd caught a couple of his friends' looks at her, and had quickly pleaded with her to dress more 'modestly'. She tried to think back on what she was wearing in the mysterious forest. Was it her green boots with the heels that made her walk more confidently or her flat black ones? She couldn't just then recall for some reason.

The techno music blasting from her cell phone's ringtone interrupted her thoughts. Kaitlin smiled when she saw that it was Sandy, her quirky best friend who now resided in New York City. Perhaps it was true that some people could sense they were being thought about and have great timing in making a call or writing an e-mail. Sandy was one of those rare people who didn't mind both the cost and time it took to invest in continuing a friendship long-distance, and Kaitlin loved how she could vent off to someone similarly disapproving of Paul's various macho, 'it's-a-man's-world' outbursts from time to time.

Glad to see she was now only a few steps near the big metal doors that led into their seaside apartment building, Kaitlin quickly took out her keys. "Girlfriend..." she exclaimed enthusiastically. "Sorry... Just un-locking the door. I'm coming home now..."

"Holla!" Sandy's chipper voice replied in feigned-slang. Sandy had moved to New York City to pursue acting after they both graduated from York University in Toronto, and although she was still waiting tables

31

after two years in the Big Apple, Sandy wasn't one to be bitter. She had managed to land a small role in a small comedic-play, which she performed each weekend off-Broadway. And though it wasn't quite the Hollywood dream she'd always imagined, she would often quote philosophically, "this must be my mission in life: to be a bigger fish in a smaller pond."

"I missed you so much, hon," Kaitlin began. "You have no idea how glad I am to hear your voice! How are you?"

"Same here, girly," Sandy responded. "How everything going?"

"It's… going," Kaitlin started, "Can't complain too much…"

"Well good, good, hon. Listen, I think I probably should just get straight to the chase as you must be busy, being married and all," Sandy chuckled, and caused the same reaction in Kaitlin. With anyone else, it may have sounded offensive and even rude, but it was impossible to be upset with Sandy. "As usual, I've got a dilemma, and I am not afraid to bother you halfway around the world since none of the superficial friends around me seem to get it!"

"Aw, don't say that," Kaitlin attempted to console her friend. "I'm sure the other girls in the show just see you as competition, with your talent! Anyway, what's up? What's the matter?"

Despite instantly realizing that she had just given her the same flattery as Marcos would have given her, in Sandy's case, Kaitlin had seen her friend perform well on stage and so she had definitely meant the compliment. She was genuinely concerned for Sandy. She was a sensitive girl, despite her funky-dressing appearance and an outgoing way of being social that could certainly be misinterpreted as borderline 'easy'. Sandy was a girl who knew how to have a good time, but also when to call it a day. Kaitlin had gotten used to Sandy constantly getting into guy-drama – even much more than herself back in the day– yet this time her voice sounded extra upset.

"The boy. And yes, the latest one. Neighbor boy. No birthday gift. Well, unless we are to count the cup of coffee he brought me in the morning with a surprise knock on my door, a kiss and some birthday wishes!"

Sandy had been dating a 'bum of a guy' who lived in the same apartment building as her, albeit with his mother. According to Sandy's emails, he was a thirty-year-old affected hard by the 2008 economic crisis in the States. She had apparently fallen for his boyish looks and fun-outlook on life, and had felt sympathetic to what the mother and son had gone through economically when he'd gotten laid-off. Kaitlin didn't know how she herself would have put up with a grown man asking the girl whom he was seeing to pay for the bill at times, let alone splitting the bill. The guy definitely had the nerve. Sandy would advise everyone to be 'ballsy', yet when it came to her own matters of the heart, her sensitive 'candle' of a friend, who shone a light of optimism on everyone's issues, just couldn't 'light' her own luck.

"Oh my God, that has got to be the last draw, sweety!" Kaitlin exclaimed, placing the phone between her right ear and shoulder to take out the onions from the plastic bag and wash the spinach. "Just coffee? What? No more?!"

"No, I know, I know," Sandy responded. "I mean, it's not like I'm the type who ever has big expectations from a guy, especially materialistic ones, but, come on, he could have at least *said* something more romantic than a simple, 'happy birthday, baby cakes'. Written a little poem? Given a card? Something! *You* sent me flowers for goodness sake, hon!"

Kaitlin tried her best to similarly put in an effort for her one long-lasting friendship left in the world, as many of her other friendships had fallen victim to the *growingly-different-places-in-life* struggles that many of them faced after graduation.

"Well, like I always say, the heaviest rains bring about the rainbows," Kaitlin tried to cheer up her friend. "Maybe this jerkoff is the *one* before *the* one, if you catch my drift, love."

"Oh, I hope so!" Sandy chuckled. "You and your nature references, Ms. Norway. Speaking of which, how are things going over there with you? Found anything fun to do yet?"

"Oh, well, at least my legs are having fun. Still jogging. And, well… yeah," she thought for a minute if she should mention the Finn-incident to Sandy. After all, it was something she could only share with her—any of her acquaintances in Stavanger would surely judge her since their husbands were in the same oil business as Paul, and gossip could breed horrendous results. She hadn't quite gotten close enough to any one of those ladies to call them a 'friend' yet.

"Well... what? Uh oh, what's up?" Sandy asked.

"Well, the strangest thing just happened ..." Kaitlin started to say, retelling the events of the previous day without giving a thought to the long time they ended up being on the phone. She'd already placed Sandy on speaker-phone, and poured all the ingredients she'd chopped into a copper saucepan along with olive oil to heat up dinner.

"That... is... strange indeed, hon," Sandy replied after a moment of hesitation. "Are you sure you didn't imagine the whole thing? You know: hit your head on a reindeer's horns as you fell in the forest and began hallucinating?"

Sandy's reindeer reference made them both chuckle, albeit with her it was more over Sandy's lack of cultural knowledge. Yes, Norway was famous for its reindeers, yet, no, they weren't exactly roaming all over the streets everywhere in the entire country.

"Nope," Kaitlin finally said. "I looked at his card again this morning. Definitely one bizarre, yet very *real* experience."

"His card?" Sandy asked with a raised voice. "Oh my God, Kaitlin! You didn't exactly meet him at some downtown networking event like you're used to, for God's sake! He's a creepy stranger you met in the woods! You should have thrown that thing out!"

"Would *you* have done so, Ms. *I-get-in-contact-with-any-new-guy-who-shows-interest-immediately-as-one-relationship-ends*? Kaitlin asked defensively.

"First of all, ouch," Sandy responded. "Secondly, uh, sorry to wake you up, but, *I'm* not married, babe!"

Kaitlin felt her cheeks grow red. Sandy was right. She had crossed the line. Well, in her reaction to her friend, anyway. "I'm sorry, sweety. You know I didn't mean to insult you. Of course you're going to date around until Mr. Right comes along. I don't know why I'm... making a big deal of this whole thing..."

"Yeah, yeah, that's alright," Sandy continued. "I'll give it to your bizarre experience. I mean, look, here in New York I must have gotten used to meeting random crazies almost on a daily basis. But in Norway? That's a country with a relatively low crime rate, right? I mean, in your shoes, but in NY, I'd be thinking 'I'm lucky this random stranger didn't hurt me, especially with no one else around'. There wasn't, right?"

"There wasn't what...?" Kaitlin started to ask. "Anyone else? No! I mean, I don't think so. Not that I would have noticed. I mean, girl, you had to see his eyes, they were almost *too* green! And almost translucent! It was like I was looking through him at the leaves all around him and behind him, it was crazy!" Kaitlin paused to take a breath. She smiled with satisfaction at the realization that she could talk to Sandy like they were still fifteen.

"His *eyes?*" Sandy responded in a more serious tone of voice than Kaitlin had expected. "Ok, hon, I hate to say it, but now this is another territory altogether. I won't remind you again of Paul. I mean, didn't you tell me about how Norway is full of random beautiful people at every street corner you turn? That if they had lived in Toronto or here or some other big city, many would have surely been picked up by a talent agency already. I mean...?"

"Yes," Kaitlin interrupted. "But Sandy, no, no, you don't get it. I mean, I guess it's my fault for not being able to explain what I'm feeling exactly. It's not like I developed some sort of crush just because I found the guy to be handsome, don't think like *that*..."

"Of course not." Sandy's voice deadpanned.

"I'm serious!" Kaitlin continued. "I'm just mentioning details because... well, there were all these details that are still fresh in my mind, and all that conversation, yet I can't seem to *similarly* recall which way he came up to me from, for example... or where he went after I turned around to leave," Kaitlin's voice was sounding panicked now. She could hear herself speak as a third person would, listening in on their conversation. "I felt almost... hypnotized or something. I can't really explain..."

"Well..." Sandy said. "When you put it like that, yes, it sounds weird, totally. And what was it you said about the long path you came across suddenly becoming a short turn right and –*bam!*– you were already downtown?"

Kaitlin sighed and looked at the time. Her husband would be coming home soon. He didn't need to hear all this. "Yeah, it definitely was a longer walk out into the trees and getting lost than it was to get back into town. But, I guess there's an explanation for it. I don't need to drive myself crazy over this, right?"

"Yeah, I mean, you've always been bad with directions," Sandy said with a chuckle. "Don't worry, hon. What else could it be? He's a ghost? Was this some alien abduction? Of course not! I mean, I hope not… Maybe with all your walking in the friggin' woods you may have been actually walking in *circles* or something. Why don't you ask Paul? Maybe he's been in that area before and can explain."

Share with her husband. Kaitlin hadn't even thought of such an option, and now her inner voice was telling her to keep this to herself for a while. The ringing of the doorbell interrupted her thoughts.

"Speaking of Paul, he's home, sweety," she said hurriedly. "I've got to go. You know he likes it when I open the door for him. I think he finds it *domestic* of me or something somehow."

"Alright… alright," Sandy said with a laugh. "Thank you again for the flowers. But… wait. You said this guy just gave you his card and talked professionally, right? The nerve! I mean, like I said, it's not like this was some networking event…"

"Hon, I told him I was just walking around and had gotten lost!" Kaitlin interrupted her friend with a small laugh, pressing the button to open the door to the apartment entrance. "On a weekday! He must have guessed I wasn't exactly employed. Who knows? Look, keep me posted about neighbor-boy. I've got to go…"

Hanging up the phone and heading back toward the door, Kaitlin instinctively turned to the silver-framed round mirror hanging adjacent to it on the wall to fix her hair. She believed in the effect of keeping up your femininity as a recipe for a 'good' marriage—whatever that was. At least it had made her feel good about herself, and this in turn would make her a more cheerful wife, wouldn't it?

"Hi," she said coyly as she opened the door for the tired yet grinning man in front of her.

"Hello, my beautiful wife," Paul quipped, kissing the tip of her nose. Kaitlin was grateful he still articulated such words. 'Happy wife, happy life,' he'd often quote.

"How was your day?" Paul asked as he began to remove his boots and took a look at their wooden dining table, visible from the entrance. They were blessed to live in a modest-sized apartment with a high-society view of the sea. "You cannot *begin* to imagine how boring the presentations were today. And how long they lasted. I barely had time to grab lunch!"

Kaitlin got the hint. "Don't worry, babe. Dinner's almost ready. We have the soup from yesterday, plus I'm heating up some spinach and there's also your favorite desert after that. We don't want any pasta or rice with them, do we? I mean, you know we have to watch our carbs…"

"…Yes, yes, my amazing trainer," Paul interrupted warmly, throwing himself on their ivory-white leather sofa. "You're right. The soup will be fine. I'll just have some bread with it, and it'll do. We are allowed bread, right? The ones we buy *are* brown, after all?"

"Yes, babe," Kaitlin said with a mocking laugh. She realized she actually felt grateful in that moment to be required to turn her attention toward something mundane like setting up the table. It surely distracted her from her conscience.

"The veggies are much better tonight, honey," Paul grumbled fifteen minutes later at the dinner table, with the food still in his mouth. "Last week they were a tad undercooked, but this time my wife's got it."

He sent Kaitlin a little air-kiss that made half of her smile and the other half of her think: *Really, Paul? The food tastes in accordance with your liking, so that's how I, as a wife, have 'got' my duty accomplished? Hooray! Well, maybe I actually like them a little more raw: preserves the vitamins. Did you think about that? So, technically, you should feel your wife's 'got it' when she's thinking of your mutual health together, shouldn't you?*

She surprised herself each time she got such angry thoughts in her head—often so quickly after thinking warm ones about what a sweet guy she had. It only took him to make a face, and open his mouth about some *old-school* way Paul thought something 'should be' and, bam! It would feel as if the love inside of Kaitlin could twist into temporary hate. Her soul would cyclically become tormented by the two opposite ends of emotions.

"We'll go out for a walk to town after dessert, OK, hon?" Paul continued. *He's trying to be encouraging now, I suppose,* Kaitlin thought, nodding with a small smile forming on the corner of her lips, but not quite in her eyes. *There it is,* she recognized: *a tad light of 'forgiveness' flickering inside, but only a tad.* She hated being 'taken out for a walk' like a dog. Not that she minded walks, loved them in fact. The exercise gave her dopamine, or endorphins, or whichever one she'd read somewhere made people feel happier. She just didn't like her husband thinking that that's all there would be to lifting her mood. He sometimes seemed oblivious to the fact that it was only a temporary solution to her boredom, when they should have been looking for more lasting solutions, shouldn't they?

Moreover, Paul had a tendency of using poor choice of words for many of his requests from her: often saying that, when married, women 'should' do something or other. Not all women were the same, and Kaitlin just hated being lumped up in the general and standardized category of *women*, and what they were *supposed* to like, and supposed to *be* like. After all, she never judged him like that. Okay, so maybe she thought he could loosen up a bit, but it was for his own good as well, wasn't it?

"Ooh," Paul mumbled through his store-bought lime pie, which had been defrosted from the freezer. "We could also run outside by our special lake. I mean we either go to cafes or shops. I feel like we haven't been out in nature in a while, right babe? This tastes really good, by the way…"

No thanks, Paul, she wanted to say to his puppy-eyed face. *I was just in the forest yesterday, and, oh, I think I forgot to mention it, but I got lost, and all time seemed to freeze in a single moment as the forest became endlessly bigger and I ran into this mysterious, handsome stranger who handed me his card to call him…*

"Babe?" Paul interrupted her daydreaming. She decided to keep her mouth shut. After all, merely withholding easily misconstruable information wasn't the same thing as lying, right? She had to comfort the guilt she felt for both the events of yesterday and for thinking such bitchy thoughts about a man who was obviously trying to make them enjoy some time together.

"I'm here, babe," she said with a smile. "Sorry, just got a little bored today at home. You're right. I mean, I ran around a little today, but didn't get too far. Sandy called to thank me for the birthday flowers, and you know how long our chats can get. So we'll do that. We can go into town tomorrow night, if anything…"

Thirty minutes later, what began as a hand-in-hand walk toward the lake from the parking lot (where they'd parked their navy-blue Volvo S60), soon turned into light-jogging, with Paul's athletic pace gradually pulling him slightly ahead of his wife.

Admiring her husband's physique, from his shapely back (with the depth visible even through his thick Hally Hensen sweatshirt), to his cute little butt, Kaitlin smiled. *What's my problem?* she thought. *So what if I ran into some strange man in the woods and for some reason the thought of him uncontrollably seems unable to escape my mind? I love this man with me, and he's generally good to me, for Heaven's sake!*

Yes, Paul could be annoyingly stubborn sometimes and raise his voice over the littlest things from time to time, especially in the realm of orderliness and housework, in which Kaitlin herself knew her inadequacy and had warned him ahead of time. Times like that made Kaitlin feel chastised, like a little girl. She had known she wanted to be *with* Paul in a romantic relationship, but *marriage* wasn't something she was exactly feeling ready for when she said 'yes'. *It was partly my mother's fault*, Kaitlin thought, for often criticizing that she was 'making a mess of her life' by not being more ambitious at work, or in regards to being unable to find 'better' men than her usual loser-jock types. She had wanted to run away from all the noise (both literal and psychological) in Toronto. Yet when Paul was now the older figure in her life doing the chastising, the *quiet* she'd found in Norway would sometimes feel even 'noisier' than her mother's bickering back home.

Still lagging behind Paul, Kaitlin's eyes lazily began exploring the beautiful scenery around her. To her surprise, her eyes scanned for Finn to appear out of nowhere among the trees like he did a day ago. *No way*, she thought. *Why the heck has this man gotten such a hold on me after only being in his presence for ten minutes or so!?* she wondered. This wasn't usual for her. In fact, she vaguely recalled ever having thought deeply about a guy who hadn't first done the chasing before becoming bored—only after which Kaitlin would then mourn the lost attention and constantly obsess over him. But this was different. She was a *married* woman now. Wasn't this what all those girls back at the office in Toronto wanted to be? What all those women's magazines (which she had to admit she too loved to follow religiously) set up as the 'ultimate goal' for women, regardless of professional success?

She decided to get a hold of herself, stop being a brat, and concentrate once again on the loving man in front of her. "Hey handsome, slow down," she called out as Paul turned around to smile at her in his special slick way.

Countless runners whizzed by them. It never ceased to amaze Kaitlin how the Norwegians viewed sports and outdoor activities as many Canadians and Americans would view going to the movies and shopping malls: an essential part of their leisurely time. In fact, on this very day, she must have seen at least three families running with their children. Not even babies were spared from the outdoors in this country—being reared to face the country's tough climate from a very early age.

"Whoa…" Kaitlin froze in her tracks when she saw Finn's silhouette staring at them just then, about one hundred meters up ahead. It took one blink and he was gone. This was definitely no tree branch or some look-alike. She could swear she had just caught a glimpse of the actual man she'd met in the woods. No way her eyes could have been playing tricks on her, could they? That's what she had told herself when she thought she'd spotted someone staring at her yesterday in the forest before actually running into Finn, but now?

Was Sandy right? Was she hallucinating? Did thinking about something very often trick the mind into somehow making it exist? Or perhaps *he* was the one thinking about *her* often since their meeting and, as she'd read in some magazine article, perhaps the 'law of attraction' had been making both of them in turn think about one another. All she knew at that precise moment for sure was that she could literally begin to feel her psyche wearing out unexplainably.

Chapter 4

A couple walking their adorable white-and-brown puppy provided Kaitlin with both a welcome distraction and an explanation for her reactionary outburst to her husband. What was its breed? She was never able to quite remember such categorical details with dogs. All she knew was that she had always wanted a puppy. Especially when her brother, five years her senior, had moved out when he turned eighteen and Kaitlin felt lonelier than ever at home. Yet her mother had insisted they would bring fleas and take too much of their time. "You're in school, and all the events we have to attend to... I mean, darling, the poor dog would simply melt away with neglect!"

She'd dreamt of the day when she'd be living with the guy of her dreams and they'd both be welcomed home by friendly licks from their Golden Retriever, but, alas, her husband's dislike for dogs in the home had proven to seal her to an everlasting dog-less fate.

"Babe! I mean, whoa, isn't that the most adorable puppy you've ever seen?"

"Oh, yeah, I see it. Cute little fella, I guess," Paul smirked in response, reaching down to hold his knees and catching his breath. "You and puppies. Is that thing the reason you stopped? Come on, hon, no excuses, let's keep running!"

"This one's absolutely *adorrrrable*, though," Kaitlin insisted as the older lady walking the dog on a leash simply smiled at them. She didn't know what it was but she sure felt this way over baby animals—more than any maternal clocks she was told she should be feeling tick away by now anyway, especially by good old Sandy back home. "Girl, don't you dare tell me you're bored," her friend would scold her. "You're in frigging paradise for Heaven's sake, while some of us are still working our asses off here in the city. I mean, do you want to know the last time I had time to give myself a waxing, a manicure, a haircut, a... anything? No wonder

I'm still single. Be thankful! Pop out a baby already!" Her frankness was one of the many reasons they were best friends, and Kaitlin had always welcomed their monthly video-chats online, aside from the occasional phone call she would get like she had that morning.

"Hon, that's what you say about all dogs. Even when, frankly, I think they look like an alien or something, but hey, that's just my sweetheart." Her husband gave her a wet kiss on the cheek.

"Yeah but, babe, come on," Kaitlin found herself insisting soon enough, as she started running again to keep up with Paul, who had already leapt in front of her about five meters. This was a surprise to her own self, and she wondered if her more-than-usual persistence had something to do with trying to push the thought of Finn from her mind. "You're at work all day and I'm left with, like, minimal human contact. You know how hard it has been for me to find work without knowing the local language, though everyone frigging understands English here, so I *still* don't get that requirement. But, anyway. I mean, a puppy would occupy my time and make me happier! Paulie?" She gave her husband her usual puppy-eyed pout which she knew he could never resist.

"But darling," Paul started, slowing his run enough to reach the top of her white-baseball-cap-covered head and kiss it. "That puppy would *precisely* occupy any time that you would have to actually go out and *make* human contact." The wink he added at the end of his sentence reminded Kaitlin of that clever, quick wit of his. "Besides, I told you, you can't avoid learning Norwegian forever. We're still going to be living here, so taking classes would keep you busy *and* be useful for working eventually."

Darn. He hadn't bought the bait. He definitely had more 'street smarts' than she ever could have thought before living with him. Her creative and hard-working brain had gotten her through school and the advertising world, yet she was ultimately 'naïve' in figuring out a stable life for herself—just like her mother had never spared a minute to remind her. This was especially the case each time she'd seen her daughter upset because some guy hadn't returned the effort she had put in making their relationship work. She preferred to think of herself as just overly-sensitive, but, whatever.

She didn't know how she could respond to her husband at that given moment, so she continued her pouting. She knew she couldn't avoid learning Norwegian forever, but had to admit to herself her pride was getting in the way: to start completely over in a new part of the world when she'd already worked very hard in Canada made her feel like those years would be going to waste.

Paul had been trying to force her to go have 'coffee' with the wives of his friends for morale, not getting it that female friendships didn't work that way—in her opinion. Their husbands may have become genuine friends through their common experiences at work, but for women to feel a bond and meet up often, they just had to 'click' over shared experiences for it to work without being fake. And Kaitlin hated being fake. A lot of his friends' wives were also older than her, and many had children, which they bonded with each other over, often leaving Kaitlin out of conversations about schools and extracurricular activities and making her feel like the 'flimsy young wife' who didn't yet live in the 'real world' somehow. At least, that's how Kaitlin felt.

"It's a lot of work, honey," Paul continued, slowing his pace to run next to her. "You know we travel often for my meetings. Who will take care of it? So don't give me that look. I mean, we discussed this, didn't we? Once we're more settled, a baby will be in the cards and until then, you have me!" It was his turn to pout and add a smile. "I'm not so bad, am I?"

That was precisely what would sometimes keep Kaitlin up at night, lost in thought. Paul's face would light up like a bright flame each time the topic of having a baby came up, especially when he would often affectionately play with his friend's babies. Though she wasn't exactly getting any younger herself, she supposed that her husband, at 35, was more ready to be a father than she was to be a mother. Baby or no baby, their situation somehow didn't feel like it could ever really be fully fair for both of them.

Their long-distance dating period had consisted of immense romanticism due to the prospect of having to part from one another at the end of the frequent yet short trips they would take turns in making. At the time, the dreams Paul expressed of getting married and having a baby were genuinely responded with a nod from Kaitlin, who thought she wanted the same thing. After all, seeing him once every several weeks increased her longing to live together and intensified her emotions, as well as her need for a secure constant in her life after so many ups and downs.

Yet from time to time she couldn't help but wonder if love was enough, and whether or not she had married for the wrong reasons. After all, after their initial introduction to one another in Toronto, she was still on the rebound from Gus (Mr. Fear-of-Commitment). She had been attracted to Paul, alright, but she had to admit she'd still thought she and her ex would get back together, and this man seemed to want to get so serious, so fast! After all, what had he to wait for? He had a good job in a beautiful country. All he was missing was a wife, and Kaitlin felt lucky he wasn't one of those men who preferred bachelorhood with a different vixen every weekend.

Paul was raised as a good momma's boy, that was for sure. Although he had apparently been engaged at one point, Kaitlin had even found out that he had fewer relationships than she'd had! Though Kaitlin wasn't exactly the one to play around either, she had certainly been a serial dater. Sandy would tell her it was the result of growing up without a father: always searching for such a figure and sometimes even just 'any man' to 'feel complete' somehow. Not wanting to lead Paul along, she had played the 'friends' card for a while.

In time, Kaitlin decided to give up reforming 'bad boys', and during one of Paul's latest 'trips back home' to Montreal, which he later confessed mostly involved his desire to visit Ontario as well since he was in Canada already, with the hope that he'd see her and she'd change her mind about him, Kaitlin had decided Paul must be her destiny. After all, he was still a single man and she had ultimately moved on from her past. In fact, she had made the first move after a night of what had started out as a 'friendly dinner'. She leaned in to kiss him in front of her door. The rest was history.

Now that they finally had one another in the same place —and in the same house, nonetheless—, it was as if something felt missing. "I must be missing something to accomplish, some *feat to conquer,*" Kaitlin would tell herself, quoting an ad for a successful campaign for women's running shoes she had once helped to prepare.

Her mother, who could never hide her disappointment in Kaitlin for not pursuing charity work like she had, would often praise the world of charitable fundraising for fulfilling a sense of 'being needed'. She had come from a line of strong, successful women, who never depended on a man for money. After her father had left them for another woman when Kaitlin was just a baby, her mother never felt the need to get remarried, and, instead, threw herself into the work with her organization wholeheartedly. Of course, they were lucky to have her grandmother's fortune be bestowed upon them. Otherwise, her mother certainly couldn't have had the luxury to go into charity work, and would have had to work heavily like, heaven forbid, Mrs. Maverick!

And, of course, how could she forget? The occasional nagging from her mother on the phone to find a 'rich husband' in her high-society circle in Toronto, so that she could have her daughter closer to her, didn't exactly make the thought of moving across the Atlantic any harder. *Oh dear.* Her dear, critical, yet naively-idealistic mother. As if things were ever that simple in life—to work out perfectly for everyone exactly as they had always imagined it.

"Okay, babe, okay, I'm not saying anything more," Kaitlin said as she increased her pace ambitiously to pass her husband slightly.

"Wow, look at you! Go babe, go!"

Paul would also advise her to join the Petroleum Women's Club, which some of the very same wives of his professional circle were a part of. At least she would have something to do every week, he would tell her, make friends, and 'feel good' because the money they would raise from the activities they prepared would go to charity. Yet a part of her refused, perhaps a bit in a rebellious spirit against her mother. Kaitlin felt that 'doing good' to 'feel good' as a selfish purpose meant your heart couldn't possibly be in the right place. That's why she had always wanted to adopt a puppy-in-need instead.

"Baby?" Paul had slowed his pace again to a walk now that Kaitlin was once again lagging behind him. He reached out his right hand to cover the small of her waist. "You're not in your usual element today. We *are* on the same page about this, aren't we? A baby, I mean…"

"Oh my god, Paul! How is it that you can bring any random topic down to a *baby*, and in such a short amount of time, and so often, too!?" Kaitlin couldn't hold it in anymore as she kneeled down to hold her knees and panted deeply. She didn't realize how angry her voice had sounded until Paul abruptly took his hand off her and gave her a hurt stare.

"I'm sorry, I didn't realize I was bringing up such a *depressing* topic up for you, so *often,*" Paul quoted Kaitlin in an upset tone.

"Paulie, I'm sorry, but think of it from my side: it's pressure." Kaitlin said.

"And a puppy isn't?" He replied.

"A puppy will not be in my body for nine months!" She was growing more and more aggravated the more her husband didn't seem to understand what she was saying. It was okay to disagree, but to see things one-sided like this?

"Wait, wait, wait… let me try to get this straight," Paul said in a serious tone, "you're comparing a baby with some sort of… monster or something, somehow 'invading' your 'body' for nine months?"

Kaitlin let out a big sigh. "All I'm wondering, Paul, is why aren't we letting time and nature take their course? I mean, I'm still trying to enjoy the thought of being a newlywed, aren't you?"

"Yeah, so am I. I just supposed that a big part of that was dreaming of a baby. I'm not saying let's make one right now," Paul's voice had quieted down to a whimper, almost child-like. "And you keep saying 'newlyweds' as if we got married last week!"

This wasn't the first time Paul had quieted her determined resolve to prolong the enthusiasm after their wedding. It had only been a year, yet she was mostly hurt since this had been his reaction during a similar fight just two months into their marriage as well. "Babe, it's been two months, two whole months, and you still haven't picked up a recipe book or looked up one of the gazillion websites teaching cooking online?" The shrill sound of Paul's disappointment over her lack of interest in cultivating domestic skills had made Kaitlin cry alone in their room then —and still hurt just as much now every time she was constantly reminded of how they still had lingering different expectations from one another.

Kaitlin sighed and tried to change the topic. Neither of them needed to hurt each other any further right now. "Look, this isn't the time for this. Everything will work out in time. We're almost near the parking lot. So, come on, let's fasten the pace! Let's go, go, go!"

"So, just one round today? Okay, you're the boss." Luckily, Paul was also eager to drop the conversation.

It was a relatively quiet walk to the car and an even quieter ride back home. The fog had sunk lower in the sky and they soon couldn't see further than twenty meters in front of them. The beautifully lush greenery around them and the reliably breathtaking and orange-pink sunset overhead could only distract a couple in yet another disagreement for so long.

Paul did have a habit of keeping appearances and going through the motions of being part of a strong union, and liked to open doors for her and pull her chair when she sat down. Though these gentlemanly gestures were more frequent when they were dating, he would still do such little things for her from time to time. This evening was apparently not going to be one of those times. Seeing that her husband had gotten out of the car with a stiff face when they'd reached home, turning his face away from her, Kaitlin knew she was getting herself out of the car like a big girl.

A big girl. That's what she told herself she had to be. It was difficult for her to hold back the tears building up inside now for too long. For the first twenty minutes or so of having her feelings hurt, she had feigned a poker face so well that she could even be mistaken for a tough woman. Yet soon enough, they would come pouring down, and they did so, as Kaitlin walked toward the sea neighboring their building and stared out into the misty waters where a ship was yet again heading away toward the other islands of southwestern Norway. Like the magical journey of this vessel through the fog and amongst the sounds of seagulls, she and Paul had everything it seemed, yet their direction was unclear.

***

Paul pressed on the gas pedal more strongly than usual the following day, a brisk Thursday morning, brisker than the norm even for Stavanger, as it was also a windy day, and the wind here could always make a comfortable couple of degrees above zero feel like ten below.

He was running late to work after sleeping through his alarm clock, and both he and Kaitlin hadn't gotten much sleep the night before. They'd managed to make conciliatory, more aggressively-passionate than tender, yet ultimately satisfying love for the first time in ten days. Their arguments, strangely enough, would frequently produce this result.

Why doesn't she attempt to understand me better and make more of an effort for this marriage to be for life? Paul thought, lowering the window to let the cold air keep him awake on his morning commute to work. *I just want us to be a close-knit family, and grow old together like my parents. They look so happy, yet it's because both mom and dad sacrificed so much of themselves to make that happen. Doesn't Kaitlin want the same thing I do?*

He often feared this day would come –as several of his friends had warned him. "She's from a broken home," they'd said. "Grew up without a father figure. And she's used to the big city: the fast pace of things in life." His good friend James, in fact, had warned him the most frequently, having gone through a terrible divorce from a younger woman. "Dude, I'm sorry, but you can't always make a good housewife from a good girlfriend."

Paul would laugh it off, saying Kaitlin was more 'down to earth' than her rather distant, elegant beauty would suggest. "You forget I was her friend for a while now. I've gotten to know her better." Although it wasn't exactly love at first sight, and Paul did have his doubts about how someone like Kaitlin could fit the idea of an ideal wife in his head with which he was raised, all he knew for sure was that he was attracted to her and her spirit more than anybody else in his entire life.

Ever since he'd started making a good living in Norway, he would often be 'advertised' as 'a great potential husband' around Canada from his well-intentioned mother and sisters. He would often be set up with 'nice' girls whom he could never bring himself to feel an attraction for, despite their prettiness.

In fact, although his mind and moral values told him he wanted someone with a traditional mindset in order to complete his dream of having a long-lasting marriage like that of his parents, he often doubted whether a 'nice girl' was indeed what it would take to make his heart pound. Their first meeting over coffee, in fact, had Kaitlin making a dirty joke, which had initially shocked Paul, though gradually titillating him. The image of her shy, blushing smile soon after her comical outburst had especially lingered in his mind during more nights than he cared to admit.

He smiled for the first time since the beginning of yesterday's jog. Those were such exciting times: growing gradually closer to Kaitlin over a period of time had him longing for more and more of her, and not just in body like most men. If he was going to have a woman like her, it would have to be for keeps. He knew himself. He would grow extremely attached to someone like her (someone with beauty, brains *and* class), so much so that he couldn't handle it very well if they were ever to break up. That's why he had popped the question not too long after they'd first become romantically-involved.

He'd wanted her to know that although he would be traveling back to Norway for work, he was for real. He didn't want any man in Toronto clouding what he knew to be Kaitlin's romantic mind, and fooling her sensitive heart. That was one of the few negative aspects of dating a long-time friend: you'd gotten to learn more about their prior relationships than you'd care to know. Yet he didn't want to judge her any more than he wanted to be judged himself: for being alone for so long, for not being as confident to go out and meet local ladies in Norway as he was in making friends to fill the place of romance, for anything for that matter.

He had taken a leap of faith in asking Kaitlin to marry him. At the time, he was almost sure she'd say something like, "Let me think about it." Yet didn't. The look in her eyes was genuine when she screamed: Yes! No one could fake that. He had seen their future together in those sparkling hazel eyes. He only wished she would come down from the clouds where he knew her mind wandered off to at times. Surely she had bigger dreams for her life back in Toronto. Yet from what she told him, those 'fun' days had ultimately left her with her heart broken and professional efforts unappreciated many times.

His instincts had hardly proved him wrong in his life. He'd had faith it was only a matter of time when Kaitlin, despite her boredom, would get used to a peaceful life, and see the same dream when she looked into his eyes as well.

***

He's just become a friendly face in this lonely town for me to think about, that's all, Kaitlin couldn't stop herself from thinking about her earlier mysterious run-in with Finn, even as she was busy folding the laundry that afternoon.

She'd spent the entire day lazily, with only a quick walk to the nearby market to pick up some groceries and a couple of overpriced English-language magazines for her guilty pleasure. She would console herself at the top of each hour that seemed to pass since she saw that glimpse of Finn again in the woods while with her husband.

Pouring herself her third cup of steaming hot coffee, she pulled one of the leather chairs from the kitchen table and sat with a loud thump, sulking her shoulders as if she'd given up. *This is ridiculous, and so wrong*, she thought, taking a sip of the drink in her hand, not caring that it'd burnt the side of her lips a little bit.

Her husband would soon be home. *Sigh*. Was she just thinking about this mysterious Finn person to distract herself from the awkward baby argument she and Paul had had during their jog? *Excuses, excuses*. For this reason or that or another, she was thinking about some inviting and handsome mystery man who was not her husband, and she was feeling like a 'bad girl', indeed, with thoughts of her mother's 'well-intentioned', yet hurtful criticisms from her youth replaying in her head. Stretching her long arms out in front of her, Kaitlin had just picked up the magazine with her favorite Hollywood actress dressed in a gorgeous burgundy dress on the cover when the doorbell rang. Sure enough, there stood her husband with his own bag of groceries in his right hand and a full smile on his face. Kaitlin couldn't help but smile back and place a kiss on his lips to welcome him in. She'd grown to appreciate Paul's ability to act as if nothing had happened after they'd spent hours apart from one another without as much as mutual text messages for communication, though it could also be annoying in the way time also allowed for unspoken grievances to sink further into her soul at times.

"Paulie, I already picked up some stuff at the Coop Mega. I texted you! Didn't you get it? You didn't have to!"

"I know, babe, but these are opportunity items for the month," Paul replied, taking off his Timberland boots. Picked them up with Tim after work on the way home."

While Paul hopped in for a quick shower, Kaitlin placed the milk, some cases of various fruity yogurt, the specialty cheese, and the eggs her husband had brought into their oversized refrigerator and peeked behind their loaf of bread on the second shelf –yup, she had indeed luckily remembered to remove their tomato/basil/mozzarella/cheese pizza from the freezer to defrost earlier. This would have to do for the night.

The ringtone sound of Elvis Presley's 'Jailhouse Rock' came to play right as she closed the oven door after placing the pizza in with some fresh toppings she'd sliced and added on for additional vegetable content.

"Honey, you've got a call," she called out to her showering husband, who sounded quite cheerful judging by his uncharacteristic whistling of some tune from a song.

"You can pick up, honey. Don't say I'm showering, though, too personal. Say I've run to the market or something and should be back soon to call them back, whoever it is." Ever proper with his manners, Paul also often made the effort to ensure transparency between them, recognizing her trust issues early on in their relationship, though he certainly had some as well from his past, and expected the same transparency from her.

"It's… never mind, I'll tell them," Kaitlin's felt her face drop and for some strange reason, a-kick-in-the-stomach feeling developed when she read the name: *Jeanette*. Without learning any more information, the name was somehow enough to make her tremble as she managed to press 'answer'.

"Paulie? You have got to hear this!" The high-pitched voice rushed straight into conversation without waiting for her to say hello.

"This is *Paul's wife* speaking," Kaitlin stated in a firm tone. "He can't come to the phone right now. May I ask who's calling?" She couldn't help but emphasize his name pronounced correctly.

"Oh, Kaitlin…" Jeanette responded. "Hi. This is Jeanette from the office. Paul's always talking so much about you! It's a shame we haven't met yet. How are you?"

The continuation of her chipper tone only managed to annoy Kaitlin further. "I'm, uh, fine, thank you. No, we haven't met yet, you're right. May I, uh, take a message?"

"Don't sweat it, hon," Jeanette replied. "I'm sure he'll call me back. Just tell him I've got *the big news*. He'll know what it's regarding…"

"Will do, sure." *How in the world are they close enough to have nicknames for each other, and I'm only hearing about this woman now?* Kaitlin thought angrily. *And like this!*

After mumbling some forced pleasantries and hanging up the phone, Kaitlin paced back and forth in front of the closed bathroom door. Her arms were crossed almost as tightly as her angered eyebrows (she could feel them tensing up, simultaneous to her stomach beginning to turn). She was actually glad for the several additional minutes it took for her husband to squeakily close the shower handle, step out, and immediately turn on the hair dryer before ensuring that his body was dry firs—one of his most annoying traits in her opinion. Why couldn't he just let his hair dry naturally like *she* did? *Whatever.*

"Who was it, babe?" Paul called out, turning off the dryer.

Damn. She was still thinking about how to best articulate her questioning without coming off as a jealous, insecure wife.

"What? Oh, some woman from work, *Jeanette,* ...apparently you guys are buds?" Kaitlin tried her best to sound unaffected, but she wasn't so sure it had worked.

"Jeanette? Uh oh, I wonder what gossip she's got now!" Paul sounded surprisingly calm about her having called, and Kaitlin was hoping this wasn't some sort of act. He was apparently cool enough to feel the matter didn't call for any further explanation, turning the dryer back on.

"You never mentioned your 'gossipy' office mate, though, babe," Kaitlin half-heartedly called out over the machine.

"What's that? Hon, I'm coming out, hold on. I can't hear you," Paul called out.

There was that word, again: *Hon.* The word had always sounded too friendly and un-special –for a significant other, anyway– to Kaitlin, especially since she and Sandy used it often to refer to each other as mates. But for some reason it was bothering her even more now after the way she'd just heard the woman on the phone also use it. *Hon.* Did Paul call Jeanette 'hon', too? Was *that* what was nagging at the back of her mind?

"We come from the same small town in Montreal and went to the same middle school, hon," Paul shook his head with a slight smile, stepping out of the shower. He didn't even need to glance at Kaitlin's face to imagine her expression. He always knew his wife was sensitive, but ever since the relative isolation she faced living in Stavanger had begun to kick in, his wife could turn into a high school girl sometimes, and he had grown accustomed to appeasing her. "I should have introduced you guys earlier, you're right. But I honestly became lazy about it, and you know how caught up I've been at work." His hair was interestingly still dripping onto the white towel he'd placed on his shoulders.

"It's not just about the lack of introduction, Paul," Kaitlin made sure to position her entire body to face him straight on, causing him to look into her eyes now. "I mean you didn't even *mention* her. Was it so difficult to remember saying, 'Oh guess what baby, what a small world, my friend from school also works here at Stavanger?'"

"Um, honey, it's not like I began working at Statoil and ran into her *after* we got married for me to point out something like that. I hadn't seen her in ages and honestly couldn't even label her a friend now. We barely get the time to chat in the office, and when we do, it's usually about business, or some major gossip, which this woman loves, my God! Which is why she wouldn't have called unless it was something major. It's probably about Tim…"

Paul chuckled to himself as he opened the hair dryer and continued drying his hair in front of the bathroom mirror. He realized it was nearly dried already, yet he was pleased he was still half naked and the hair dryer's sound could still be used as an excuse for a moment's distraction from having to continue this conversation with his wife.

"Paulie, look at me, please…" Kaitlin reached out and shut the machine off. She had to shift her approach. "I think your hair's dry enough," she smiled as she combed her hand through his wavy hair. She knew his scalp was a sensitive spot for him. "I just find it weird that I've neither met nor at least heard about your other colleagues, that's all. What's more natural than that? Put yourself in my position…"

"She's… like one of my sisters to me. But I… I didn't think you guys would hit it off, alright?" Paul blurted out, taking Kaitlin's hand and placing it to her side, gently.

"Wait… *what*? What in the world is that supposed to mean…" Despite the tender expression on her husband's face, she wasn't exactly liking his little confession.

"…It means I was sure you'd look down on her, okay? You'd say something about how plain and boring she is or how… how… silly it is that she's into traditional-cooking the way she is and what a countryside type woman she is, etc. I mean, the woman gets homemaking magazine subscriptions at work, for Heaven's sake. I know you, babe. Don't deny it, you would make fun of her!"

Kaitlin was suddenly at a loss for words. This was not the sort of thing she expected to hear.

"Don't look at me like that," Paul continued, lowering his voice now and inching closer to Kaitlin. "It *is* what you said about Scott's wife, Tonya, when they came over for dinner, remember? Saying all she seemed to talk about was cooking? And even Lars's wife, too…"

"I went *shopping* with Lesley," Kaitlin protested. "…and I never bad-mouthed her to you! I can't believe you think I'm such a… such a… friggin' snob!"

"Well, yes, you went shopping with her, but only after her, like what, *third* invitation? You just didn't want to be rude. And you *did* say how bored you were that you guys were only able to go to that one store at Kvadrat since she constantly attended to her baby, didn't you? That you guys could barely even down your coffee?"

"Wow," Kaitlin said, offended. "I am officially at a loss for words at how, how, mean and judgmental you are being with me right now…"

"I'm just telling you what I see, what I can observe from your actions," Paul continued. "Look, Jeanette is sincerely a nice lady and she wanted to meet you countless times… I just…"

"Ok, Paul. Just stop it, ok? I'm sorry you apparently don't think that *I'm* as 'nice' a lady as your office buddy is!" Kaitlin stormed off into their bedroom without even a single glance at Paul, who just stood with his mouth and arms open wide in silent protest.

"Aren't you going to come out and have this pizza with me?"

***

Paulie! Kaitlin remembered suddenly. One of the last thoughts she had before drifting off into a restless sleep after exchanging cold 'good nights', as well as a 'you're overreacting for nothing, babe' from Paul before he turned his back to her and inched closer to the edge of his own side of their king-size mattress.

Paulie. The 'hon' thing was no longer bothering her as much in comparison. Though Kaitlin didn't quite like how childish it sounded,

Paul had insisted sometime soon after they'd moved in together that she had used it once, and that he had really liked it. She had told him she loved when he called her his 'darling', and had asked him in turn which of her nicknames for him was *his* favorite. "Paulie, baby," he'd replied. "I really love it when you call me that."

Chapter 5

Groggy after getting less than her ideal eight hours of sleep, Kaitlin woke up the following morning feeling decisive in joining the famous Petroleum Wives Club she'd been told so much about. She needed a social life outside of her husband and his circle, and she needed one as soon as possible if she didn't want to lose her mind, she'd decided.

The phone call from her husband's female colleague and 'friend' (that was what he had called that Jeanette woman) had gotten to her more than she cared to admit. So she had gotten him to suggest that Jeanette was somehow 'domestic' and 'plain', supposedly non-threatening, though Kaitlin always trusted such girls less, whom she felt would do even more to steal a man's attention.

She never thought she could feel jealous of other women around a man who had chased after her devotedly for so long, hence seeming 'safe'. Yet, he was a man (*her* man), and Kaitlin's paws were out. She also knew she wanted to meet this woman in person.

Throughout all of this, if one good thing came out if it, Kaitlin decided, it was that she found herself feeling less guilty for Finn having occupied her thoughts over the past couple of days. If her husband could have a female 'buddy', perhaps Finn could just be hers.

Yet a part of her also was feeling 'punished' somehow by the universe for having thought so much about Finn. At least this Jeanette woman and her husband were childhood friends, and the possibility of a friendship seemed more innocent (the rational part of her mind thought) than her thoughts of Finn after just one meeting.

She searched online for the PWC website and found that, coincidentally, their first meeting was being held that Friday evening at five. She could consider it. What great timing this was. Surfing it for a bit, Kaitlin saw that the website was full of photographs of the group's activities from earlier years. This clicked something in her brain—she could similarly check out the local website for Paul's workplace!

Kaitlin opened up a new Tab on the Internet Explorer screen in front of her. Statoil's Stavanger website popped up several seconds later. What would she be looking for exactly? Pictures of her husband sharing a drink with certain 'coworkers' over the company's Christmas dinner? This was no Women's Club. This was a professional website regarding oil technology and operations. "Don't be silly, Kaitlin!" she warned herself out loud. Yet, as usual, her self-awareness did not stop her curiosity.

"Investor Centre... News & Media... About Statoil... Careers..." Kaitlin suddenly had an instinct about the 'About Statoil' tag: it could very well have photos of employees. Her own photo, after all, used to be on the website of the last company she'd worked for in Toronto.

"Eureka!" she mimed to herself in silence when she spotted the tag for 'Corporate Governance', pausing to take a sip of her coffee.

Kaitlin sighed as she only saw the names and pictures of Executives. *Certainly this bitch couldn't be the Vice President or something, could she?*

"What's this? 'Public Relations', Let's see here. 'Sarah Singh... Tony Mitchelson... Helge Dodson... Jeanette Andrews...'" As soon as she saw the name she was looking for, and the brief image of a buxom blonde appeared from the waist up, Kaitlin reflexively averted her eyes to the side of the computer screen. Was she ready to see this? "Oh, what the hell!"

Looking at the picture of this woman in a skintight black top, flashing something a little more than a bright-orange stone on a gold chain around her neckline –a little too low for work, in her opinion–, Kaitlin felt the skin under her neck begin to flush, as it often would whenever she felt nervous. So this woman was attractive, yet a little older-looking than she'd imagined. At least it appeared to be true what Paul had said, that this could very well be an old classmate of his. Glancing now at her piercing blue eyes (highlighted by smoky makeup), Kaitlin wondered whether her husband had had a crush on her then. Was this the 'plain' woman Paul was afraid Kaitlin would belittle? Was he kidding her?

If this was a sign she needed to get up and get out of the house, and outside of her negative thoughts, Kaitlin would accept it gladly. She needed to dress up and leave the house to increase her self-esteem. She clicked off the Statoil website and left only the Women's Club site to take another look at the address provided. She then called her husband at work to let him know she would be attending a club meeting, so they should 'eat dinner out'. Eating out wasn't a prospect Paul liked to do too often. The city was irrationally expensive, and, despite his comfortable paycheck, according to Paul, their money was to be used to 'save up for their future as a big family'. And, of course, according to him, with Kaitlin being home, she had no excuse not to cook, unless she was really sick or something, did she?

With a loud sigh, she put on her favorite DKNY suit, which she had brought with her from Toronto the year before with hopes that she would wear it to various 'fancy' events. Usually, she would get her frizzy, wavy hair blow-dried straight and her nails manicured before such an event, but she wasn't exactly in her 'usual' zone—neither geographically nor mindset-wise. She didn't exactly want to become like those women who just didn't give a damn about their appearance once their social life became limited to domesticity, either. Kaitlin never wanted to give up making an effort to look her best, regardless of whether or not the event she was attending was high-scale, like the ones she was used to in the big city. It was for her own well-being, after all, she'd decided.

Putting on some matching eye-shadow to her navy suit and her hair up in a high ponytail- achieved by teasing the top of her head with a comb-Kaitlin put on her black wedges and headed out the door. That was another thing about her life in Norway: she could no longer wear her favorite pumps on the hilly and stony city sidewalks if a car-ride wasn't involved. Paul would always warn her of the constant possibility of icy roads and difficulty walking through the cobblestone streets in her favorite heels. She still preferred to avoid the flats he'd often advise, though: she hated feeling less feminine than she was accustomed to.

Taking the bus to the building located in the district of Forus, as Paul had taken the car, Kaitlin decided she was going to involve herself in whatever boring activities these ladies would plan. She didn't want to be too prejudiced; perhaps they could even manage to have some fun alongside doing meaningful activities after all. Yet, she knew how these things usually went—from her mother's circle. She was practically raised amongst ladies bringing baked goods to sell for fundraising. And the idea that a woman's biggest 'contributions' could consist only of her cooking or child-rearing, or any other 'traditional' concept for some reason irritated her to her very core. "You feminist!" Sandy would tease her. Perhaps she was, Kaitlin decided, though she was educated enough to know that ultimately it depended on whose definition of feminism one was looking at. If one were to ask a high-ranking businesswoman in New York City, for example, she herself may be looked down upon as (the horror!) a 'woman who had left her professional and social life to follow her husband into his world'.

The scenic bus routes of Stavanger had always been a welcome distraction for her, and luckily they did not disappoint today of all days either. She stepped out of the bus after arriving across the mainly-glass, four-story building with burnt-orange colored tiles to see two rather dressed-up young women, a slightly overweight but very striking one with curly blonde hair and an elegant brunette with her sleek hair obviously styled at a salon, head into the same building as she was. *Maybe I could make cool friendships here after all,* she smiled to herself. She was beginning to feel the eager-to-fit-in-school-girl inside of her awaken.

Room 402. She showed her building ID to the Security Officer after the revolving glass doors –one she had as Paul's wife–, and entered behind them. The place smelled like fresh paint and the voices of the two ladies that had entered right before her were echoing throughout the main corridor.

Stepping into the same elevator, she gave them both a smile which was greeted with a smile back and a nod from the brunette. "PWC, yes?" The brunette asked.

"Yeah… yes. How did you guess?"

"Well it *is* 5 pm, and we all know no professional activity really lasts *this* long in this city," the brunette said with a smile, bringing on a smirk from her blonde friend.

"Yeah, you can say that again I suppose. The 4th floor will likely be the loudest one in this building!' Kaitlin immediately wished she had been able to come up with something wittier than that, but it was the best she could do. To her luck, these ladies hadn't yet found her corny enough to drop their smiles.

"I'm Sibel, and this is Jamie," the brunette extended her hand.

"Kaitlin… nice to meet you, ladies," she shook both of their hands. *Si belle*, she pronounced in her head, *translates to 'Rather very beautiful' in French, which this lady certainly is.*

"Uh, here we are. Joy!" Jamie mocked, leading the way to the room, which was luckily close to the elevator, as Kaitlin's heels were already beginning to pinch the sides of her feet. *Damn!* Normally they wouldn't have hurt this much this soon, but she *had* of course been out of practice walking in them lately.

Kaitlin knew what had made *her* come to the meeting that evening, but why were these other ladies here? Especially as Jamie's sarcastic tone of voice echoed her own suspicions over whether or not they would actually manage to have a good time.

As if hearing the question inside her head, Sibel turned to her friend and whispered. They were now within hearing distance, and Kaitlin could have sworn she could make out the words, "It's going to work, trust me."

Stepping into the room, she saw that, as fate would have it, the three of them were seemingly the only women under forty there. Kaitlin wasn't ageist. She could never forget the divorced, loud, yet fun-loving Mirabelle back in Toronto whom she had met at her last job, and had enjoyed several after-work cocktails with, despite at least a decade between them. Yet looking around at the casually-dressed older women at the roundtable in the brightly-lit room, she couldn't imagine having anything in common with these particular ladies.

Kaitlin took a seat next to a curly-haired blonde and a rosy-cheeked woman of at least fifty, wearing a bright green sweater that not even her mother would be caught dead in. She was beginning to feel overdressed, that was for sure. Even sarcastic Jamie was wearing jeans, she just noticed. She was glad Sibel at least had on a knee-length black skirt under a trendy lemon-colored blouse.

"Hello, ladies, welcome!" a cheerful voice came from a slim, curly-haired woman with a face full of lovely freckles which accentuated her mocha-colored skin and laugh lines one could tell were the result of many genuine smiles over the years.

"My name is Ann, as many of you know, though I am seeing some new faces this year," she looked in the direction of her and her elevator mates. "Welcome, ladies."

Looking first at each other and then at Ann, the three of them muttered their thanks. Apparently they were the newbies. Kaitlin immediately conjured up a small fantasy in her mind that maybe they would be like those 'cool', 'rebellious' girls from those high school movies. She chuckled to herself. The few cold stares she consequently received made her clear her throat, putting on a serious face and reminding herself to grow the heck up.

"I would like to begin with, you guessed it, my favorite thing in the whole world: a presentation on who we are, what we do, and all the things we have accomplished in the last year," Ann was smiling as she set up the projector and pulled down a white screen at the back of the room. A few loud grunts were heard, but hearing Ann's laughter confirmed Kaitlin's suspicion that it was for show: these ladies were actually loving this stuff they were apparently accustomed to!

The presentation was luckily a lively one, full of colorful pictures from the Club's previous activities and music in the background, taking Kaitlin back to her days creating power point presentations in college. She never thought the day would come when she'd be missing those days of working on something, then presenting it in front of a large room full of all eyes on her. Though quietly-dispositioned in general, a wallflower Kaitlin was not.

"I hope you're still awake ladies!" Ann joked, causing laughter to erupt from all of the twenty-five or so ladies in the room, according to Kaitlin's count. She decided she actually liked this Ann lady.

"Before I take your questions, I would like to point out some of our goals for this year, which we voted on at the end of last term…" Ann read aloud a long list of such goals: 'have more dessert sales' (since they were apparently a big success last year), and the 'babysitting club' (since the ladies apparently loved having their children watched voluntarily by Club members on busy days).

After a long round of introductions, it was Kaitlin's turn.

"Well, hello everyone!" Kaitlin tried her best to put on her friendliest face, yet surprisingly felt her heart patter with nervousness, something she wasn't used to when she was in her usual element. *Come on, you can do it, you rocked the world of advertising in Canada, for goodness sake. Sell this!* She encouraged herself.

"My name is Kaitlin Maverick. I arrived in Stavanger last year due to my husband's job being here. He's in the oil business: it's mostly either that or NATO families here, as you all know!" Kaitlin chuckled, hoping to get a similar reaction from everyone else. *Nothing.* She felt eyes on her from the left side, and saw that only Sibel was smiling at her.

"I'm originally from Toronto, Ontario, where I worked for several years in two major advertising agencies…" This last tidbit of information brought on an 'Oh wow' nod of interest from Ann, easing Kaitlin's nerves. Yet she had now come to what she believed to be the hardest part of introductions like these. The other ladies had mentioned their children and their various volunteer activities –only Jamie, the blonde, was apparently a working woman– and even she only worked part-time at some retail store.

What would Kaitlin say? What *was* she doing exactly, besides having listed all her accomplishments from Canada that had seemingly come to a halt when she'd gotten married? She didn't need anyone to feel sorry for her—including herself. So she tried to look on the bright side of things.

"I wanted to come here and check out this club because my mother instilled in me a love of charity since I was a child, and, since I haven't yet found work here, I wanted to contribute to my new city through any way I could." Now all of the ladies seemed to smile at her. *Approval. Yey*, she thought.

"Welcome!" bright-green-sweater called out, to which Kaitlin mouthed, "thank you."

As Ann took questions from the ladies, Kaitlin realized she had gradually begun to stop listening, yet forcing her eyes to stay open and blinking rapidly must have made her look rather aloof. "Are you ok?" Jamie asked her in a low voice, to which Kaitlin nodded reassuringly.

"I think I know how you feel," her next-chair neighbor continued with sympathetic light-green eyes, looking over her shoulder to make sure they weren't causing too much of a distraction from the lady in the green sweater now asking her question to Ann. "Lord knows I only joined to get out of the house. My mother-in-law has been with us for the past six months, ever since she lost her husband back in the States, and it's been driving me insane!"

So *that's* what Sibel must have meant by the words she whispered to Jamie right before entering the room. Kaitlin found herself instinctively reaching out to give Jamie's arm a touch of comfort; though she liked the sweet old lady that was her mother-in-law enough (the very woman who seemingly didn't have any aspiration in life other than to be able to cook enough maple-syrup pie for all her neighbors come Easter), she couldn't imagine her staying with them for so long. "Six whole months, you say? Oh my goodness, that actually makes me appreciate the absolute *boredom* I've been feeling being home *alone* most of the time!" They both giggled.

"Trust me, you're much better off bored than absolutely *annoyed* to death!" Jamie complained.

Two of the older ladies sitting closest to Ann turned around to give them dark looks, making Kaitlin feel like a troublemaking-student. Ann, however, continued talking uninterruptedly, much to Kaitlin's both surprise and gratitude.

Kaitlin took a look at the clock hanging on the wall. Five minutes until seven. She was surprised to witness how two hours could have gone by so fast. Wasn't she supposed to be having fun for that to happen? Luckily, she saw that everyone had started to place their hands on their jackets. It was apparently over. *Paul must be fuming*, she thought, waiting for her at home, where they'd last agreed he'd head straight to after work and wait up for her to come and join him for some takeout Thai he was supposed to bring over. If anything, she would just microwave her Pad Thai. After all, she wasn't a nit-picky eater like her husband.

"Thank you for coming, hope to see you in the new year, ladies!" Ann exclaimed. "Don't forget in the new year we'll be meeting at our regular headquarters in Sandnes, every other Tuesday. Now this upcoming Tuesday is too soon, and the Tuesday after that is Jul[4]! So I'll see you all in the first week of the new year, okay? Merry Christmas! God Jul! Happy New Year!"

"It was great meeting you, thank you!" Kaitlin smiled as she too reached out her hand toward the Club President, after she saw Mrs. Santa Claus in the bright green sweater do so. Alright, so maybe she was being

---

[4] Jul: Christmas season in Norwegian.

too harsh. At least she was having social interaction with friendly ladies. She actually was beginning to look forward to sharing the details of her day with Paul over dinner and was surprised that this was making her feel somewhat rather accomplished. Keeping the smile on her face, Kaitlin noticed that the two women she had spoken to earlier were heading out, ahead of everyone else in the room.

"Hold the elevator!" Kaitlin's leather shoes were hurting her feet even more now and she was pretty sure it showed, for she felt herself wobbling while running to the elevator.

"Kaitlin! Slow down! I got you! Don't break your foot or anything," Sibel was smiling from ear to ear while pressing the button to keep the door open. *Is she just trying to be friendly or is this woman this annoyingly cheerful all the time?* Kaitlin thought. Either way, she was glad her name was remembered.

"Argh, thank you so much. I could not bear to wait here for even another minute for the next elevator." Kaitlin had to place both hands on her chest to try to catch her breath.

"You were that bored, huh?" Sibel turned to fix her hair in the full-length mirror. "Come on, it shouldn't be that bad. A friend of mine was a member before moving away not long ago. She always spoke of good things. Besides, it's a non-profit, so they, well, I suppose I can say from now on *we* do donate a good percentage of the income from various sales and memberships to charity each year. Last year, in fact, I believe it was to a shelter for women mainly suffering from domestic abuse. It's good work."

"Wow... women get beat up in Norway, too? Seems so peaceful here." As soon as the words left her mouth, Kaitlin feared having sounded ignorant or insensitive, but their conversation was flowing smoothly, so she had just spoken without thinking.

"Well, uh, yeah, unfortunately it happens everywhere." Sibel allowed Kaitlin to step off the elevator as they walked to the main exit. "It's not just domestic violence, either. Lots of economic woes also place them there I suppose."

"Where did your friend go? Jamie, I believe?" Kaitlin inquired.

"Oh, she headed straight to the bathroom to fix her hair," Sibel answered. "Her husband is picking her up for dinner. Apparently it's his mother's birthday or something, so we parted ways for the night. I had to head down right away to meet *my* husband. We only have the babysitter until seven thirty, so… oh, there he is!" The striking brunette's smile now seemed to stretch even higher than her ears as they passed through the automatic doors to the right of the revolving entrance doors. She waved enthusiastically at the man waiting inside the black Sedan, who waved back with a smile just as warm. "He arrived just in time. I'm so glad. You have a ride too, right?"

How Kaitlin wished now that Paul could pull up behind Sibel's husband as soon as the question had been asked. She regretted just then not taking Paul up on his offer to pick her up, insisting the bus ride wasn't a problem. "Unfortunately, Paul, my husband, is still at work with some overtime stuff to do, and he has our car. I took the bus, so…" Kaitlin still couldn't manage to tell the truth: that her husband was waiting for her at home to have dinner, which innately sounded strange to share.

"…Oh, I see… but wait, do you live nearby? We can drop you off if you want!"

"Aw, thanks. But the bus stop to the city center is right here and it's not a long ride…"

"…It may not be a long ride, but it may be a long wait," Sibel interrupted enthusiastically. "These Norwegians are always on schedule, I know, but the traffic at this hour can get ugly! We live on Hundvag island, you'll be on the way if you're near the city center, it's no trouble! Come, come, let me introduce you to my husband…"

Sibel led Kaitlin softly toward the car before she could protest. As soon as the introductions were made between her and the tall dark and handsome man in the driver's seat, who stepped out of the vehicle to shake her hand and identified himself as Engin, Kaitlin took her seat in the back of the car like a happy little kid.

"You ladies enjoyed the meeting?" Engin asked, leaning in to give his wife a kiss on the cheek.

"Oh, *hayatim*, I've gotten used to what was awaiting us since, as you know, Leyla would tell me about this organization all the time. But you had to see Kaitlin over here! She practically fell asleep!"

"Oh, no, it wasn't that bad for me either, don't worry," Kaitlin chuckled, blushing. "I was just, I don't know, expecting to see some sort of a... cocktail hour, appetizers and background music playing or something like that I guess..."

"Ooh, fancy, is that how it's done back in... where are you from?"

"She's from Canada, *Engincim*," Sibel told her husband, placing a strand of silky hair behind her left ear with a perfectly-pink-manicured hand.

What language are they speaking? Kaitlin thought. "Toronto, Ontario. In Canada. Yeah. Definitely had a good time when I was working there... And you guys are from....?"

"Canada. Nice. Nice," Engin chipped in. "We're from Istanbul, Turkey. But I've been in Ontario before, for a meeting. Visited Niagara Falls. Spectacular! How long ago were you there last?"

"Fourteen months ago," Kaitlin stated. Yes, she had been counting the months *exactly* since she'd come to Stavanger soon after their wedding. "Sibel, have you been there as well?"

"Oh, no, no. I wish! I was home taking care of the kids! These men, so lucky sometimes! *Degilmi canim?*" she tickled her husband's chin, as he let out an endearing laugh.

How in the world do they manage to stay so in love? Kaitlin thought. And with children too! They were apparently also calling each other some endearing nicknames in their language.

"I take it your husband's in the oil business too, with you participating in the same Club as Sibel and all?" Engin asked her, looking at her in the back seat from the window mirror.

"Yup, that's correct. Statoil. And yourself?"

"Nice," Engin smiled. "That's where I initially applied, remember, *canim?*"

"Yes, yes," Sibel picked up where her husband left off. "Engin's at Aker Solutions..."

Their conversation lasted a bit longer than expected as they got stuck in a sea of Audis and Volvos. How a city as small as this managed to attract so many car-riders that flooded the main highway during rush hour was still a mystery to Kaitlin.

"That's going to be... my stop... right there!" Kaitlin exclaimed twenty minutes later. "Before that turn on to your bridge. You can drop me off next to the market, it's fine!"

"You sure?" Sibel asked her from the rearview mirror right before Kaitlin got out. "Ok. Oh Kaitlin, by the way, I try to hit the gym every Monday, Wednesday, and Friday. It's when our little ones are in school, so I try to make the most of it. I was going to go today actually, but, alas, Women's Club was tonight and I was feeling too lazy to step out of the house twice today! Care to join me tomorrow afternoon for my make-up session?"

"Tomorrow?" Kaitlin asked. "In town? Which gym?"

"You know *Elixia*, right? By the Clarion Hotel?" Sibel asked.

"Yeah, I've been there a couple of times myself actually," Kaitlin lied to Sibel for the second time: she'd only been there once, and the only exercise she'd gotten was going up the stairs inside to fully check out the premises.

"Great! You have membership? I can let you in as a guest… Oh! That is, if you and your husband don't have early Saturday plans together? Sorry! Where are my manners?"

Engin shook his head side-to-side playfully. "My wife's become so obsessed with the gym lately, she forgets not everyone else is like her! Luckily it's become routine. I love spending that extra time with our babies whenever I can."

"Aww, it's a good thing, then," Kaitlin said as she smiled, inching closer to Sibel now in the front seat. "And, yes, I do. Have membership, I mean. And I think we're free tomorrow during the day, so it probably won't be a problem. But I haven't been there in a while. You could tell I'm in poor shape from the way I was back in the elevator, couldn't you?" Kaitlin laughed.

"Oh, hush, don't be hard on yourself," Sibel said with a smile. "You'll show me your stuff tomorrow. What's your cell number? I'll give you a ring, and we can record each other's digits."

As they saved each other's names on their similar, white-framed smart phones and waved goodbye, Kaitlin stood outside by the entry to their building a little longer before going in. She put her arms around her body tighter to warm herself from the sea breeze, and smiled at a passing swan, thanking her lucky stars for what must have been the umpteenth time for living in a fairytale setting such as this.

Making a new potential friend didn't hurt her upbeat mood either: she was still surprised at how smoothly their conversation seemed to have flowed. Sibel must have felt the same genuineness coming from her herself to invite her out like that so soon after having met each other. She felt good that, for the first time since she'd arrived here, she'd be meeting up with someone because she'd befriended them, not because they were simply a spouse of one of Paul's friends.

Maybe hitting the gym more often and feeling productive doing any sort of activity at the PWC would help cure her boredom after all; and she could forget about Finn easier, like she knew she should. Maybe she could finally shake off the image of his curly blonde hair, his carefree way of speech, and those eerily piercing eyes.

Chapter 6

"Hi! Sibel? Good morning, it's Kaitlin from yesterday..." Kaitlin tried to keep her voice leveled as she didn't want to seem too eager for a new friend, though her calling first had thrown *that* out the window now that she thought about it. She waited until her and Paul were on their second cup of coffee after breakfast to call her.

"Oh, hi, Kaitlin. How are you? You mean good afternoon, don't you? It's almost noon," Sibel's voice chuckled, though without a tone of mal-intent.

"Oh, you're right. I guess you can tell I'm not exactly a morning person!" Kaitlin looked at the glass clock placed above their living room's television set. 11:50. *Umm, isn't 'noon' 12:30?* Or was it 12? She often found it tended to depend on different people's views rather than general acknowledgement. Whatever the case, she felt sure this chipper lady on the phone must be a morning person.

"Hope I didn't catch you at a bad time. Just wanted to take you up on your offer of hitting the gym today, that is, if you're still interested or available, you know." *Argh, why does attempting to meet up with a new acquaintance always feel like an awkward dating situation?* Kaitlin thought. How she missed the days of environmental friendships that formed naturally on their own through people working or attending classes together.

"Yeah, yeah. I mean, no, of course not! I'm good to go, I mean! In fact, I was going to call you!"

What a cliché, sure you were, Kaitlin thought as she caught Paul shooting a curious look in her direction from the corner of his morning paper. "Great, sounds good! So, what time should we meet? And where?" As Sibel suggested they meet in front of the *Domkirke*[5] in the city center at 2:00 P.M., Kaitlin repeated the details looking at Paul, who nodded with

---

[5] Kirke: 'church' in Norwegian

encouragement from his favorite one-person couch in their living room. He was apparently going to take this opportunity to work on a report he had had due, and then meet up with his colleague and friend Tim. They decided they'd later be joining each other around six for drinks at *Timbuktu* —her pick, as she enjoyed the lounge music they played.

The thought that Little Miss *Jeanette* might also be joining them burned at the back of Kaitlin's mind, but she didn't dare verbalize it. She was grateful her husband had suggested spending some time out before dinner at home; and having drinks together in town would be nice for both of them. Of course if they were going to have early drinks, they weren't going to follow it up with dinner out unless it was a special occasion to celebrate. No. That would be too much 'unnecessary spending'. *Whatever,* she thought with a sigh. She was determined to just enjoy herself a nice Saturday despite the paranoid workings of her brain as of late.

***

Two hours later, the two women were jogging side by side on the treadmill on the premises located among the few high-rise buildings in the region, right behind the lakeside *Radisson Blu*. More particularly, Sibel was jogging while Kaitlin was attempting her usual, comfortable zone from back home: jogging moderately for five minutes only, then walking it off for ten minutes. She'd started exercising in Toronto right before her wedding, where sometimes her ten minutes of walking off her running would become fifteen minutes, or even longer, and soon it would have been at least half an hour and Kaitlin would then call it a day.

Something told her Sibel was not intent on allowing her new gym buddy to slow her down. In fact, she seemed determined to have Kaitlin be the one to speed it up to rise up to her level.

"Oh, come on, I've seen you run faster to the elevator in your heels yesterday!" Sibel stated with a smile (miraculously not out of breath despite doing a marathon on the machine non-stop for fifteen minutes.) "If you're doing the stop-and-go thing, you have to run for two minutes then walk for one: *that's* the fastest way to burning off calories."

"Are you kidding? I wish I was in good shape like you. And you said you have children? That's, simply, wow, amazing!"

"Yup, yup. Thanks. Hakan is three and Aylin is two. They're both at the British school: the only one that allowed them to be schooled at that age." Sibel said, lowering her eyes, which had until then been glued to the television screen. "Aylin actually did the sweetest thing this morning. I was having my second cup of tea when…"

Kaitlin looked at Sibel in amazement as an adorable-sounding scene of a little girl trying to get her mother's attention was being recollected. She realized s*he* wanted to have things to talk about as well, and more opportunities to have people to share with. Her rather pessimistic outlook perhaps *may* just have been what increased the distance between Paul's friends' wives and herself, she sometimes thought. But Kaitlin just hated being fake: that was all. She'd simply been unable to have as warm a conversation with any of those ladies as she managed to have with this person besides her after just one day.

She also never thought she'd miss the days of being in front of a computer all day, working, doing *something* requiring *some* intellect and thought, benefiting *someone*. Often terming her days as a student-intern in college as 'boring office work', where she often couldn't manage to stick out through an entire semester, Kaitlin now felt longing for those days of at least having some place to dress up and be motivated for every day: returning home feeling tired but accomplished.

Paul was always talking to her about the crazy things his colleagues said and did throughout the day. He was mistaken if he thought that his closeness with his male buddies automatically meant their wives would also be close. She yearned for social interaction and having events to look forward to more than she cared to admit. As temporarily fun as her husband's 'cheer up' weekend shopping sprees with her and their time trying to do sporty outdoor activities together were, they just weren't cutting it in the long-run. And this twice-a-month woman's club thing didn't look like it was going to be enough to excite her, either.

Sometimes Kaitlin feared she was thinking too selfishly, especially when she heard from the still-struggling single friends of hers like Sandy; and thought maybe she really *should* humbly be looking forward to motherhood and becoming the best homemaker she could be. After all, there were also stories around her of couples trying for years to become pregnant, to no avail. It wasn't like there was a guarantee she would be able to tell Paul one day "Ok" and then, poof! Magically that night would lead to pregnancy—and she knew that. Nevertheless, times of such thinking would often be followed by silly arguments over housekeeping or budget-spending with her husband, as well as swallowing her fears with ice cream and self-pity on days when Kaitlin realized she'd just spent an entire day watching three soap opera episodes back to back. And, just like that, any desire for having a baby with him soon would then disappear.

"They're my reason for waking up every morning, I'm telling you..." Sibel continued, finally lowering the speed of the treadmill by several decimals until she could walk without panting. "...You'll always regret it the longer you wait."

"I can imagine it's great despite the challenges, yeah," Kaitlin said, insisting on her average-paced walking. "But, like I said, it's only been a year of marriage for us, and I still want to work or at least be a little more active outside the house first, so..."

"...It's none of my business, you're right," Sibel interrupted. "So please don't misunderstand. It's just, I don't know, I just feel like I understand where you're coming from already, though we've just met. Maybe it has to do with what you shared yesterday at the meeting. About your previous career? You don't know this yet, but, I was actually involved in a major catering organization in Istanbul for two years before coming here. I was fresh out of university then, and had quite a few suitors. Engin saw me at an event and, that was it! He asked my father for my hand in marriage and snatched me right up! I became a young mother when all the girls at work were telling me I was crazy! But I caught up with some of them online recently, and with an exception or two, I'm still seeing that they're bar-hopping at thirty! Looking for guys! I mean, I don't want to judge, but it's crazy to me..."

Kaitlin nodded politely, but secretly wondered whether a little jab was also being thrown her way. She wasn't exactly bar-hopping anymore, but she sure was nearing thirty. Sibel looked to her to be around two, maybe three years older than herself. Sure, she realized she similarly felt bad for her friends like Sandy at times, still trying to find Mr. Right. But wasn't Sandy also doing something meaningful still pursuing her dream in New

York City? *Everyone dreams of time off when leading busy lives,* Kaitlin often reasoned, *yet when free time is 'all' you have, you can tend to feel like a loser.* "To each their own, Sibel. Not all women have motherhood as their first priority. As for me, I guess I'm still trying to see things out…"

It was now Sibel's turn to smile politely and continue her work-out. *I hope I didn't offend her,* Kaitlin thought. "So, what do you think?" Sibel finally asked later, ever-so-slightly out of breath, pressing the 'cool down' button that slowed the treadmill's speed even further. "Think you can handle this with me a couple of times a week?"

Kaitlin looked at the screen in front of her: she'd managed to get 3.5 miles to Sibel's 5. That wasn't too bad, was it?

"Well, I've got to give it to you: you're my new inspiration, Sibel!" She chuckled while placing the white towel she'd hung on the machine's handle on the back of her neck to absorb sweat, right before hitting the 'cool down' button. "It's been fun and I'd love to definitely do this at least *once* a week with you, for sure." Yes, some harsh realities of life were discussed, but, so what? Kaitlin realized she enjoyed Sibel's sincerity with her, which hit her like a breath of fresh air after too many forced conversations with other friend-candidates she'd met in Norway.

"Boo! Only once?" Sibel started, reaching over her head to fix her ponytail. "I'm just kidding, no problem. I guess I'm just looking for a partner-in-crime to be as obsessed as I am! That is how my husband put it, didn't he? You heard him."

Kaitlin nodded and smiled at her while secretly wondering just why someone fit and seemingly happy and her-hands-full-with-kids like Sibel was so attached to going to the gym. Did they have something in common? "I take it that it must be nice for you just to get out of the house too, yeah? Coming here so often, I mean?"

"Exactly, yeah," Sibel replied. "I mean I love my angels but I *do* need the time to get a little break now and then, definitely! I can't deny that! They can be a handful!"

"But the gym?" Kaitlin continued, eyeing her slim yet curvy physique ever slightly enviously. At 5'7 and 135 pounds, Kaitlin wasn't exactly pudgy, but she definitely knew she could use a firmer tummy and buttocks area.

"Oh honey, let's be real. Where else am I going to go in this town? How many shoes and tops can a woman *really* buy?"

"I hear that," Kaitlin chuckled in response.

"And besides, I guess it's the satisfaction of knowing I'm doing something good for *myself* after trying so hard to look out for Engin and our angels, you know?" Sibel said.

"*Me* time," Kaitlin nodded. "I get you." She wondered if Paul would be cool with them having a regular babysitter too if they decided on having children—when they weren't in school, anyway. One of the best things about living in Stavanger was the high wages that took some of the shock off the expensive cost-of-living. Yet Paul had been raised to save up for 'the big house back in Montreal' he idealized for when his Norway contract was over—for them and their 'at least three' children that he would always tell her he imagined. Kaitlin sighed.

Arriving home at a quarter past three, Kaitlin plopped her tired body on the flat surface of the wooden shoe-rack by the entrance. She stared at her reflection from the mirrored-closet across from her: her cheeks were pink with blood and she had genuinely gained a cheerful disposition. *It couldn't just be from the exercise*, she thought, though it undoubtedly must have helped, as she often did that outside alone or with Paul, albeit at a much slower pace. No, this inner sense of satisfaction also must have come from the social aspect of her day with Sibel. It had been especially fun to drop by a local seaside café/bar afterward to continue their girlish chit chat.

Social contact. *From contacts I've made on my own*, she thought. *Oh, what a concept.*

Kaitlin pulled open the closet to place her running shoes and immediately spotted the black running-jacket she had on the previous Tuesday. Smiling with excitement, she reached inside its right pocket. There it was still. Finn's card. She recalled better now: he had definitely mentioned there being some sort of group in the forest he was working with. How more *unusual* would it be for her to want to get to know more about those people, as she had just tried to do with this Women's Club? It could be harmless, too, couldn't it?

Besides, she doubted it'd be a volunteer thing, if a company name like 'Inc.' was involved. That's why he had given her his card, wasn't it? He might have been an employer who was also responsible for recruitment, or something of the sort. Perhaps earning some cash would make her feel good. She had to at least try and satisfy her curiosity. What harm could getting in a little more working-girl-time for herself (before becoming a mother) bring?

Whether or not to dial the number ran through Kaitlin's head the entire fifteen minutes she was in the shower, preparing to doll herself up to meet Paul for pre-dinner drinks later. Feeling energized and pumped up from both the amount of socialness she'd just experienced and doing physical activity, "oh what the heck," Kaitlin told herself. After all, though she was sure it was nothing even if Jeanette *had* joined Paul and Tim for lunch, she was feeling that her husband apparently would have continued to hold it from her for whatever reason.

Reminded of how awkward she'd felt upon discovering her husband's apparently secret friendship with his middle school 'buddy', Kaitlin felt the final kick of motivation she needed. With her hair wrapped up in a white towel and trembling fingers despite the courageous decision she'd just felt she'd made, she took a deep breath and dialed the number on the card. Right then and there she had a thought: that the risk she was taking calling up some mysterious stranger in the forest would either be the end of her sanity or the beginning of it, if it indeed led to some cool work and interaction. It took only two rings before his husky, deep voice picked up the receiver. "Hello?"

Kaitlin realized suddenly she had become incapable of letting out a sound, preparing herself to hang up. He didn't know her number, after all, so she still could.

"Ms. Kaitlin Maverick, are you there?"

***

With the smell of the burning logs complementing his earthy cologne, Finn took a deep breath as he glanced again at the number on his smart phone. 42 37 41 86. *Yup.* It was Kaitlin's number alright. The one he had known even before her encounter with him the other day. But that didn't matter. Even if he hadn't known her digits, he could instinctively feel the presence of her shy and reluctant energy mixed with brave spirit—even before she'd uttered any words. He was planning to wait another day or two before making up an excuse to have located her number, but luckily he didn't have to as she had called him, just like he knew she would.

She hadn't yet hung up. Finn didn't want to miss the chance to make her feel at ease.

"Ms. Kaitlin, is it you?" he feigned again, as if he didn't know. "Can you hear me?"

"Uh, yes, yes, hi, Mr. Du Feu. It is, indeed. How did you know it was me?"

How adorably naïve she sounds, Finn thought with a smirk.

"Well, you *are* the only one I gave my personal card with my personal number to recently. And regular clients often call from office numbers, which show up as such on my line, so…"

"Office numbers?" Kaitlin asked. "Do you mean landline numbers? People still use those these days?"

"Well, some still do, yes," Finn chuckled. *This Kaitlin sure doesn't seem to miss the chance to turn the topic of conversation away from herself,* he thought. "But some cell phone numbers are also used purely for business, which you must know. Mine, I use for both personal *and* business. But, hey, anyway. I'm glad you called, Ms. Kaitlin. How have you been?"

"I've been alright, great, in fact, thanks for asking," Kaitlin responded nervously.

Undoubtedly, she is questioning herself as to why she is even calling a strange man she just met. A peek at the antique mirror stretching horizontally throughout the entire region above the fireplace allowed Finn to see that his smile still had not left his face. He was glad he was enjoying himself, despite performing a duty.

"And yourself?" Kaitlin finally asked. "How have you been? You disappeared pretty quickly after helping me find my way the other day."

He knew this would come up. "I'm doing very well, Ms. Kaitlin. I'm much more glad that you're well, though. You looked pretty down that day. Well, more *pretty* than *down*, but, hey, I can still tell when a lady is upset." All women liked compliments, Finn knew, but especially the truly pretty ones like Kaitlin. They always ironically seemed to need it more than the others, in his experience.

"Well, thank you," Kaitlin responded. "But yes, I'm fine. And no. I wasn't feeling down or anything that day. I was just downright lost! Come on! I was also shocked, frankly, to find myself in a forest just a few-minutes-walk from the town center…" She was sounding a bit more relaxed now. "Which brings me to my question, the one you still haven't answered. How do you explain the distance factor and where exactly did you go so fast after dropping me off?"

"Is this an interrogation, Ms. Kaitlin? I helped you, as you say, and yet you're not satisfied? Am I getting this correct?" Finn waited patiently for her to snap, to put her wall down and give in to him. After all, he knew mind games worked very well on sensitive women like Kaitlin.

"Wait a second. What? I'm just curious," Kaitlin said defensively. "Since I'm not very familiar with the area like you are. And just what do you mean by…?"

"…Calm down, Ms. Kaitlin," Finn continued, chuckling, "I was just busting your chops. Curiosity killed the cat, they say. Look, you seem to have a lot of questions, and I can't blame you. But, yes, you're right. I really *am* more familiar, like you said. I was just returning from town when I saw you. You looked lost, and I wanted to help. And I just hurried back to the cabin after bringing you to safety. Didn't want to keep the gang waiting."

"The Group, Inc. you mean? You, guys, live and work together if I remember correctly?"

Finally. She seemed to be over his little disappearing act. "Yes, yes. Everyone's like family here. The cabin has become our home away from home, truly." Finn really hated chit-chatting for a longer period of time than he had to. He preferred getting straight to the point. "You have to come check it out sometime. And, not to worry, Ms. Kaitlin. We would welcome you at our office on the main floor. Our personal rooms are upstairs and in the basement. You wouldn't feel awkward or anything. You'd just be like a regular client, visiting to discuss paper shipment details".

"I'd be like a regular client, you say," Kaitlin's voice had lost its enthusiasm. "Right, right, well, thank you for your invitation. But, I actually…"

Did he hear a tone of disappointment in her voice? "Well, not like just *any* client, Mrs. Maverick. You'd be a… guest of honor, what with your tales of fancy Toronto, we would *love* to hear your stories of the big city. Gee, I hear they've got buildings as tall as trees o'er there!" He did his best imitation of a farmer he saw from the movies.

Kaitlin finally managed a laugh. "Yes, Toronto's great, but Stavanger has got mountains to take on our skyscrapers! Anyway, thank you, again, for your invitation. Like I was saying…it's why I wanted to call, actually. I mean, I'm sort of in-between jobs here. I was wondering if you, guys, or any company you may work with, I don't know, had any positions available. You finally put a name to it by the way: a paper shipment company, you say? Well, either way, do you guys require Norwegian like almost every other company here?"

Finn had to fight the urge to burst out laughing. She was actually kind of sweet, this one, he decided. And proud, too, apparently, coining her situation as 'in-between jobs' when in reality she was obviously a kept woman.

He was accustomed to Daddy's girls: rich, educated, yet aimless. This was new territory for him. *A bored housewife*, he thought with a smile. He had to play along. "No, no, English is fine. As you know, almost every Norwegian speaks it fluently. And we have more of an international clientele, so, just English is sufficient. But, hey, why don't you come in and we can all discuss this in person. It'll give you a better idea of what we do, and how you can contribute, if you choose to. It's a lot of 'home' work, phone calls, seldom trips out to companies, other cities, etc."

"Yeah, you know, I was actually going to ask about that as well". Kaitlin continued in a calmer tone of voice, once again. "How come your office is in the woods and not in the town center or near any other business buildings in other parts of the city?"

"Well, Ms. Kaitlin, as I believe I've just explained, we mainly work from home," Finn said impatiently. "And we love it. When you're doing work involving nature, like we do with our paper, being amongst as much green as possible, for both work *and* as a living arrangement, it's indescribably amazing. Once again, you just have to see it for yourself!"

"Ok, ok, I think you've convinced me!" Kaitlin exclaimed. "You've convinced me. Norway consists of amazingly beautiful natural scenery, so, yes, I can understand. I think. When can I come in? Do I bring a CV? But, oh wait!"

Excited like a fresh-graduate out looking for work for the first time, Finn thought. *This is starting off even smoother than expected.*

"I don't exactly know the address, do I? How do your clients get there? There aren't street coordinates in the woods, are there?"

You're a classic, Ms. Kaitlin Maverick. Of course not. "I usually meet a client, or a new *friend,* somewhere else, and we walk to our cabin together. It's much easier that way, you're right. But once you come, I assure you, it'll become very easy to keep coming after that. How's Monday for you?"

"Mmm… Monday?" Kaitlin stammered. "Hmm, let me see…"

Yeah, ok, Toronto. Like you have somewhere more exciting to be on a weekday when your husband is at work. Finn had to admit he was enjoying moments like this more than he'd care to vocalize.

"I think I'm free around noon," Kaitlin finally exclaimed.

No, no, you're not going to call the shots. "At noon I have to be somewhere. How about at 2:00 p.m. sharp. By the statue I dropped you off the other day?"

"Ok, but, you or someone can escort me back to town afterward, right?" Kaitlin asked. "I mean, I can only stay around for an hour. I don't want to get lost or get home too late, you know?"

"No problem. Will do. So, see you Monday then?" He wanted to cut it short and sweet. *Mission almost accomplished.*

"Alright, thanks for offering to pick me up. I'll see you there. 2:00 p.m., with my CV!"

Her CV. Cute. "Until then, Ms. Kaitlin."

***

Kaitlin paid special attention to cooking some of her husband's favorite dishes that evening before heading out to meet him for pre-dinner drinks. She started with tomato soup, his favorite. And, of course, he enjoyed two sides besides the main dish. Usually Kaitlin just conjured up a salad as the second dish next to the pasta or rice that was already accompanying some cooked vegetables or chopped meats in sauce, but not tonight. Tonight, Kaitlin made sure she also cooked some soy beans in the style Paul liked. Besides, she was still a little buzzed from the surprisingly fun time she'd just enjoyed with Sibel, so she was in good spirits to cook.

She was possibly going to find some work on Monday, and she didn't intend to share the details with Paul. Not until she was sure of what in the world she herself would be doing, if anything, anyway. So she figured she'd tell him she would be lunching with Sibel this time. The concept of fibbing made her feel guilty like hell and so she wanted to make sure she did something good for him; and for her husband that tended to be more of eating his favorite dish than being greeted by his wife in sexy lingerie or something of that sort. He'd once even dismissed doing the latter as 'trampy' the one time she'd tried it for Valentine's Day. Though she now recalled the way he *had* enjoyed it quite a bit soon afterward. *Sigh.* He often killed her buzz for nothing.

"Ok. Get it together, Kaitlin," she told herself. "Concentrate on how you're going to handle this."

She was hoping he wouldn't become upset when he found out she'd possibly be working from a remote location. She didn't even dare imagine sharing the exact truth of how she'd come to meet her boss or one of her colleagues. *Damn it!* She wasn't even sure what Finn's position was! She assumed he was in charge, but whether or not there was a higher-up, she didn't yet know. All Kaitlin knew was that she didn't feel any sense of danger in meeting him again. She was excited by the intrigue he was presenting, and was certain this was perhaps a good sign, despite involving something seemingly mundane like logging and paper.

It is Norway, after all, she told herself. This might not compare to the ads she had to work on in Toronto, but she'd gladly take it even if it promised to be half as much fun.

Toronto. Toronto. What *was* it about Toronto that was bugging her at the back of her mind since her conversation with Finn earlier? Toronto. That was it! He told her she would be an 'honorable' guest because she was from some cool city like Toronto or something like that.

Had she even *told* him she was from Toronto? Or even Canada? For the life of her, Kaitlin couldn't recall. She must have mentioned it in passing that day in the woods—probably something about her being lost since she wasn't from Norway. Something like that. Could that have been it? It had to be! How else could there have been an explanation for it? As far as Kaitlin was concerned, there had also yet to be an explanation for other things as well that she still couldn't figure out. They would have to wait. She didn't want to think too much. She didn't want anything to dampen her excitement. Not yet.

Chapter 7

Standing between the glass exit doors of one of the indoor shopping centers in town, Kaitlin glanced at her reflection. Her hair still seemed to be in place, as did the tight-pulling of the belt she had added on to her navy blue, furry-hooded Canada Goose parka coat, highlighting her thin waist. Paul tried countlessly to convince her the additional belt wasn't necessary in the style of the jacket, but Kaitlin knew he was just annoyed with the curvier way it made her body frame appear, and so had stuck with her own taste in the styling of the coat anyway. She stared down at her matching boots that wrapped tightly around her legs and reached her knees over her skinny jeans—they appeared clean despite stepping on some leftover muddy-mixture from the early morning snow.

She hoped that the jeans weren't too casual. It was apparently a cabin, after all, and there wasn't an official job position to discuss yet. Besides, she *was* wearing a white button-down tunic over them, just to be safe. She just needed to outwardly come across as presentable as she felt.

Yet feelings of guilt were also panging somewhere deep around her ribs even stronger now that she and her husband managed to have themselves a nice weekend together. They'd had a laughter-filled evening Saturday, as well as a cozy Sunday indoors reading books and watching both an action-packed movie and the softly-falling snow outside their living room windows. Not a single argument had occurred. It had been remarkable.

She had deviated from her originally-planned lie of 'lunching with Sibel', which had certainly sounded more realistic to her, as they'd just gone to the gym together. But somehow her nerves got the best of her and she ended up telling Paul over their Sunday brunch that the two would be simply going to the gym, again. "Already?" he'd asked. "Didn't you guys go just yesterday? But, hey, you ladies seem to have hit it off, so I'm glad, honey." Kaitlin had felt his sincerity.

Although his criticisms and expectations were what caused her fleeting moments of unhappiness at times, that man truly wanted her happy, didn't he? She knew that he knew the mostly-solo activities they did as a couple over the weekends wouldn't keep her satisfied in the long run. What a funny thing love was.

And love indeed is a 'thing' all in itself, isn't it? Kaitlin pondered. *Like an offspring, resulting from a twosome's union: a relationship forms love. And when that relationship dies, it must very seldom be due to the death of love. In fact, at times that love can be felt as a stander-by surrounding the periphery of a couple in dispute-watching with a disappointed pout. Like a child, or even the beloved family pet, when that same couple is in a happy mood and is able to get along, it too is happy, walking besides them with a smile. No. Relationships seldom die due to love's death. So why do they?*

Cotton-snow covered the top of the trees aligning the long coastal road of wooden panels, with various shipping and fishing boats Kaitlin had to walk past before making a turn toward the main harbor downtown. A ray of sunshine hit her eyes, promising warmth that never came in Stavanger—not even when the sun set well after 10 o'clock in this region during the summer. *How dare I complain of boredom when I feel so awed by the unique beauty of this land?* she pondered with guilt. *And how dare I even think of relationships dying when ours has no palpable reason to...*

Then she had another thought. What if *he* was similarly bored from their lack of close coupled-friends with whom *both* of them could derive social pleasure without the need to meet separately? Maybe she needed to give Paul's friends' cooking-loving wives another chance. Or even meet this Jeanette woman, in a guise to 'befriend' her, of course. How did that saying go? Keep your friends close, your enemies closer?

That did it. Her last thought helped to ease her guilt for planning to come home before 4 o'clock to change out of her non-gym clothes, so that Paul wouldn't become needlessly suspicious. *The damned interview in the woods better not last too long,* she thought, still squinting her eyes.

It's just temporary white-lying, Kaitlin further pressed her psyche, as yet another doll-like Norwegian baby with white-blonde hair smiled at her as he passed her by, holding his mama's hand. *If I actually start working with them, I'll tell him; and the whole thing will then cease being a problem,* she comforted herself.

Checking her wristwatch and taking a deep breath, Kaitlin started walking toward the statue where Finn said he would pick her up at 14:00 sharp. Usually someone who never looked straight at the crowds of people passing her by in the busy streets of Toronto, here in Stavanger she had gotten accustomed to looking at everyone in the eye, mainly because it felt instinctively like the right thing to do due to some inner need for human contact. *It's as if all of our fates have seemingly become intertwined enough to make us all be present in the same small city at the same time,* she'd often think.

Today, Kaitlin was looking all around her for another reason: she didn't want any of Paul's colleagues or their various professional acquaintances to see her meet a strange handsome man and get any wrong ideas. It wasn't exactly after work hours, but one could never be too careful. There were more cries coming from the seagulls surrounding Stavanger harbor than any of the numerous amounts of children walking past her with their mommies or even daddies likely on paternal leave: most of them much younger than herself, as the government here was actually assisting wed or even unwed couples in every way imaginable in order to encourage reproduction for population growth.

Norwegian babies seemingly did not cry in public. *Yet another reason to be in awe of this place,* Kaitlin thought as she passed by more smiling babies. *Maybe I just need a good cry...*

Chirpy barking coming from a small dog in the arms of a fashionably-dressed young blonde to her left made Kaitlin turn her body in the direction away from the harbor; and sure enough, there he was. His back was turned to her, and he was leaning against the statue of the old man: some historic writer and contributor to the city or whatnot from what Kaitlin had read somewhere. His dark leather jacket seemed too light for the rough weather that day, yet fit perfectly across his muscular arms which were amazingly visible through the thickness of the material. *Ahem.* Kaitlin cleared her throat, both as a warning to him that she had arrived as well as a reminder to herself to stop thinking such thoughts.

"Ms. Kaitlin…," Finn turned around without a single hint of any surprise that she had arrived. "It's 5 past 2 o'clock. You're a little late. I'm shocked."

"Oh, five minutes doesn't count," Kaitlin teased back. "I hope, anyway. I mean, you know, for those of us from a big city it's always more fashionable to be at least 15 minutes late, actually."

"Yes, but for a job interview, Ms. Katlin?"

Kaitlin was stunned. Oh, darn. Had she gone too far into friendly conversation with a potential professional contact? This was very unlike her. "You're right, Mr. Du Feu. I, I was kidding, of course. You know, the icy roads sort of make it difficult to walk very fast…"

"Ms. Kaitlin. I was kidding as well, come on," Finn told her. "Relax. And, please, it's Finn. Right this way."

Immediately Kaitlin felt herself relax again, as she followed him past the town lake, and in the direction of houses that stood higher on a hill than the rest of sentrum. "Just follow me." There was that soothing tone of voice again, lowering her defenses. He was walking about three steps in front of her, looking back at her from time to time without a sound, motioning her with a tilt of his head toward the direction of the right back corner street from behind the statue.

Anyone else walking ahead of her would have annoyed Kaitlin deeply and made her feel like some little kid being guided, but in this circumstance she put up with it and didn't attempt to walk up to his side. After all, he would have allowed for that to happen if he had wanted to chat, wouldn't he? Maybe he really *was* being professional, taking this 'job interview' idea more seriously than she'd instinctively given him credit for. Besides, what did the two of them really have to talk about? The weather? Was their random chitchat as pure strangers the other day what had perhaps caused Kaitlin to confuse all sense of direction when he'd walked her back to town in the first place? This time Kaitlin made sure to keep her attention very focused on their surroundings. She had to solve the mystery still lingering in her mind.

"We're here!" Finn exclaimed in what only seemed to be another five minutes or so. To Kaitlin's surprise, the walk to the cabin area took a much shorter time than she remembered—and they had walked only about three blocks past some private houses from what she counted. Not too difficult for her to retrace their steps if she were to come to the cabin again. Also, not as woodsy an area as she recalled, either. *Although I never did exactly see the cabin the other day when we met*, she reminded herself.

Her mother always *did* tell her she often had her head in the clouds, oblivious to her surroundings, making her appear aloof to potential friends and naïve to 'predators' like her toxic ex-boyfriends and two ex-bosses who had hit on her. She was angry with herself at the time for having shared so much information with her mother, yet now she was glad, since everything her mother had warned her about had annoyingly come true. She was actually missing her being so far away. She was glad her big brother Aidan was working at a law firm in Toronto now, taking care of their mother, she herself being now so far.

"It's not as far as I thought it would be," Kaitlin said, stopping in front of a grand two-story, red-brick house with a vivacious garden full of many different kinds of flowers typical of Norway, and classical Roman-looking statues, which were not. She felt all her homesickness temporarily fade now as a deeper sense of intrigue took over. Was *this* majestic beauty what Finn had simply called a 'cabin'?

"You got the idea of how to get here now, I imagine? I hope I didn't walk too fast for you. I want to introduce you to The Group before they head out. I think Tan should be here with Meredith; I think you'll love them the most," Finn said with yet another characteristic wink, ringing the doorbell to the right of intricately-designed doors in a stand-out shade of crimson red different from the rest of the house. Kaitlin smiled back reassuringly, though she was kind of beginning to hope Finn's winking had become some sort of tic throughout the years, and that he didn't mean anything else by it.

"That's odd," Finn said, ringing the doorbell again as Kaitlin had her eyes fixed on a particularly charming marble statue of an adorable cherub.

"Coming!" a husky male voice resounded from just behind the door. Kaitlin could make out additional footsteps descending some sort of stairs. They were definitely women's heels.

"Dude, you didn't tell us we had company today," the muscular man wearing only a white undershirt and shorts claimed, giving Finn some sort of a bro-hug.

What is this? Some sort of frat house? Kaitlin thought, trying to plaster on a polite smile.

"Oh but I did, I did, my man," Finn told the guy. "How can you forget? Tan, this is Kaitlin. Ms. Kaitlin, this is Tan. You have to excuse his unusual lack of clothing and manners today."

"Kaitlin! Oh, that's right! Your visit was today, wasn't it? Nice to meet you," Tan reached out his hand. Peeking behind his shoulder at the young woman wearing an oversized man's t-shirt over nothing but burgundy pumps, Kaitlin wasn't sure where that hand had just been, so she shook it as lightly as she could.

"Uh, yes, you, too. Thank you," she replied. "It seems like we must have caught you at a bad time. I was thinking these would be your working hours. Mr. Du Feu…"

"Finn," he exclaimed, rolling his eyes this time. "Ms. Kaitlin, no need…"

"Oh yes, yes, *Finn*!" Kaitlin teased. "Yes, thank you again for walking me here, but, really, I think I can find my way back now, and just come back another time when everyone's more…"

"Nonsense!" Finn cut in again, "You have to excuse these lovebirds: working from home gets them distracted sometimes."

"Hi, Kaitlin, was it? I'm Meredith," the child-faced young woman finally spoke, inching closer to the door. "Please, come in! No need to feel awkward. We apologize for losing track of the time. Come in, come in…" Looking at Meredith's casual way of flipping her long, straight brown hair over her shoulder (so at-ease in front of strange company despite obviously having been just caught sleeping with her lover), Kaitlin began getting a strangely off feeling at the bottom of her stomach. Yet another part of her was telling her that she had come too far to chicken out now. And the presence of another woman there *did* somehow relax her –away from any feeling of immediate danger, anyway.

"Ok, if you guys say so, thanks," she smiled, taking off her coat to hang it on the reindeer-horned coatrack just behind the door, and carefully removing her boots. She'd learned by now a lot of people in Norway took their shoes off upon entering each other's homes. When she turned around, she guessed that all three of them had already gone into what must have been the living room, for the sound of the television was on. Something told Kaitlin it wasn't exactly unusual for these people, for some reason, to entertain visitors in such a casual manner.

Glancing at all the modern art hanging on the walls, Kaitlin followed the sound of a news anchor saying something in Norwegian and was surprised to see all three of their attention on the screen, and not on her: their 'visitor'. *Some 'home office' this is*, Kaitlin thought. There were modern touches like oblong-shaped vases and little decorations of stone owls and horses that Kaitlin noticed —typical of simple Scandinavian design. Yet they were strangely positioned in front of rather extremely antiquated furniture. Kaitlin couldn't help but especially notice the golden-rimmed furnace positioned right between the entrance and the living room, as well as the two matching classical armless burgundy armchairs with golden rims at either side of a spacious and modern-looking black leather couch. As Kaitlin continued looking around, something felt missing or out of place, yet she couldn't quite put her finger on it.

"Kaitlin, come on, don't just stand there. Come take a seat!" Meredith called out, heels still on, which Kaitlin guessed must have been used only indoors, as the two men had slipped into house slippers. She was glad she decided to wear her matching navy socks that morning and not some old white ones she'd almost put on, thinking they wouldn't be visible inside her boots.

"Ms. Kaitlin is a professional and a very polite lady, unlike you, Mer!" Finn teased. "Ms. Kaitlin. Please. Do come and sit down."

"Of course, yeah, thanks everyone." Kaitlin stammered as she flopped down on one of the burgundy seats, feeling more lost than she was in the woods the other day. "I'm so amazed by the lovely place you've got here."

"Do you speak Norwegian, Kaitlin?" Tan turned his attention away from the television to her. She was surprised at how comfortably both he and Meredith were just sitting there, half naked in front of both her and Finn—dressed up formally and to the nines in comparison.

"Uh, no, no, I'm afraid I don't," Kaitlin responded. "My husband has learned it quite well though!" There it was again, she realized: her marriage brought up in conversation, unasked for. "Mr... I mean, Finn, told me it wasn't a requisite to work in your business. Am I correct?"

"No, of course, English is fine," Tan continued, with a smile playing on the corners of his mouth now. "Your husband, so I take it, he's not Norwegian. Where's he from?"

"He's from Canada, like me; though his parents migrated to Montreal from Budapest sometime after the second World War, I think," Kaitlin stammered. "Mine have been in Ontario for generations, with the exception of my grandmother. But, yeah, like I said, he knows a little Norwegian since he's been in Stavanger for over three years now."

"I see. And you, Kaitlin, how long have you been here?" Tan continued. Kaitlin noticed Finn clearing his throat, causing Meredith to abruptly get up to fix something in the open kitchen just behind the living room, right in front of a set of stairs leading to the second floor.

"Oh, me, I've only been here a little over a year now. Yeah. We officially got married in Toronto late last summer, and, here we are! But anyway, I do speak *French*, though. My late grandmother migrated to Toronto from Nice. She and grandpa would speak it all the time to me when I was growing up. I also took it in school, and, well, of course, when you're brought up in a place like Canada..."

"...He must have a good job here, then," Tan cut in.

"I'm sorry? Oh, my husband." Kaitlin continued. "Yes. He's at Statoil. He's a computer expert. He's very good. So the company snatched him from Canada straight away!" Kaitlin didn't remember talking about Paul this much so early in conversation with anyone else. She decided to switch the topic to why she stated she was there in the first place. "But, I majored in Communications in college, and worked in Advertising for a few years in Toronto before coming here. I brought my CV to give you, guys, a better idea of myself..." Kaitlin reached nervously into her large shoulder bag containing her thin pink folder. Miraculously, the sheet of paper still hadn't gotten wrinkled inside. *Good*, she thought.

"Ms. Kaitlin likes to get straight to business, something I liked about her right off the bat," Finn said, winking at Kaitlin, much to her chagrin. *How can his wink be both annoying and simultaneously charming?* she thought.

"I can see that," Tan affirmed, "yet, did you tell her about what it is that we do here, Finn?"

Good question, Kaitlin thought, one that *she* should have asked in more detail before running her mouth about her language skills and her husband's line of work. "I was just going to ask that myself, yes. I mean, I know you guys work with... paper..."

"...Working with paper, huh?" Tan laughed, cutting in before she could finish her sentence once again. "But so does almost every other company out there in the world using documentation, now don't they?"

"Well, yes, but *we* deal with its actual *literal* production, Tan," Finn addressed before Kaitlin could say anything. "Now, don't be a wise ass. You're confusing Ms. Kaitlin here." It was the first time she had heard him utter foul language. Although it didn't exactly suit his refined appearance, it sure added a certain appealing toughness to his personality.

"You haven't met Bjorn yet," Finn continued. He's gone skiing in Sirdal with Anja at the moment. They're our other housemates. Now, he and I are the ones in charge of the logging from this cabin. We deliver to several paper mills connected to Norske Skog."

"...Which is the largest paper company in the world, located in Oslo," Tan interrupted. "...Yes, yes. And that concludes the boring introduction, folks!"

"Tan!" Meredith turned her fit torso away from the kitchen counter to shoot him a raised eyebrow with a stern expression that belied her almost fragile, girlish voice.

"I'm just trying to explain playfully, guys," Tan snickered, "we don't want Kaitlin to become bored with all this paper talk, do we? There's *more* to us, after all."

"He's been in too much of a playful mood today, guys, as you can tell," Meredith called out, setting some cutleries on a plastic serving tray. "I apologize on his behalf."

Kaitlin noticed that the girl's cheeks were blushing with pink, adding an extra soft quality to her petite facial features. "Oh Meredith, you didn't have to!" she called out, standing up from her armchair. "Do you want me to help you with anything?" She was surprised at how relaxed she was feeling with these people already. This was no typical job interview, that was for sure.

"No, no, thanks, Kaitlin. It's just pre-prepared banana cake. I just heated it up a little bit. Don't worry about it," Meredith came back to the living room and set white porcelain plates with exquisite designs in front of all of them –albeit Kaitlin found it strange that she served them with a plastic set of fork and knife in contrast. *Probably to dispose of quickly after I leave*, she thought. Apparently, she was not eating herself. "I forgot to ask, how does our guest take her coffee?"

"Plain with no sugar is fine for me, thank you," Kaitlin responded.

"Not even a little bit of sweet nice sugar, Ms. Kaitlin? Come on! Are you sure?" Finn teased, bringing on a smirk from Tan.

"I'm positive, Mr. *Du Feu*," Kaitlin teased back, highlighting his last name again. "The cake will be sugar enough, thank you."

"We're back to formality, I see," Finn said.

"Well, why is it ok for *you* to formally call me 'Ms. Kaitlin' when I've been asked to call you Finn?" Kaitlin shot back.

"Because, you're a lady. Look at you…" Finn replied, making Kaitlin blush further. She was certainly not expecting such a response. "I can't help but address such a lovely lady in that way. Besides, if I wanted to be formal, I would technically use your last name."

He had a point there. And why hadn't the heat in her cheeks cooled yet? She was hoping they weren't showing like Meredith's were. After all, Kaitlin could see she had at least four years or so on her, and was of course a married woman. "Thank you, that's very sweet."

"You don't have to feel embarrassed, Kaitlin," Meredith chipped in, bringing a tray with four cups of coffee. "Here we're all like family, and we believe that the best way to be productive is to be amongst those you care about, and those who care about you. If you work with us, you can be assured of that." The look she gave Tan at the end of her sentence, as if seeking approval, gave Kaitlin the feeling that this was some sort of rehearsed speech.

They must be used to explaining themselves and their peculiar work environment for every business associate or newcomer, Kaitlin tried to comfort herself.

All she could make out in response was a 'hmph' sound, followed by a nod and a smile. Having gotten the chance to look around more now, she suddenly realized what she initially found to be missing: there were no personal photos (or any other personal items, in fact, that would typically reference anything professionally related to any company, or even to these people's regular abodes, families, or backgrounds). She instinctively felt it to be rather odd.

"Well, since our charming Finn says that our *lady* guest here likes to get straight to business, why don't we do just that?" Tan said with cake in his mouth. "This is so good, honey." He blew an air kiss at Meredith, who winked at him.

What is with these people and winking? Kaitlin thought, sipping from her lavender coffee mug. She also realized she'd been so lost in observation that she hadn't even touched the cake.

"Ms. Kaitlin, you didn't even touch your cake yet." Finn said just then, making her jump in her seat, almost spilling the coffee. *Damn it,* Kaitlin thought. *I swear it's like this guy can read my mind or something.*

"I… I was just getting to it," Kaitlin managed to say. *Why haven't they asked me for my CV yet?* She'd taken it out of her bag and laid it on the table in the middle of the room where it was still untouched or even peeked at. Picking at a bite-sized piece of the beige-colored dessert, Kaitlin was surprised that it didn't taste nearly as exquisite as the plate it was served on or the fancy living space it'd been prepared in. But, she knew her manners. "Tan is right. It's absolutely delicious, thank you."

"So, Kaitlin, you said you know French. Can you read and write it comfortably as well?" Tan definitely seemed to take her professional presence there the most seriously, contrary to his jokes and the half-naked Casanova impression he'd made on Kaitlin at the door.

"Yes, yes, I can. I mean, I haven't used it much here in the past year, to tell you the truth. But, like I said, it's almost like my second native language, just like English is for most Norwegians here. So, yes, I believe it shouldn't be a problem."

"Well, good," Tan continued, "because we sure have a lot of documents here that need translating. We surprisingly have a lot of customers in France, the Pacific islands and even several African nations. They communicate with us all the time, and we've been in need of someone with a proficient knowledge of French, actually."

"Oh, yes!" Meredith chimed in. "I mean, so far, we've been getting by using online translation websites to the max! But it would definitely save us the extra time and trouble!"

"I believe I can be of help, then," Kaitlin said. She was secretly hoping she could do something dealing with her expertise area of Advertising or Communications, as stated on her CV. She had even been thinking in the back of her mind that she could perhaps come up with a campaign to make their paper business in the woods sound more interesting to woo outsiders, but, who was she to complain? *Besides, translating clientele documents could be more impressive on a CV than an empty slot to show for what I've been up to recently if needed in future job interviews, couldn't it?*

"But, please, explain to me, again, the working conditions. I mean, not everyone you work with lives here, right? Finn told me you guys were working on this floor..." Kaitlin's eyes looked around to find some sort of a classic office environment on this floor which Finn had called their main work space, yet couldn't.

"No, no," Finn laughed. It had been a while since he spoke, Kaitlin noticed. She realized she had purposely not turned her head in his direction while talking to Tan, though she could certainly feel his eyes gazing at her again, almost probing her skin. "Our main office is based in Oslo, with a lot of people working from home, as you will be, too, if you'd like. But here in central Stavanger there are five of us who work with paper, six if you include the homeowner, Lar."

"Lar? Is that short for Larry?" She had to admit she was rather impressed with the level of comfort this business had accomplished among the workers. She also hadn't missed the fact that Finn was talking to her like she was already hired as far as they were concerned. Back home, despite her credentials (and her mother's top-notch contacts), Kaitlin always had to go through several interviews and sometimes even various examinations to be hired. After a year of being home, causing her more intellectual boredom than she thought possible with all that free time which overworked professional women tended to dream about, this was a refreshing surprise.

"No. He's a very cool gentleman. A professor in fact. Yet he's always been more like a father figure to us. He likes everyone to just call him Lar." Finn's eyes remained intense, his tone serious.

"You don't ever question a man like that, Kaitlin, believe me," Meredith added. "He's so kind and so smart, so accomplished. I've been with The Group here for three years now, ever since I absolutely fell in love with his Philosophy lectures back in Trondheim."

"A professor at a university up there, I presume? How did he come to create a paper production company then?" Kaitlin asked, ever so confused.

"Yes, that's right. He's a lecturer…Very popular…Well…" Meredith started, yet Tan cut her off.

"…It's a rather long story, one you can ask him yourself when you meet him, as I'm sure you will, as a new employee. He's mostly in Oslo, but should be back next week, actually. He trusts us to do the hiring. Particularly, the job falls on myself. I'm the one in charge of, what was it that you guys called it? HR? Human Resources?" Tan turned to Finn to get an affirmation, and it was just then that Kaitlin noticed that he spoke with a unique accent, despite his perfect grammar.

"Yes. Human Resources," Kaitlin answered, along with Finn's nod. Apparently, it was Tan in charge of the hiring, and not Finn, as she had initially presumed. "Where are *you* from, Tan?"

"Originally? I'm from Turkey. But I went to both university and graduate school abroad, so…"

"Turkey! Oh wow," Kaitlin exclaimed. This was two Turkish people in a row she had met that week. *So random.* "I just made a new friend from there at this non-profit club thingy I've started attending. Cool!"

"Oh yeah? What's your friend's name?" Tan asked.

"Sibel".

"Nice name," Tan said. "My sister has the same name. They live back home, though. Is she married, too?"

Kaitlin was just beginning to ponder why on earth he would be asking that when Meredith, who visibly looked upset, cleared her throat, and then smiled just as soon as she noticed that she was being glanced at for a reaction by both Kaitlin and Finn.

"What? Nothing is coincidence, Meredith," Tan insisted. 'Maybe we're meant to include a 'new' friend of our other new friend Kaitlin here in The Group, as well, no?"

Include? That's a strange way to term business colleagues, Kaitlin thought. *Had he not meant 'hire'?* She was just starting to get an uncomfortable feeling again when Finn spoke.

"What Tan means is he's homesick for the land of his childhood," Finn smiled. "Come on, man. You don't necessarily need Turkish colleagues for that. We've got plenty of kebab stores here in Stavanger, too!"

"That's offensive, man," Tan, who wasn't laughing like Meredith was now, said with a smirk. "Turkish culture is much more than kebabs and *baklava:* your favorite."

"He's kidding, Tan," Meredith assured him with an air-blown kiss. *How quickly her look of jealousy faded,* Kaitlin thought. She was suddenly reminded of her own feelings when she'd heard the voice of that Jeanine or Jeanette or whatever 'coworker' of Paul's on the phone. She was suddenly feeling like maybe she'd overreacted a teensy bit with her own jealousy.

"Well, anyway, yes, Sibel is married, with two lovely babies. She showed me their pictures," Kaitlin explained. "She's got her hands full with lots of activities, so, I doubt she'd want to do any part-time work like this. By the way, this *does* sound like some sort of a *part-time…* arrangement… since it's working from home. Am I correct?"

"Well, yes, technically. And if you're asking about the pay, Ms. Kaitlin, it's project-based," Finn stated.

"Project-based… as in…"

"Sibel's got kids. Bummer. Motherhood kills youth, right babe?" Tan interrupted and turned around to Meredith, who just looked straight at him with no expression whatsoever. Kaitlin definitely thought it strange that a man who looked to be in his thirties could talk so judgmentally and immaturely, like some macho frat boy. *How in the world could this guy have gotten through advanced education?* Meredith, on the other hand, looked to be in her early twenties, and certainly more fragile than any stereotypically-confident, sorority-type girls in university would be. It was definitely a mystery to her how these two managed to get with one another.

"Guys?" Finn continued, "Ms. Kaitlin asked something. Well, project-based, as in: we give you a task and you get paid 1,000 Kroner when it's done," Finn continued. "Like Tan explained, we went over our workload last night. For the time being, it seems that we'll mostly be needing your translating services, so that would go for when you turn in an assignment, and…."

'Don't worry, they're usually only a couple of pages at a time," Meredith cut in, trying to reassure Kaitlin, whose face must have visibly sulked after hearing the rather low figure for the Norwegian market. 1,000 Kroner was less than 200 Canadian Dollars, after all. But then again, it was home-based work, and, what else did she really have to do? If she managed to turn in a couple of such 'projects', she could definitely buy some shoes from *Skoringen* in season or a couple of *Match* sweaters on *salg* with that kind of cash—without having to ask her husband for money.

"I understand," she said. "I think I can manage that. But I also wanted to ask about taxation and a work permit which I believe I need to apply for to get paid in Norway. I remember Paul told me…"

"…No, no, it's all cash payment until your trial period ends and you meet with Lar, so you won't need to worry about all that official stuff yet," Finn assured her. Kaitlin let out a small puff of breath. That sure fit better with her plans to delay having to share her new work situation with Paul. He would surely know everything she was up to if she were to do things like apply for a work permit from Oslo, have their response arrive in their mailbox, etc.

Kaitlin was just about to ask just how long such a 'trial period' would be when Finn slapped his thighs loudly with his palms.

"So, anyway, Ms. Kaitlin," Finn started, eyeing the entrance door to the cabin, "I believe you don't have much time, right? And we're pretty much done with telling you about our little home-slash-office here, unless you've got any other questions? Do you want to see our backyard? It's got the most amazing, peaceful vibe. It's where we spend most of our free time."

"Backyard?" Kaitlin asked, wondering how that would be relevant to attracting her as an employee. And, why exactly *had* they been doing so when they still hadn't even checked out her exact qualifications on her CV nor had she met the mysterious CEO of the company? Who was to say she wouldn't be using those very same online translation services herself? They didn't know her well enough to trust her credentials as far as she was concerned.

"Yes, and it leads out to the most amazing spot in these woods," Meredith said excitedly, adjusting the t-shirt she had on over some jeans she had apparently gone to put on while Kaitlin was discussing her wages. "Ah, it's beautiful Kaitlin! You cannot even begin to imagine…"

"Ok, sounds good. I'm in. Thanks. As long as I can…"

"…I'll walk you straight into town afterward, Ms. Kaitlin," Finn finished her sentence again.

"Exactly. Lead the way, then," Kaitlin nodded with a smile.

Walking on yellow leaves and fresh-smelling fertilizer, the four of them were soon accompanied by the sound of birds' chirping that sounded familiar to Kaitlin, as she saw a pair of unique black and white beauties with orange beaks taking off from a nearby leafless tree branch. Instinctively, she was feeling she would always associate the sight of such birds around her days in Norway with the cabin and The Group, already.

Kaitlin turned around to face the cabin again, but it was no longer in sight. "I think we've walked a little bit farther than just your backyard, am I correct?"

"About 20 meters or so, yes," Tan stated.

"Lar always says that we need to feel the grass beneath our feet and be one with nature, at least once a day..." Meredith's voice was dreamy, yet also a bit robotic as if she were reading from some playbook. For some reason Kaitlin found herself feeling sympathy for this young woman, who appeared so out of place and lost, despite her words stating the contrary.

"Well, we have to do the latter part daily, anyway. Be one with nature. After all, we can't really feel the grass beneath our poor bare feet on frozen ground in winter, can we now?" Tan chuckled, along with Finn, who was gazing into Kaitlin's eyes as if gauging for a reaction. All she found she was able to do just then was nod politely again and smile at another lovely bird flying by the top of her head.

"Our higher-level capacity for thinking and feeling is the only thing that separates us from animals, Ms. Kaitlin," Finn said in a smooth tone of voice as he inched closer to Kaitlin, his hands in his pockets. He too was following the trail of the birds in the air. "Sometimes we get so wrapped up in trivial earthly matters. We either *think* too much or *feel* too much. And it affects our lives very negatively, if you think about it. We really do have to sometimes take a cue from the animal world. At how *simple* things are for them, yet they always appear content in continuing each day just as long as they can fulfill their basic needs."

Kaitlin wasn't sure what to make of all this sudden rush of lecturing she seemed to be getting, so she nodded as she rocked her body back and forth in unison. Finn *did* have a point in that she herself was increasingly feeling like she was overthinking things more than usual lately.

"Animals and plants don't have any higher ambitions in life than having their basic needs, like nourishment fulfilled," Tan continued after Finn, with a growingly solemn tone. "They're not like humans."

"So how do you guys try to do that on a daily basis, then?" Kaitlin asked, genuinely curious now, "Get in touch with nature, I mean. I mean, you guys live smack in the middle of the woods, so I get *that* part. Does it help? I mean, *I*, for one, try to jog or at least walk fast-paced into town, at least every other day, when I feel too bogged down inside the house..."

Finn and Tan looked at each other. Kaitlin looked behind Tan to notice Meredith's still-dreamlike expression on her petite face, reaching out her French-manicured fingers higher on Tan's shapely arms. She definitely appeared to be the 'more-in-love' one in their relationship—the nature of which she still couldn't clearly figure out. Regardless of their woodsy lifestyle, one thing was sure: these people sure dressed in brand labels and took care of their appearances—not a very common trait amongst the more casually-dressed outdoorsy people Kaitlin often saw in Stavanger. She wondered whether they came from wealthy backgrounds or whether or not their marginal professional arrangement even brought in good revenue.

"Well, getting out of the house on a daily basis is all good, of course..." Finn began, "...especially as nature is luckily all around us in good old Stavanger. But it takes more than that to 'connect' with nature, as we say, and definitely more than that to connect with our *own* natures. Come, let me show you something."

Finn led the way as they all walked over a heavy load of twigs that cracked underneath their feet, and arrived in an area with a higher concentration of birds in song than the rest of the forest.

Finn placed his hands gently on Kaitlin's shoulders. "Look!"

"Where...?" Kaitlin started to ask, yet immediately didn't require an answer: a sudden ray of golden sunlight snuck between the high-rise trees and she was faced with a spectacular display of two small waterfalls leading into a small stream. The breathtaking view was further complemented by the skyscraper mountains miles behind them. What she saw looked as if it could definitely be of an area near a fjord, somewhere between Preikestolen and Kjerag, both of which were at least an hour-drive from town, as she knew from her and Paul's several trips there. So how could *this* have been? Such exquisite beauty relatively so close to town.

All logical thought stopped there: Kaitlin could now only sense her physical reality. She was still out of breath, felt her jaw still lowered in amazement. She reminded herself she had to breathe, and took a deep breath—inhaling the wonderful aroma of pine and flora surrounding her.

She faced Finn excitedly. Seeing his green eyes light up further in response to her enthusiasm gave her a sense of familial closeness to him as he gently removed his hands from her shoulders. Kaitlin imagined him as a fatherly figure who had just succeeded in amazing his baby daughter. She dared not to imagine a non-platonic alternative.

Turning back around to face the scenery, she also thought it peculiar that the mountains weren't snowcapped as they would typically be for December, and even for the spring months leading up to summer, since it would often snow in higher mountainous regions near Stavanger.

"Take in another deep breath, and… just… don't think," Finn's voice mesmerized her soul as Kaitlin found herself closing her eyes and doing just what he instructed… without question.

"This is too wonderful…" Kaitlin whispered. "…this place should be on a touristic brochure!"

Finn chuckled playfully, along with the others. Kaitlin opened her eyes and tried to bring herself back to reality. Did she just imagine it or had Tan really just whispered, 'She's like you…' to Meredith, with a mischievous smile and a chubby index finger pointed in Kaitlin's direction?

Did Meredith join them in a similar way to Kaitlin? *Join them.* Had she? The concept of them as a 'group' became clearer to her just then, and she was just starting to feel suspicion over their professional façade again when Finn spoke. "I'm glad you like it."

"I'm starting to see why you guys would want to live here. I want to take a picture…"

"Don't!" Tan interrupted suddenly as Kaitlin was reaching into her bag. Was that slight panic Kaitlin heard in his voice?

"I mean, like you suggested, this isn't exactly on some average tour of Stavanger, and we want to keep it that way. We don't really want to be disturbed here in our little piece of heaven so close to the city, you know?"

"I see," Kaitlin stated, still taken aback. "But what harm could possibly come from a picture, I mean…?"

"You need to learn to just *live* some things, Ms. Kaitlin," Finn cut in. "That's all. It'll allow your time here to be more special. I mean, think about it. Who goes to Paris, takes a picture in front of the Eiffel Tower, and then keeps looking at it, wishing to go there again? By taking a photograph most people just feel satisfied knowing they've checked off something on some mental or social to-do list, and that picture just stays catalogued, or perhaps just immediately shared on social media, the actual moment, never really savored."

Kaitlin truly wasn't getting what the big deal was, but she didn't really want to press the issue any further either. Especially as she was seeing, now that she'd checked her black leather wristwatch, at nearly 16:00, the sun was beginning to set. "Ok, guys. You win. You win. No photos. But, yes. It is *indeed* absolutely breathtaking; especially as it was so unexpected and out of place. Thank you so much for this experience then. But I really should be getting back to town. It's getting late. Now, how can I…"

"As promised, I'll walk you again this time, no problem," Finn said excitedly. "But only because we've walked a little farther from the cabin. I mean, after all, I know from now on you can probably figure out the path on your own from the cabin, so we'll walk from there."

"Thanks Finn. Sounds good. So, back to the real world after all that beauty, the work that needs to be translated? My initial job for you, guys?" Kaitlin began skipping on some of the small heaps of rocks and twigs around her. She was glad her boots had plastic soles that allowed her to do so with ease, suddenly feeling grateful for Paul's constant nagging to choose practicality and comfort over style.

"I'll e-mail you the latest letter we've received from Senegal—they insist on their correspondence in French," Tan said, linking his arm with Meredith's and tilting his head toward the cabin as they all started to walk. "I mean, what year are we in? They're no longer under occupation. Don't they realize the world does business in English now?"

"Well, it's just that *one* small Senegalese company we work with," Meredith said teasingly, tugging on Tan's arm. The wind blew her long brown mane, highlighting her striking bone structure even further with the last glimmers of sun still able to cut through the trees. "We don't exactly work with the more professional companies," she added.

"Meredith!" Tan tugged her arm a little too roughly in Kaitlin's opinion. "Don't belittle what we do in front of our new friend here!"

"Oh, no, I don't think there's any shame in that or anything, working with smaller companies," Kaitlin said, trying to give Meredith a reassuring look. "Some of the best ideas we got for our top projects back at the firm I worked for in Toronto came from some modest sources."

"I'm sorry," Meredith just said, looking down at her red Converse sneakers. Kaitlin definitely wasn't approving the imbalanced power Tan seemed to have over this woman, not even one bit. She had definitely looked more confident wearing the pumps she had back in the cabin—after an apparent fantasy session with her man, Kaitlin imagined.

"Well, not all of us can be big and mighty, like BP or Stat Oil, can we?" Tan asked rhetorically, following his statement with an audible smirk.

Do these people have something against oil companies? Kaitlin thought, confused. *Were they or their family members previously fired from them?* That reminded her of something she'd been meaning to ask. "So, Tan, I understand your family is in Turkey. And Meredith, yours are in Trondheim, I presume? How about yours, Finn?"

"Why does it matter, Ms. Kaitlin?" Finn asked rather sternly. "We're all independent adults here, aren't we?"

The harsh look that appeared in Finn's glance toward her sent a chill down Kaitlin's spine. That was surely a surprising response. "I'm just trying to get to know everyone better. I mean, you guys asked *me* about Toronto..."

"Sandnes," Finn cut in, "Belgian and Scottish immigrants."

"Sandnes," Kaitlin said. "Oh wow. Isn't that...?"

"Very close to here," Finn completed, "Yes, but we don't really see each other. Everyone's got their own thing, their own mission in life."

Kaitlin knew how to take a hint. "I see."

"Well, here we are," Meredith chirped happily once again as they all gathered at the now familiar red doors. "It was a pleasure meeting you, Kaitlin," she said, reaching out her hand. "I hope to see you around again."

"It was great meeting you, too, Mer…" Kaitlin started to say, shaking her hand.

"Oh you will, Meredith," Tan interrupted. "I'm sure we'll all be seeing Kaitlin again."

Finn must have sensed the discomfort level Tan was too often starting to raise, since he attempted to interrupt it with a feigned soft laugh. "What he means is I'm sure Ms. Kaitlin here will do a splendid job on her translation and we'll all be in need of her services more often."

"Well, I don't know how much better I can be than the *gazillion* online translation services," Kaitlin said in a soft tone, feeling herself blush, but immediately regretted saying it. Didn't she *want* some work to keep busy? Why was she sabotaging herself? She often felt this way: that the polite and modest manners she was raised with could at times come back to bite her.

"Nonsense," Tan said, inserting the key to open the doors for him and Meredith to go in. "Those *never* quite translate in the correct, daily-usage context. Do you think you could get the document in by the end of tomorrow if I send it to you tomorrow morning? Oh, by the way, I guess I'm going to need that CV of yours for your e-mail."

"Certainly!" Kaitlin exclaimed, taking the sheet out of her bag once again and handing it to Tan. It still hadn't gotten wrinkled. Good. She was glad she'd had the wits to place it back into her bag as they were heading out. "If it's a page or two like you said I'm sure I can even have it in by the afternoon!" She knew she had to cook something up and do laundry, but those things could be taken care of with a little break for work.

"Sounds good, then. You guys go ahead. We'll see you later, man," Tan and Finn did some sort of brotherly handshake goodbye as Tan went in—reminding her once again of those frat boys back in college. She had often tried to stay away from those, yet somehow couldn't. They could basically *sniff* out sensitive girls like her as their prey.

Meredith smiled and went in after him, slowly closing the majestic red door.

"Well! There we are! That was just some of The Group members and, of course, employees. What did you think? … Let's go," Finn started to head off in the more familiar direction to the left of the house—the same path from which they'd arrived earlier. Kaitlin followed, looking around her to familiarize herself more thoroughly in order to come by herself next time, if need be.

"They seem nice, especially Meredith," she said.

"Oh, you don't want to comment on Tan, do you?" Finn said teasingly. "I don't blame you. He's an odd one. But we love him for who he is. Just like we all love and accept one another here." Fallen leaves continued to crackle under their feet. Heavy snow hadn't yet come to Stavanger like it had the winter before, so the foliage was still lovely and kept up an autumn feel.

"Speaking of The Group," Kaitlin chimed, noting an especially tall tree with three thick branches that she told herself she'd seek when trying to locate the cabin the next time, if she needed to, "How many of you are there? I mean, six in the house, you said, but..."

"We have two more cabins of six in Rogaland, right outside of Stavanger: one in Sirdal, and, well, the other one is closer to Sandnes actually, near Dalsnuten..."

"Oh we *loved* Dalsnuten," Kaitlin interrupted, choosing not to share how difficult it'd been for her on her first mountain climb—although the city view at the top surely had been worth it. Without those hills for experience, she certainly never would have been able to climb the other higher and tougher mountains overlooking the fjords. "Paul's climbed it like ten times already, in fact."

Finn smirked. "Right. Well, that's where the third cabin of friends is, like I said. They all contribute to our paper business from time to time, though they each have their own."

"Their own?" Kaitlin was genuinely more confused now if that was even possible. "Something aside from paper production?"

"Well, the guys in Sirdal, for example, make a great living as ski instructors. And in the summer they rent out canoes for the main lake there; basically profiting from their surroundings and the seasons in any way they can and, well, ah, it just works out amazingly for everyone!"

"Oh," Kaitlin said, perplexed, seeing the last rays of daylight coming in through increasingly disappearing trees now, signaling they'd neared town. "So the Group isn't just *one* business?"

"Nah, more like a lifestyle, with various earnings on the side. A philosophy, if you will," Finn stated proudly. "Like I said, when you meet

Lar, he'll be glad to tell you more. Well, here we are... there's your old man."

That explained the lack of detail on his 'business' card, Kaitlin thought. "And this Lar person," she insisted, though Finn had clearly signaled they'd reached town by pointing at the bronze statue of the man with the top hat that had apparently become both their meeting and drop-off point. "You said that he was like the main 'philosopher' of this whole, multi-field working concept and living arrangement you guys have going, if I've understood correctly. So, *he's* in charge of those other cabins, too?"

Finn squinted his eyes at her as he smiled. "I'm rather enjoying your curiosity, Ms. Kaitlin. You could definitely have been a journalist. And, yes, Lar owns all of the cabins and technically controls and distributes all of our profits too. It's so very humble of him to just share the wealth he's accumulated over the years with younger people trying to make a living and enjoy life, isn't it?"

"I suppose so," Kaitlin stammered. She didn't quite know what to make of this mysterious Lar character yet, though she'd be lying to herself if she said she wasn't disturbed slightly by the way they all seemed to idolize him. She wondered what in the world *he* got out of this arrangement, but of course did not yet dare ask. Who was he? The Norwegian Bill Gates? She hoped she'd find out soon enough.

"Thanks again for everything. Really. It's been a lovely experience, especially discovering that waterfall area! I mean, I know there are lots of little waterfalls around the region but *that* was something else! It should *definitely* be publicized more."

"You and advertising," Finn cut in, laughing. He checked his watch and started walking backwards. "You're a funny one, Ms. Kaitlin. Don't forget the translation tomorrow, OK?"

Kaitlin took the hint that she'd been rambling on excitedly. They had definitely stayed out later than intended. "Definitely not! Thanks again, Finn. For the professional opportunity, I mean. I guess this really *is* a small city, isn't it? Glad I ran into you."

"Like we stated earlier today... *Nothing is coincidence*," Finn told her with a wink as he waved goodbye hurriedly. Kaitlin waved back, and was just about to start her fast-paced walk home past the busy bars at the harbor when she got the urge to turn around to see Finn walk off. Would she catch him leave this time? Or would he mysteriously have vanished on her again? What *was* this guy doing apparently running back so fast? It's not like he had any obligation to return so quickly, did he? Wouldn't he have preferred to grab a drink or check out a store since he'd already walked to town? Something inside her told Kaitlin what she'd be faced with when she turned around, but she did so anyway. Yup. Sure enough: Finn was gone.

Chapter 8

(December 11, 2010)

Placing her body as neatly and quickly as he could inside the beautifully-carved wooden coffin (hidden away under many layers of wool blankets) he'd placed in the back of his pick-up truck, the boyfriend buried it where he was sure no one would find it. After all, he wouldn't be that cruel as to never pay her a visit. He'd even add in a few prayers for good measure, he decided. Would God answer the prayers of a sinner like him? A murderer? He certainly hoped so. He wasn't evil—he had simply been serving a greater purpose. God would surely understand and forgive him.

He congratulated himself on a job well done. Yet it wasn't enough. It was never quite enough for someone to accomplish something so brave, yet not be able to share it with anyone, was it? So he'd called the one person who would understand, just as soon as the burial was over. His new friend: a very powerful man. Just like Linette's precious John, but even more so. He was extremely glad this man had come into his life recently, becoming an older brother figure to him. No. More than that. He had become his hero, with his quality clothing average people could not afford, and fancy slicked-back, jet-black hair; and deep, charismatic voice. This was a guy you wanted to be associated with. This was a man who had gained many riches in life, yet had never forgotten humanity. A spiritual man, he believed in love and respect for all of nature's beautiful creations, as the creations of God. He believed in the value of wealth through hard work—never promising instant wealth like some scumbag gurus he had heard about. He wasn't stoic though, he did occasionally reward good behavior through gifts. This man was real: supra-human, in his eyes, yet simultaneously down to earth and gentle.

He met him at an academic lecture he had come across while trying to earn his graduate degree in order to gradually accumulate an elevated status of sorts that Linette could brag about. But, of course, Linette began acting as if she would not be able to wait for him while he pursued his own road to success.

Initially supporting him, his sweet angel had gradually started accusing him of wasting his time, taking out loans for a 'useless degree' in today's 'networking-valuing world'. But not Him. His words, that magical spring evening, were inviting in tone and appreciative of hard work: "higher education is an end in itself, in becoming a more elevated and beautiful creature of God." He had spoken those words precisely at the perfect time in his life. He had become so impressed by him in fact that he'd gotten in line to buy a signed copy of his book just to meet him.

"You have the godlike power inside you, lad, to achieve anything you desire," Lar Iktar had told him, leaning closer and staring deeply into his eyes.

Around fifteen people in front of him in the queue had bought the book, yet he'd observed that Lar hadn't paid as much attention to any of them. Lar was a worldly, accomplished man. He knew things, and he was always right. "I can see it. You just have to rid yourself of everything and everyone misleading you from your true path."

And so, he had.

Chapter 9

$\mathbf{S}$taring at the fuchsia-tinged sky preparing to set, Kaitlin nervously flipped through the contents of her bag as she arrived at the entrance door of her apartment. Once inside, she took out her glitter-case-covered smartphone, which she realized she hadn't even taken a peek at back in the cabin. 4:45 in the afternoon. Paul had sent her a text message. *Shit,* she thought. She'd had her phone on vibrate throughout her 'interview'. She took a deep breath and already prepared her 'I didn't hear your message with all that music in the gym' message in her mind when she was pleasantly surprised by what she actually read.

[I hope my baby's enjoying her time at the gym… Can't wait for her to show me her aerobic moves later tonight! ;) <3]

This was odd for Paul. He'd sent it just a little over half an hour ago, and would be home in another twenty minutes or so. Kaitlin was suddenly not appreciating her husband's early-return-home work schedule. If they'd been back in Canada, a man in his managerial position certainly wouldn't have been able to get home before at least 7 o'clock in the evening. How would she be able to so quickly take in everything she'd just experienced and be able to greet her husband as if everything were normal at the same time?

And that expectative message of his. Cheesy and flirty, yet romantic. Like a teenager, almost. He hadn't sent her a text message like that since they'd first begun dating. *Those were the days,* Kaitlin recalled. Their passion had felt all-consuming, especially since Kaitlin was taken aback by connecting so deeply with a man she'd never brought herself to see as more than a friend for a long time.

It wasn't the weekend yet (that's when he tended to be well-rested and have the most energy for making love), so his come-on message seemed early. *Did he go to the gym at the office? Pumping iron always does seem to make him more turned on than usual,* Kaitlin thought. Or was this something deeper? Had he finally recognized the disappointment she had been facing in all the activities, like the women's club or tea with his buddies' wives, which he had encouraged for her? Was he trying to spice things up? Why was it that people in relationships appeared to make more of an effort *just* as the other person had stopped trying themselves? *Had* she stopped trying?

No, she decided. She had just begun exploring other venues to keep herself busy. That was it. That had to be all.

For some reason it was questions like these that had been bugging her mind over the fifteen-minute walk home ever since Finn dropped her off. She knew she should have been going over the rather peculiar circumstances she'd just faced instead: going to a job interview in the middle of the woods, in a home-office environment where people felt comfortable enough to answer the door half-naked, with a mysterious company president, a spectacular view that was to be kept secret, and so on and so forth.

Leaning back against the Spanish-tiled kitchen counter and looking at the ships go by from outside the main windows, she finally began reflecting on what she had just faced. Was it an interview for some work to do or admittance into some friendship circle? She could not be sure. Perhaps it was both? Meredith *had* said they'd wanted to capture a 'family-like' business environment. For some reason, she and Tan reminded Kaitlin of hippies from the 1960's she'd read about in school and witnessed on stage during several musical productions.

Finn, on the other hand, was something else entirely, that was for sure. So refined, so reposed, he belonged in that main office in Oslo they'd mentioned. What was he doing with these free-spirited, casual folks in the woods? Then again they *did* appear to all have higher education in common.

Oh well. For the moment she decided to just concentrate on the piece that Tan was going to send her for translation. She'd get to it after seeing Paul off to work tomorrow morning. She'd already decided not to tell him anything for a while—at least not until she ensured that she was taken seriously and was getting paid.

How had these people been so quick to accept her linguistic services just by the word of mouth of one man, who had only known her for one day? How was *she* so quick to trust this man to walk with him to some strange 'home office' cabin? Why weren't these people working straight from a paper mill?

None of what was happening made any sense to her, yet Kaitlin had to keep telling herself this was to keep busy. To do something social. To get out of the house. Besides, who ever *really* knew their coworkers and the personal lives of their higher-ups?

And, of course, a woman with plans became a better wife as well, not nagging her husband to be her only source of fun, didn't she? Isn't that something countless blogs and women's magazines had been telling women like her? "How to overcome newlywed power struggles", "What educated housewives can do", "How to make sure your life isn't over just because you got married". Even Kaitlin herself had begun asking Google things she could never ask the acquaintances she'd made in her new setting, since they could always gossip to their husbands which would get back to poor Paul. It would make her lighten a certain load off her chest from time to time, at least.

She had done it. Changing into her black slacks and baby pink t-shirt, and once again being glad their apartment had an excellent heating system to encourage lighter clothing despite the bitter cold outside, Kaitlin congratulated herself on her time management. *Poor Paul*, she thought, looking at his message once again. *Look at him, so believing in his wife, with whom he's still flirting, despite the hectic schedule I know he is having at work this week. What is wrong with me?*

[I've *just* come home after a whole hour on the treadmill, honey! Can you believe that? Took longer than expected since Sibel was so nice; we ended up having quite a long lunch as well. You would have been proud if you saw me run ;) See you tonight, kisses!]

Sent.

She walked into their cozily decorated kitchen and turned on the kettle for some hot water. Some instant coffee would have to do. She knew she'd be making the better stuff after dinner—in the foamy latte way to enjoy with Paul.

Despite petty arguments from time to time (and slight nabs such as the one over children they'd had the other day while jogging), deep in her heart, Kaitlin supposed she and Paul were probably doing fine compared to a lot of married people. She wasn't abused or cheated on, she comforted herself. She was also living a life far above many people's reach in the world and she knew she should be thanking her lucky stars more often than she had been lately, having settled into the *routine* of it all.

"That must be it," she told herself, stirring some cinnamon into the coffee mix inside her navy-blue mug before pouring in the hot water. Routine. That's what had to be bothering her. Lord knew she hadn't had much of it in Toronto. Even when she had been at one job for a while, she had always had some sort of romantic or friendship drama that would rock things—always some possibility of upcoming change, for better or for worse. Yet here, mundane chores seemed to have a darker effect on her psyche than she ever thought possible: crushing that sense of *hope* and *dreaming of a 'bright future'* she'd always had since she was a little girl.

She used to fantasize that she could handle her 'wifely duties' with finesse—doing housework in her playful, Kaitlin way. Picking up sexy-maid costumes to vacuum clean the house and later welcome Paul home with them on. Looking up fancy cake recipes, only to smear it all over each other's mouth and then kissing the pieces off after her dessert-trial would result in an unattractive cake. None of these scenarios had really happened: they'd come close, but Paul had always managed to find a way to take things more seriously than she could have imagined. He'd say things like, "that underwear's material is not hygienic honey," and Kaitlin's heart would drop. Her enthusiasm would dampen. And she'd pout the entire night, which would upset Paul, who seemed oblivious to why she would 'overreact' and 'act like a child'. And, so on and so forth.

Dinggggggg

The obnoxiously loud doorbell buzzed Kaitlin back to the moment. They'd e-mailed the real estate agent to have that changed, hadn't they? The damn guy hadn't gotten back to them with a response yet, as far as she knew.

Clearing her throat and throwing her hair back behind her shoulders, Kaitlin smoothed her shorts and opened the door half-way. "Who could it be?" she teased.

"Darling? You look very energetic for someone who spent over an hour at the gym!" Paul eyed his wife up and down before leaning in to give her a sensual hug, his nose touching her nose.

"Oh, baby, you have no idea how many cups of coffee I've had today. It's insane!" Kaitlin hugged back, placing her head on his right shoulder and staring out the window. At least that part had been true. "The caffeine definitely must have helped me out!"

"But darling, you know that's bad for your heart. Be careful."

"I know, I know," Kaitlin said as she watched Paul head into their bedroom to change out of his two-piece black suit. She noticed he was wearing the red tie she'd gotten him for his birthday, and considered following him in and tugging on it teasingly, but then stopped herself. That would have to wait.

Instead, Kaitlin proceeded to head to the freezer and remove a pack of fries she'd decided she'd serve with gravy and cheese: good ole Canadian *poutine,* one of her and Paul's favorite comfort food which she liked to spice up with some red pepper and onions. She felt they could both use it tonight. She decided to serve it with a side of rich salad which would hopefully suffice as fulfilling the daily-vegetable requirement, and they'd be feeling less guilty for going heavy on the carbs.

"Mmm, is that what I think it is?" Paul noticed immediately, sure enough, whispering into the back of her neck and blowing air into her ear. "My baby's fixing us some yum yum?"

Kaitlin turned around to face him and rolled her eyes playfully. "Yes, yes, babe. Now behave or no yum yum of *any* kind! Have a seat, it'll be just 15 minutes, 20 with the salad." She was glad their hormones both appeared to be on the same page that evening.

"You don't need to bother with the salad, honey." Paul muttered.

"That's ok, it'll be quick. I wish I could have been home earlier to have it all prepared already, but you know…"

As twenty minutes became forty, Kaitlin was glad Paul was lost in reading news articles on the computer to notice the time too much, though she was sure his stomach had taken note, and his face had no longer exactly been smiling either.

"This is delicious, baby. I've missed this! Mwah!" Paul managed to make out through a full mouth later when they'd both sat down to eat.

"Bon appetit, babe," Kaitlin returned his kissing sound. "Worth the wait?"

"Ahh. Yes. So tell me more about your day," Paul started after he'd had a couple more fillings of creamy potatoes in his mouth. "How did your time with your new friend go?"

"Oh, she's awesome. A great runner! And that figure, even with two kids. So inspirational!" In her mind, Kaitlin was running through all the details of her *actual* and *only* date with her new friend from the previous day.

"I can tell you girls had fun, that's great," Paul muttered. "After all, it's not exactly like you to socialize yourself two days in a row like this, babe. I mean, why, it'd take from a day of pampering your nails or hair or something, wouldn't it?" Paul chuckled playfully and went on to sip his orange soda.

"It's not *like* me?" Kaitlin wrapped her right fingers into a fist and hit the table with it, the fork still in her hand. "What's that supposed to mean?"

'Whoa, there! I'm just saying. You know. You would usually say, after going out for coffee or something with the other ladies here, that that was enough for the week! You know, since it took time from 'mending to yourself' or whatever, didn't you?"

"Oh, wow," Kaitlin said in a lower voice that emphasized her offense. Why in the world had he changed the topic like this? "Thank you, Paul. Truly. Thanks a lot. Apparently a wife that takes care of herself isn't relevant to you. And, if you must know, like I *also* said, those other 'friendships' you tried to force on me felt exactly that: Forced. So *forgive* me if I wasn't as *enthusiastic* in meeting up with *them* so soon after having grabbed a drink together somewhere or for some other tea or cake-baking session they'd invited me to!"

"We're back to mocking baking again," Paul had stopped eating now as well. "I'm sorry babe. You're right. You're *above* all that. Going to the gym and things like that are 'cooler' activities. You don't want to become the 'typical' married woman, wasn't that what you'd told me? You have the soul of a, what had you called it, a 'teenager'. That's right. My mistake."

"Wait, *what?*" Kaitlin almost spilled the large gulp of sparkling water she'd just drunk out of her mouth. "*Where* is all this coming from, Paul? I don't understand! I thought you'd said you were happy for me."

"Nowhere! *You're* the one overreacting!" Paul took a deep breath as he saw Kaitlin face the window, avoiding his eyes and keeping her lips and chin clenched.

"Look, I didn't mean anything deep by it," he continued. "It's just… Lars gave me a call today. We had a nice chat. But… apparently Lesley was wondering why you hadn't returned her call yet. I mean, I just don't want my wife to be viewed as rude. Is that so wrong?"

"Umm, when exactly did she supposedly call me and I didn't return her call?" Kaitlin was peeved. "You think if I'd actually *received* a call from her, that I wouldn't return it? Even if just to say 'hello' back, and politely turn down any offer to hang out again that she may or may *not* have made? You're not asking *me* first, me, your *rude* wife!"

"That's *not* what I said. Look, these are just genuinely nice people, and I've known them since I came to Stavanger," Paul continued. "They really helped me out when I was alone here. You know that. I mean, how well do you know this *new* lady you've met? And then you complain about our social life here. I mean, I'm just saying maybe you should finally realize that…"

"Realize what Paul? That since I'm married, apparently I can no longer decide for myself who to befriend or not? Apparently, *you* have to know their husbands as well and approve? Is that what it is? I see! Great!"

"You're doing it again!" Paul said. "You're not letting me finish…"

"Finish what?" Kaitlin asked. "Finish what? Turning what started out as a romantic, nice dinner into a fight over nothing?!"

"Why are you shouting, babe?" Paul asked calmly. It only took one glance into his eyes, and Kaitlin knew he was being strategic again. She absolutely despised having her buttons pushed, only to be met with an annoyingly calm and passive-aggressive reaction from her husband. To be made to look like the problematic one.

"Ok. Ok. I'm shouting," Kaitlin said with angry sarcasm. "Yes. You're right, *babe.* You've done nothing. I'm the bad guy."

"You realize you're never able to take constructive criticism, don't you, honey?" Paul added calmly.

"Constructive criticism… oh, right!" Kaitlin exclaimed, suddenly feeling like she'd lost her appetite. "What *perfect* timing you have!"

"There would *be* no problem with timing, if you didn't insist on overreacting to every little…" Paul started to explain.

"Since all this 'domestic' stuff is *so* important to you, more important than a loving relationship with your wife, whom you don't even care that you're hurting, maybe you should have just married someone like, like, your 'plain' Jeanette!" Kaitlin suddenly couldn't believe the words which had just escaped her mouth. But they had.

"Whoa… what?" Paul asked with a shocked look.

"You heard me!" Kaitlin continued… on a roll. "You're such a jerk!"

"Oh yeah?" Paul asked, angrier.

"Yeah!" Kaitlin responded.

"Maybe I should have then!" Paul exclaimed, pounding his fist on the table.

The sudden silence became louder than any words that could still be spoken, if only they could.

***

Kaitlin went on to prepare their routine after-dinner coffee: partly to keep busy and partly to at least attempt some sort of reconciliation. After all, as angry as she still was, she'd go absolutely insane if she ran out of one more person to talk to in Norway, she decided, especially one she was living with. If he could do strategy, so would she.

She peeked at their dinner table, which hadn't been cleared yet. She'd headed into their bedroom immediately after Paul's last comment and thrown herself onto their bed in frustration—such had become her usual reaction whenever he said something he knew would hurt her, but also silence her when she'd been nagging.

The loud exaggerated clapping of the audience to some mundane 'talent' some group of contestants were supposed to have was enough to tell her Paul was watching what had become his favorite nighttime show as of late, much to Kaitlin's dismay. She'd usually retreat into their room and pop open one of the several novels she had a habit of following simultaneously. This attempt at distraction would often prove futile: the thought that they had little in common in regards to hobbies would scream at the back of her mind.

Tonight was a different kind of night—one of those rarer occasions when Kaitlin would head alone into their bedroom way before bedtime for another reason besides idleness. They'd usually bicker about some little thing or other: sometimes she'd even wonder if it was intentional, just to add some spice. At first, Kaitlin would cry, sometimes audibly, in order to lure her husband to come after her and comfort her. He never would. So she gradually learned. She learned that he was different from the loving and apologetic man she'd always idolized in movies— apologizing immediately, coming home with flowers, the whole works. Isn't that what a man who genuinely loved his wife was supposed to do once he's realized he'd been hurtful? Forgive and laugh off any of her childish whims and be the 'bigger person'? Not Paul. He was proud, sometimes *too* proud. She'd grown to bury her tears and his accusatory words after a certain point; and, despite the pain, attempt to at least consider his critical points, if not respect and obey them blindly.

Maybe Sandy was right in what she had once said, and astrologically speaking, Libra Kaitlin and Cancer Paul were simply incompatible. Period.

Or perhaps her own mother was right. Maybe she truly did go into this whole marriage thing without thinking about whether she was ready for it or not. Or maybe she just thought that marrying an older man automatically meant he'd baby her and she could get away with some caprices and feel ever young in return.

She decided she'd try to hold back the tears for as long as possible tonight. Jeanette and domesticity: the words were haunting her brain and she instinctively felt a pull toward the kitchen. Speeding past Paul, who was still glued to the television set as she saw from horse-sight, she reached inside their wooden cupboard farthest to the right of the counter. Six minutes later, she was placing two cups of steaming espresso with frothed milk poured over it to make it her 'special K-latte', as Paul liked to call it, on their marine-themed serving tray. The two cups were now adjacent to each other on the small table in front of the main couch where Paul was seated.

"Thank you, ma'am," Paul said in a soft tone, looking up at his wife sheepishly after first looking at the solo sofa she usually chose to sit on, lost in a book or whenever the cold distance between them was palpable enough to drive them away physically as well.

Kaitlin plopped down next to her husband on their leather couch with a smile, making sure limb contact was established. She was not going to give in. "I'm sure it's not as tasty as your potential-wife Jeanette would have made it, but…" Kaitlin cooed playfully. Paul initially shot her an angry look—placated immediately as one look at her flirty pout told him she had laid down the artillery for the night.

Paul rolled his eyes and let out an extremely long sigh. "No one can be like my baby," he faced Kaitlin, placing his hands on her shoulders. "I see her potential and believe in her more than she believes in herself sometimes. That is all. And about Jeanette, really, I *have* to finally introduce you two. I truly see that now. You have to finally come visit me at work and see how much you've been overreacting over nothing, once and for all."

Kaitlin felt unable to choose between being appeased with his seemingly reconciliatory response or being annoyed by the stubborn way in which he continuously managed to urge her to somehow change herself. But the events of where she'd been earlier in the day (unbeknownst to Paul) helped to keep her mouth shut. *Tonight, I will let it go*, she thought to herself, giving Paul a smile and taking a sip of her latte. *It tastes pretty darn good*, she thought. *Screw the way any other woman who may or may not be interested in my husband would have made it.*

"I'll have to do that honey, you're right," Kaitlin nodded. "And no, not to check up on your friend or whatever, but to visit the place in general. I mean, seeing the inside of Statoil for the first time for the Women's Club the other day made me even more curious."

"Mmm," Paul said with pleasure as he sipped the drink himself now. "This is going especially well after that heavy yum-yum!"

"Mmm," Kaitlin repeated with a wink, excited at his usage of those childish yet flirty words again.

"Let's put on some music, shall we?" Paul suggested, placing his cup on the coffee table and picking up the remote control instead. They enjoyed a media system where various international radio stations could also be followed through their television set. Immediately as Paul switched the channel, the small area on the bottom of the multimedia screen showed the channel 'NRK 1', where the local news was on. Paul listened for a couple of seconds, and Kaitlin noticed he hadn't even placed the cursor on the radio yet.

"Whoa," Paul muttered, enlarging the screen for the News channel.

"Honey?" Kaitlin called out. "The radio?"

"One second," Paul mumbled, taking a seat on the edge of the solo sofa closer to the television set.

"Paul? Are you OK?" Kaitlin asked.

"…Just… turning the volume up… hold on, babe," Paul's hand was visibly shaking nervously while he pushed various buttons on the remote control until he got to the right one, as if he'd never used it before.

"Did something major happen?" Kaitlin got up to take a seat on the high edge of the couch now to come closer to both Paul and the TV. She hated feeling out of the loop whenever Paul spoke Norwegian somewhere or watched something in the language, as was the current case. She also didn't enjoy having her husband know something she didn't: one more thing they would not be able to share together.

"I really wish I'd begun those Norwegian classes we always talked about. You know more and more jobs I've been looking into require it, so perhaps…"

"…Kaitlin! One second!" Paul said, emphasizing each word to make a point: he'd raised his voice without looking at her. His eyes were dead fixed on the photo of an attractive brunette now shown on the corner of the screen where a waif blonde woman was anchoring the news. The anchor's lips pursed as she made an upset 'hmph' sound before continuing with the story. Kaitlin assumed something bad must have happened. "Linette Peterson," the woman stated the name of whom Kaitlin assumed to be the victim (since the name appeared below the photograph now) articulating her name in a way that Kaitlin could make it out, despite the rapid Norsk[6] being spoken.

"Did something happen to that woman, Paul?"

"The police have just released her name after some new conclusive evidence that helped to identify the body," Paul began to say in a somber tone, his face still glued to the television set. "Apparently, the body itself

---

[6] Norsk: 'Norwegian' in the local language

was discovered about ten days ago in Trondheim, buried inside a coffin somewhere woodsy where a local company had just begun to dig deep for construction. She's apparently been dead for a while, but, like I said, they were just able to use forensics to discover the identity…"

"I see," Kaitlin stated, walking up to Paul and placing both her hands on his left shoulder. "Poor thing. But, what's the matter? With *you*, I mean? Have you been following this story or something?"

"Hmm?" Paul stared up at her, heaving his shoulders. "I, just, I don't know, Kaitlin. I mean, this is Norway. It's supposed to be one of the safest places on earth. And I'm out of the house a long time sometimes when you're here, alone. In this case, they haven't caught the killer yet. That's another thing. And listen… Hmm… An autopsy report apparently concluded she must have been poisoned somehow… They're also ruling out suicide, as she'd been placed by someone into a coffin…"

"Right… how tragic… and strange…." Kaitlin said, shaking her head in disbelief.

"What if something were to happen to you and I wasn't there? I couldn't…" Paul wiped a tear from his eye and sniffled as he finally turned around to look at Kaitlin in the face. "I couldn't bear it, baby," he said, kissing her cheek tenderly. "I couldn't bear it if anything were to happen to you. Do you *understand*?"

Kaitlin nodded somberly and kissed him reassuringly and long on the lips. "Shh. Don't think about things like that. Let's go finally clear the table. It'll get your mind off." Kaitlin loved it when he helped out around the house occasionally and she wasn't about to miss this opportunity to do something together with him around.

Throughout the wiping and the dishwasher-loading, Kaitlin count-lessly looked at him straight in his eyes. She couldn't come up with a single thing to say, and he wouldn't exactly meet her gaze. It was an endearing thought, for one's husband to be concerned for his wife, sure. But why had Paul reacted so deeply to *this* story in particular? Similar stories of the victims of crazies were on the news all the time, weren't they? Yes, Trondheim was a little closer to home. Yet Kaitlin couldn't shake the feeling that something was off all the way until hitting the sheets that evening.

She cursed her luck for the bad timing of the news, and how it seemed to have affected Paul. She could tell that right before dinner and soon after the coffee, despite their heated argument, they'd both been looking forward to something good come bed time. But a "Phew, I feel so tired" from Paul heading toward their bedroom made it obvious that his mood had certainly passed.

Kaitlin had no choice but to wash her face and put on her casual pajamas. The black-laced slip she'd been planning on would have to continue to wait a little longer. She'd tried to change his moods before when he had been down, and she'd learned by now that it would be to no avail.

Picking up her cellphone to place it on the charger and plugging it into the outlet over her dresser, she saw that she'd received a text from Sibel, inviting her out for coffee Wednesday afternoon. She texted 'yes' back enthusiastically, despite realizing that to Paul this would be their 'third' almost back-to-back meeting, when in reality that wasn't the case. She just had to take that chance. *I'll tell him tomorrow*, she decided.

Once in bed, the look on Paul's face: eyes-open and still frozen in distant thought as he kissed her goodnight before turning around to sleep, only seemed to confirm her fear over their lack of action that evening. At least he'd kissed her again despite their silly fight-of-the-week. She had learned to try to become thankful for what she could get. Dreaming of more than that never helped anyone, did it?

***

"Earth to Paulie!" Jeanette cooed, waving her self-manicured hand with chipped red nail polish in front of Paul's face. "What on *earth* could have you *so* distracted when you know we've got a big one comin' up!"

Paul shook his head and smiled at his friend. Good old Jeanette from one of the southern American states she'd mentioned before, though he'd forgotten which one and decided would be impolite to ask again. She had basically grown up in Canada since middle school yet had somehow never lost her slight drawl. "Jeanette, I've already prepared the files we need in the presentation. I just have to edit them by today and I'm done. Don't sweat it!"

"I know, I know, Mr. Dependable. We know. But come on! Don't keep a girl wonderin'! Because you know I'll be comin' up with the wildest theories in my mind if you don't tell me what's actually goin' on!" Jeanette smiled a toothy smile, which showed the gum she'd audibly been chewing. This was one of Paul's biggest peeves in a woman: he couldn't believe Kaitlin had seemed almost jealous when Jeanette called the other day. He chuckled to himself. If only she had met her.

Jeanette was an attractive woman alright: curvy and with baby blue eyes. Yet she was one of those people who would be more attractive if they never opened their mouth to speak. Not that it mattered much to him. He sincerely wished she'd find the man of her dreams already and they could all attend a nice wedding. He knew she always had good intentions, and loved her like the sisters he missed from back home.

"Now, now, Jeanette. It's nothing juicy, so you can stop those crazy gears in your head from spinning any further! I'm just a little worked up about the news from last night, I guess. Have you heard about that young woman? Crazy things going on near Stavanger."

Paul turned his swiveling chair back to face his computer screen, hoping Jeanette didn't catch a hint of his personal feelings over the events. He opened up one of the files he knew he had to edit and started playing with the mouse to make it look as if he had actually begun concentrating on work. He knew Jeanette long enough to know she wouldn't be offended, and would go on talking anyway.

"Oh, you mean that murder on the news last night, right?" Jeanette didn't disappoint. "…The body of that poor girl being discovered in Trondheim? Oh Paulie, it's not *that* close to Stavanger. And it's only one body. Maybe it was somethin' personal. I mean, *of course,* I hope they catch the son or daughter-of-a-gun who did it! But you don't have to worry your sweet lil' head, as if some serial killer will now be goin' after your Kaitlin or somethin' like that!"

"Yeah, I guess you're right," Paul turned his head to smile at her. She smiled back and retreated to her seat at her desk five meters away from his. He truly wished it were that simple. He truly wished he hadn't recognized Linette in the photograph. Had he done the right thing by not opening up to Kaitlin about it? He realized he still harbored some feelings of guilt about the events of the past. He decided it was best to keep his past to himself for now.

Kaitlin was suffering enough at home, so far from her loved ones during his long hours at work, despite the happy face he was glad she was usually putting on for him. It would break his heart even further if he caught her crying again; like she had done several times when she was feeling most homesick during the first few months they'd arrived in Norway following their Parisian honeymoon.

She'd also cry and react, way too much as far as he was concerned, at his attempt to make her realize she'd chosen a different life for herself now compared to the party-woman-in-business life she'd had back in Toronto—a life that had ever so intimated him in the beginning. At least she no longer cried as much, not in front of him, anyway. He was hoping she'd gotten used to some things, like most people did.

Surely, they faced difficulties here and there, but they were happy, weren't they? Wasn't *she*? Regardless, it didn't mean he could stop trying. Maybe if she could become even *happier*, she could consider a baby more, wouldn't she? Was that not the natural womanly thing to do?

He had to try. That reminded him. "Hey, Jeanette?"

"Yes, Paulie?" She murmured enthusiastically, "you finally decided to tell me what's *really* bothering you?"

"Jeanie, I told you, nothing more exciting to share! Sorry!" Paul laughed. With anyone else, he would find her quirkiness extremely annoying. "No, I was actually going to ask how the decorations and preparations for the Grand Ball are coming up?"

"Oh, the New Year's Eve Ball is in less than two weeks, that's right! I was going to tell you: Tim's thought of the most *wonderful* theme!" Jeanette's eyes lit up each time she mentioned his name, and Paul knew she'd had a crush on their book-worm colleague for a very long time. Though he liked the guy, he never could quite see what it was Jeanette found in someone seemingly as dull as Tim. Maybe it was just the fact that they were the only single people at the office at the moment. *Whatever,* he decided. *What do I know?*

"Oh yeah, what is it? And, most importantly, is it hopefully not *too* 'grand' so that we can actually accomplish this 'ball' in less than two weeks?" Paul picked up his favorite red pen and started chewing on the plastic around the handle. He always got nervous with deadlines. For some reason the three of them had been placed in charge of the Ball-Prep Committee—on *top* of the Annual International Petroleum meeting that was also coming up soon in January. Their boss must have liked their tendency to get along the best: with all his emphasis on 'teamwork' throughout various meetings they'd had.

The ballroom in the nearby *Scandic* hotel had already been booked, but none of the details, including the catering, were ready. They'd been holding things off until the day neared and they could get a better count of how many people had RSVP'd; and would actually be attending. In truth, he feared any suggestion Jeannette or Tim would have, as he was sure it would be something 'over the top'. Things should be celebrated as simply as possible, as far as he was concerned.

He was, after all, raised in a family that didn't even celebrate birthdays after a child's certain age. A fancy dance was definitely over his head. He had grown bored of going to these things every year, especially as he was always alone. Last year, during what would have been their first attendance as husband-and-wife, Kaitlin's mother had gotten very ill and she had to fly to Toronto that week. He knew how much she'd been looking forward to a fancy attendance together. "Oh, babe, it'll be like *Prom!*" She gasped when he'd first mentioned it to her earlier that fall. She had even bought the dress she was planning to wear: a scorching reddish number, yet somehow in time they'd both forgotten about it.

Paul knew his wife would be spending the following day having coffee with that Cybill lady or whomever she had recently befriended, which he was glad about, especially since she told him during their weekend breakfast that this woman seemed happily married, with children. He was actually hoping she'd be a good influence on his wife. He decided to call her on his lunch break to discuss their long-awaited ball attendance, eager to hear excitement in her voice.

***

"Well, Tim definitely felt that a futuristic *space* theme would be great for this year, as we already did 'Historic Characters' last year; so this would be just the opposite. But we *have* been contemplatin' between a realistic one with stars and planets, and a fictional one with fantastic elements, such as…" As Jeanette went on to describe her preference for a futuristic *Jetsons* theme that would suit some dress she had found on sale, Paul took out his cell phone from the back pocket of his dark grey suit trousers. He nodded like a bobble-head at Jeanette to avoid being rude, all the while thinking about the happy look on Kaitlin's face as they'd be dancing under some sort of starry decoration on the ceiling of the ballroom: a sure thing, regardless of what version of space they would ultimately choose.

"Paul? So, realistic or futuristic? What do you think?" Jeanette asked eagerly.

"Oh, uh, I think I'd go with *realistic*. I mean, last year got a bit too "costume-y", and you know Phelps didn't like it." The head of their division was one tough-to-please man. Despite the tremendous money they raised (which had gone to the Petroleum Women's Club, in which he was glad his wife had finally gotten herself involved), and the relatively high turn-out they'd obtained, Phelps had decided to get paranoid and feel that outside onlookers had been mocking them when guests began to arrive at the hotel dressed as characters from Hollywood movies, with even one freakishly-tall Napoleon Bonaparte who seemed to get a lot of coverage in the local press.

"Tim said the same thing!" Jeanette quipped. "I'm outnumbered! Ok, Ok, so no alien make-up and elaborate collars, fine. *Realistic*, it is. But I'm still wearing my metallic-colored dress. I just hope Tim likes it!... Umm, that is, I mean, I hope he and Phelps don't think it's too much or anythin'. I mean, you know…"

Paul raised an eyebrow at his friend and smiled. "Yes, yes, Jeanette. Don't worry, I know."

Chapter 10

Kaitlin hung up the phone with her husband feeling giddy like a seventeen-year-old girl who'd just gotten asked out to the prom by her senior class' hunky football quarterback. They were finally going to the famous annual Ball she'd been 'teased' but 'not-yet-pleased' about!

The shiny velvety red gown she'd bought for last year's Ball was the one she now couldn't wait to finally get herself in. She made a mental note to get to the gym again (for real this time) and check her weight to make sure she hadn't gained too many kilograms since last year when they'd bought it. She had refused to keep a scale inside the house out of fear of possibly growing numbers lowering her self-esteem. After all, there was only a short time left until the ball.

Paul had sounded so excited and so eager to receive a joyful reaction from Kaitlin that she actually felt a single tear drop from the corner of her right eye onto her cheek. She sighed heavily and lowered her face to rest her chin on her right palm, wiping the tear away with her pinky finger.

She supposed the tear was one of emotion for the loving gesture by her husband, yes, but then she had another thought. What if it had been a result of guilt? After all, when he called her, she *was* busy going over the translated sheet she got to work on for The Group straight after her breakfast. Only mere minutes had passed since she'd pressed 'Send' on her internet browser where her e-mails had been opened, and headed to her room closet to check out what she could wear to her *actual* lunch date with Sibel tomorrow, when she heard her phone ring.

She didn't recognize the number. "Hello?"

"That was fast!" an excited male voice said immediately on the other line.

"I'm sorry. This is…?" Kaitlin asked, confused.

"Oh, sorry. It's Tan, from The Group. So, thanks for the translation, Kaitlin! Looks great!"

How in the world did he manage to read it over and decide it was 'great' so fast? Kaitlin thought. *Especially as they apparently don't fully understand the translated language of French (using online translation services and all), do they?*

"Ah, I see. Thank you. Of course. Just keeping my promise. Doing my task. You guys are the fast ones actually! I just hope I didn't send it too soon before proofreading…"

"Oh, it's fine," Tan assured her, "Finn looked it over. He knows a little *Francais* from growing up with his Belgian dad and all. We appreciate your dedication, Kaitlin."

"You're very welcome. I hope…" Kaitlin started to say.

"So, how're you doing, by the way?" Tan cut in, "Have you gotten used to Norway? And do tell us more about the Mister who brought you here, Kaitlin. How'd you guys meet?"

Kaitlin was truly taken aback now. Even Sibel hadn't gotten around to asking her that question, yet! "Uhh, long story, I guess," she started, deciding to answer anyway to be polite, keeping things general. "We were introduced back in Canada, were just friends for a while, so on and so forth, heh. Why do you ask?"

"Just making conversation. I just find this stuff fascinating."

"This… stuff? What? Girl talk?" Kaitlin tried to hold her laugh in.

"Marriage," Tan answered in a serious tone. "Are his parents still married, Kaitlin? Are yours?"

"Well, *his* are, yes," Kaitlin was just about to recite how she had grown up without her father, but stopped herself, noticing he hadn't continued to ask, even though she'd paused. It was as if he had already gained an answer he was looking for. For some reason she felt that his interest was on her husband, rather than on her. *Weird,* she thought. *Definitely weird.*

"What kind of work did *he* do before coming to Norway?" Tan continued. "Your CV showcased *your* brilliance in having had two ad creations make it in top magazines, but *his* accomplishments? By the way, I hope I'm not keeping you from anything. I just miss phone conversations. No one much to call, as I pretty much live with everyone I know in Norway," he chuckled.

Awkward, Kaitlin decided. "No, it's alright. It's just that I have to meet my friend soon, so…"

"You're meeting Sibel today?' Tan asked eagerly. *Too eagerly*, Kaitlin decided, not caring to correct her lie by saying she'd actually be meeting her the following day.

"Oh, but wait. It was *momma* Sibel, wasn't it? Oh, wait, wait. I think someone wants to talk to you, hold on…" Kaitlin was hoping it was Meredith: a female and his girlfriend. Things needed to become less awkward… and fast!

"Ms. Kaitlin?" Finn's voice sounded raspy.

"Finn?" *Oh boy*, she thought. "You sound sick, are you okay?" As soon as she asked, she regretted it. Who was he for her to sound so concerned? She felt powerless over her words with him for some reason, as if she were bewitched. How could she *feel* such a rapport with him when her mind was definitely telling her this was insanity? Unfortunately, feelings affected her body much more than her mind could, so the excited yet guards-down state she always seemed to be in when talking to him managed to clear her doubts each time.

"Better now that I hear your concern," Finn continued. "Listen, we don't want to keep you from any plans. Just wanted to say 'great job' on the translation. And so quick! I mean, yes, we only sent you one page this time, but those were some unnecessarily big words those Senegalese used! Really, small company or not, they use more professional French than even our Parisian clients. It's remarkable!"

Kaitlin smiled proudly. She was definitely more flattered when congratulated on an ability rather than her looks or some other trait which she had no control over. "Thank you. But I *just* sent it. It's rather quick of *you* to have read it already. Either way, thanks again."

"We're impressed!" Tan screamed enthusiastically into the phone. Finn and Kaitlin both laughed; though for her, it was more out of slight ridicule. Were these guys *serious*? The piece she had to translate had really *not* been as complicated as they were making it sound: it was something about being pleased with the results of a shipment of two different types of paper used, and a detailed order for more. It hadn't appeared to Kaitlin to be above high-school-level French. Were these people really *that* bad at translations and language fluency, or was *she* really just that good? *Either way, it feels refreshing to be complimented on some service I'm able to render*, she thought.

"We sure are, Ms. Kaitlin," Finn continued, his throat still sounding hoarse and dry. "And we'd like to work with you officially. Anja typed your contract and we would like to have you come in this afternoon to sign it. As you may be able to tell, the others are back. You'll also be meeting with them. It'll be fun."

Anja. *A woman's name,* Kaitlin thought. Apparently now there would at least be two other women besides herself there: a reason to feel less nervous about Paul finding out. The whole thing would be like making friends at work (like Paul had), wouldn't it? After all, he had his, what was it, close buds Lars, Tim, and, oh yes, how could she leave out *Jeanette?*

"I appreciate it, thank you, but…" Kaitlin started to ask whether going to meet them tomorrow would be better. If she went later that day, she'd be leaving the house for two days in a row without an explanation. That would make Paul suspicious. After all, she had already gone to the gym *and* would be meeting Sibel tomorrow. She supposed she *could* say she was going shopping; yet that was something Paul knew she'd be doing to blow off steam when she *hadn't* been out of the house for a while, which uncharacteristically hadn't been the case recently.

Argh, Kaitlin thought. *I hate having to do these things. I never want to be like 'those' women—like my mother terms women of 'loose morals'. But I'm almost forced to lie like a teenager under these circumstances. Paul isn't exactly an open-minded man: he wouldn't understand this unorthodox professional arrangement.*

"Would it be possible for me to stop by tomorrow afternoon?" Kaitlin suddenly blurted out, counting on the good mood Paul's voice was in on the phone earlier, and keeping her fingers crossed. "That is, if you don't mind. I mean, today there is this, family thing, so."

"Family," Finn started to say, with an audible smirk. "I see… well, actually, we're having a celebration tomorrow for Anja's birthday; so maybe that would work out better, right guys?" Kaitlin heard some mumbling in the background as Finn addressed his housemate-colleagues. "Ok, so, no problem, then. We'd love for you to come right before, say, around 4 o'clock? That is, of course, if you wouldn't mind being around our preparations for the evening and such." *Hmm,* Kaitlin thought. *That would mean going there after lunch with Sibel. If I stay for an hour, I could be back home by 5:30. It could work, I suppose.*

"That sounds perfect. Thanks for your understanding," Kaitlin exclaimed. "Now when you say 'contract', I haven't yet met Mr. ... what was his name... Lar? Yes? I mean, would *he* be okay with that? Also, it wouldn't be full-time or anything like that, right? I mean, you have to understand, as a married woman I can't exactly go into a home-like environment for work very often..." Kaitlin let out a nervous laughter, biting her lip as two wooden fishing-boats treaded behind one another outside her window view.

"It's a temporary contract, Ms. Kaitlin," Finn interrupted matter-of-factly, as if he were prepared for such a speech. "Like I told you. It's project-based, so you'd mostly be translating online and would have to come in very little. We wouldn't want to disturb Mr. Maverick or anything. Don't worry."

Had he gotten a little offended or was it just her? She hadn't meant to sound unprofessional. "Alright, then. I'll be there at 4. Thanks again."

"You can come by yourself this time, right Ms. Kaitlin?" Finn asked.

"Sure thing." Kaitlin responded.

"Alright, 'til then. Give us a call if you get lost." Finn said as he ended the phone call.

All Kaitlin could suddenly think about as she hung up the phone was the beautiful-smelling flowers and the dreamlike fountain she was shown... with Finn's warm hands on the back of her shoulders.

***

Opening the entrance door of the local French Café, Kaitlin peeked in to see that Sibel had arrived before her. Her new friend had on a long-sleeved, deep green tunic which highlighted her hourglass figure, over shiny black stockings and knee-length black leather boots. A black pearl necklace complemented by black dangly earrings peeked through her shoulder-length chocolate hair, as she stood up to welcome Kaitlin with a warm hand grip with both hands.

"There you are, honey. I was just going to send you a text, to make sure everything was alright."

Kaitlin was amazed at how sweet this woman appeared to be. She didn't yet know whether their recent acquaintanceship would bloom into a close friendship, but Sibel's company sure had come at a poignant time in Kaitlin's life: when she'd wished for such a social distraction, mostly for her mental health!

"I pace-walked as fast as I could," Kaitlin was still out of breath as she placed her other hand on Sibel's. She mentally applauded herself on deciding to wear her casual wedge boots over her pumps at the last-minute right before leaving the door, despite the professional outfit she'd had on for the cabin later.

"You're starting to be out-of-breath less and less, though," Sibel smiled and pulled her chair back in. "It's a good sign. I mean, you're not a smoker, right? A few more full days at the gym and your body will get accustomed to speed in no time."

"I sure hope so," Kaitlin responded, running her fingers through her hair. "And no, no, I don't smoke. So, what's good here, what are we drinking?"

"Well, I have my go-to latte. The ones they serve here are absolutely delicious. Do you like lattes?" Sibel asked as she took a small, delicate bite off a chocolate-drizzled croissant. Then added, "I'm sorry, I already ordered. I hope you don't mind. Did you eat at home?"

"That's Ok. I'm good with just a latte, thanks. But Sibel! My goodness, you surprise me. How many calories is that?" Kaitlin always hated it when topic of conversation somehow always ended up with someone's weight control, yet watching one's figure was the only thing the two of them had so far shared.

"Ah!" Sibel waved her off with her French-manicured hand. "We can reward ourselves once a week if we've been good for the remainder of that week, can't we?"

"You're right, you're right," Kaitlin nodded with a smile, standing up to order a latte from the friendly Arab-looking man at the counter. The international quality of this city had indeed been one of the biggest surprises for her. The truth is she had expected everyone to be blonde and light-eyed. "I'm just not really a sweets person, so…" As soon as she said it, the image of the fruity cake Meredith had served the other day came to her mind. She truly wasn't a dessert person, yet she sure had eaten at the cabin without protest, hadn't she? *Enough self-guilt-tripping,* she decided. *That was to fit in for professional reasons. I'll consider it my 'weekly-allowed-indulgence'.*

"I hear goodies like these will also be served at our subsequent PWC meetings from now on too," Sibel continued, reminding Kaitlin of the other thing they had in common to discuss. It felt funny just then to realize how the whole 'Group' surprise had taken precedence in her mind over the Women's Club she'd finally managed to get herself to the previous week. "Speaking of which, you're coming again to the next meeting up in January, right?"

"I hadn't really thought of it, actually," Kaitlin answered truthfully, peering over her shoulder. "Will you two be going?"

"Us two?" Sibel looked quizzed, yet immediately a look of understanding washed over her face. "Ah, you mean Jamie." She threw her head back with a wide-mouthed smile, staring up at the Parisian-themed wall behind them. "I don't know if her mother-in-law will let her. It's a crazy arrangement she has in that home of hers. Poor thing."

"I guess everyone has their drama, don't they?" Kaitlin asked over her shoulder, nodding thankfully at the raven-haired man as she went on to pick her latte up from the counter.

"Uh oh," Sibel said, raising one eyebrow at Kaitlin when she sat back down. "Is there anything *you* would like to share? I mean, I know we haven't known each other long, but you can tell me anything. Believe me, I know how boring and lonesome it can get in this city at first."

"It's not the city! At least, I don't think so…" Kaitlin *cut her off.* Sibel's invitation to open up to her fulfilled such a necessity to share all that was bursting inside of her with someone, that she'd temporarily shelved away any misgivings and logic as to their friendship being new.

"Something's bothering you," Sibel quipped. "Look, I know I may seem like I've got it all under control now, with Engin and our babies. But trust me, it wasn't always like this. Believe me, we went through some *real* difficulties to get to this stage in our lives."

"I appreciate you saying that," Kaitlin said. *Screw logic.* "It's just that Paul and I feel so different from one another sometimes. I can never fully be open the way I want to with him. For example, a few days ago, I was in town and all of a sudden I came across this man…"

***

It had been only a half hour or so since she'd come home after Kaitlin confided in her about her secret 'work deal', yet Sibel still couldn't figure out what it was about this 'Finn' person that was bothering her. It wasn't like she knew Kaitlin very well yet, but their instant bond was strengthened, at least on her side, due to her empathy towards her.

She threw the whites into the laundry and hit 'Start'.

I went through the same emptiness and boredom she is now going through, she recalled. Currently she and Engin were luckily doing much better, especially with their daughter Aylin and little Hakan—a Turkish name they'd given their son as it sounded similar to the Norwegian word for 'king'.

During her husband's first year in Norway, Sibel stayed behind in Istanbul with then newborn Aylin. She'd wanted to be close to her family for their support with the baby, and thought that she and Engin would make it through the long distance okay. They hadn't been able to make trips out to see each other as frequently as originally planned, however; and things gradually soured between them. When Sibel decided to take Aylin and move to Stavanger, everyone told her she was crazy. "It isn't worth your effort," her family would tell her. "He hasn't been good to you. You can't trust a man who values his career over his wife's feelings."

Yet Sibel had refused to give up hope and chose to have faith that they were going through a temporary period in order to create a more secure future for their family. Their hot-and-cold cycle had initially continued once they were under the same roof again in Stavanger, but with time, and many days of long conversations, including an important intervention by her father to warn Engin on his negative attitude, they seemed to be on track again. Hakan was born and his name would remind them of their 'finding each other again in Norway', they'd decided.

Sibel recognized the eternal optimist in her wanting Kaitlin to similarly conquer her demons and grow more satisfied in her new life. *That is probably why this Finn person is bothering me*, she told herself. *I just don't want some other man to cloud my new friend's mind needlessly.*

Yet she also couldn't shake off the feeling that there was something else in what Kaitlin had told her that was bothering her. Was it the fact that she was keeping this 'new job' a secret? Was it Finn's unusual occupation and circle, and their secretive life in the woods? What was it that sounded so familiar to her? For the life of her she couldn't just then figure it out. Oh well. She would have to wait until it came to her. In the meantime, she was just hoping that her new friend (aside from her need to tell her husband the truth, in her opinion) wasn't in any major trouble.

***

"How… in the world… did I just reveal The Group to Sibel?" Kaitlin asked herself under her breath, causing a couple of older Norwegian ladies passing by to stare at this fast-walking lady that was talking to herself. She must have looked crazy to them, and she was no longer sure she truly wasn't.

Often preferring to be upfront with people, Kaitlin hated having secrets. She'd learned throughout the years that she wasn't even *able* to lie efficiently since her body system often literally broke out in dark pink hives whenever she got nervous and did so. Surprising herself for what must have been the umpteenth time in the past week, she walked toward the path to the cabin.

She would just sign their contract, meet the others politely, and leave as promptly as she could.

***

"There she is… dear Ms. Ca-na-da…" Tan sang her welcome to the tune of what Kaitlin was sure had originally been 'Miss America', as he opened the red door of the cabin to greet her. Kaitlin chuckled. Gratefully he was fully dressed this time (and surprisingly in professional attire at that), with a crisp, white button-down shirt and a designer-label green vest over dark trousers.

"Hello… hello… thank you," Kaitlin cooed, beaming with the admiring look-over he gave to her own 'professional-as-possible-without-going-overboard-in-a-cabin-environment' combination of a silky burgundy top she'd bought on *salg* at the local *Gina Tricot* store, over slim navy pants and her matching wedges.

"Is this our translator? Hi! Welcome!" A cheerful blonde woman with a modern, shoulder-length haircut and sparkling blue eyes came to her with arms open for a welcome hug.

Oh dear. Kaitlin thought. *A hug?*

"Oh, hi, thank you, yes," Kaitlin hugged back to be polite. "Are you…"

"Anja. The birthday girl. That's me!" Anja exclaimed, with an over-the-top smile. "I'll put away your coat!"

Damn, this girl is bubbly: the very opposite of Meredith, Kaitlin thought.

"Oh, yes, yes, Finn told me. Happy birthday!" Kaitlin walked in and removed her trench coat, handing it to Anja. "Thank you. Is he here, by the way? Finn? I actually came in today a little early to discuss the contract, which I believe *you* have for me…?"

"That's right, Kaitlin," Anja said excitedly. "I have all that prepared for you to sign, don't worry about it. But, look, business later. Come on! Today is a birthday! It's a good day!" Kaitlin secretly wondered how old this woman-child was turning, exactly, with her overly playful attitude: sixteen?

"And not just because it's my own," Anja continued. "I mean, birthdays are great in general. When's yours?"

Apparently their small talk was to continue. Kaitlin saw that the living room was empty except for some party decorations, although she could hear noise from upstairs. "Me? Oh, mine is on October 8th…"

"You're a Libra!" Anja said, almost immediately. *Damn this New-age-girl is good*, Kaitlin thought. *She'd get along with Sandy.*

"I'm a Sagittarius," Anja continued. "It explains why I'm so active all the time, right baby?" Anja turned around to face a fit young man, who had just then climbed down the stairs dressed in a casual shirt and beige trousers, with slicked-back hair and chiseled jawline.

This guy didn't look the least bit amused, giving her a raise of the eyebrow and an aloof nod. "Hey, I'm Bjorn. Nice to meet you, Kaitlin."

"Likewise," Kaitlin responded, shaking his now outreached hand. *Damn, the guy sure has a firm grip.* He'd definitely shaken her hand for a good ten seconds or so longer than normal, as far as she was concerned.

She turned around to face Anja, who was eyeing their hands intensely. The woman appeared to lighten up however when Bjorn then gave her a brief kiss on the cheek.

"Well, I don't know if *I* carry any of my sign's supposed characteristics, but, yes, I am indeed a Scale!" Kaitlin attempted a forced laugh after her own little joke, but it seemed to have flown by over their heads. She certainly didn't yet feel herself quite click with this particular couple.

"Look who we have here," Finn exclaimed, eyeing Kaitlin up and down as he also now came down the stairs, with Meredith following close behind. "Welcome again to our humble abode, Miss."

"Thanks," Kaitlin smiled, clasping her hands together in front of her and playing with her thumbs.

"Hi Kaitlin," Meredith kissed her cheek 'welcome'. It felt odd to be physically this friendly with this girl when she had known Sibel for about the same amount of time, yet had not yet done so, despite having shared much more with her.

"Did you guys wrap up those preparations upstairs?" Bjorn asked Meredith suggestively, raising his eyebrows twice in a row.

This guy is apparently on a similar mindset as Tan, Kaitlin thought.

Meredith just laughed off Bjorn's question, but it occurred to Kaitlin just then that she and Finn *had* descended the stairs together, with Tan and Anja now working on something together in the kitchen. Kaitlin wondered how long they had all actually known each other in order for everyone to be so close. "What's so interesting upstairs, you guys?" she asked, deciding to play the 'naïve' card.

"Oh, Kaitlin," Tan waved a hand dismissively. "Be patient. You are just beginning here…"

"Is it a surprise for Anja?" Kaitlin insisted.

"Well… if it were… you just ruined it for me, didn't you?" Anja turned around from the kitchen counter and laughed, stirring laughter from everyone else.

"Oops! I guess I did!" Kaitlin said sheepishly. "Sorry, guys, I'll just change the subject. So, Anja…Finn mentioned you and Bjorn are doing your work out in the lake by Sirdal?"

"We sure are," Bjorn answered for the both of them, raising an eyebrow at Anja. "It's great fun."

Weirdo, Kaitlin thought. "It's beautiful there. My husband and I visited it twice last winter. Although we have yet to see it in the summer…"

"It's much prettier in the winter," Anja interrupted enthusiastically now, wiping her wet hands with a towel and walking next to Bjorn. "It's a scene straight out of the Winter Olympics, isn't it?"

"I'm sure it is," Kaitlin replied, as Anja put her head on Bjorn's shoulder and he landed a loud kiss on her forehead in return. "Paul and I absolutely loved it there! Paul, he's..."

"Your old man, I know, Kaitlin," Anja smiled.

"Ahem," Finn cleared his throat from one of the burgundy arm chairs, rapidly closing the cover of a photo album he'd been looking at. "I discussed all of your details with the Group, Miss Kaitlin. You're almost like *family*, already."

As soon as he spoke the words, a cold chill went up Kaitlin's spine, though she feigned an uncomfortable smile. Five pairs of eyes were all now fixated on her. This was beginning to feel like too much, too soon. Was she overreacting? Was this simply the 'friendly', 'European' way of making new acquaintances? She still had so many of her questions unanswered; and Kaitlin wasn't one to let things flow when she wasn't feeling on top of events.

"Umm, thanks. May I take a look at that album, Finn? If you don't mind..." Kaitlin requested.

"What album?" Finn jumped and placed the leather-bound album inside a drawer close to the television set. "It's nothing interesting, just some pictures from various meetings we've attended."

Kaitlin couldn't help but notice a pleading look Finn's green eyes shot at Tan.

"Come on, Kaitlin, since you're going to be leaving early, allow us to give you a preview of the fun we'll be having outside tonight," Tan indeed cut in, jumping from his seat and walking toward the door. "We'll take much cooler pictures there... we light a fire, roast sweets... it's an awesome time."

"After you, Kaitlin," Meredith chimed in as she grabbed a short, beige coat and headed toward the door. Kaitlin knew she didn't exactly have a choice in the matter. She'd come this far to the cabin: and of her own volition. She'd play along and head out with them before referencing the contract again—and head back home at the first opportunity.

"Come on, let's get started!" Tan was motioning for everyone to pose in front of a fire he'd set over a couple of logs almost immediately once they'd all walked toward one of the towering evergreen trees close to the cabin. The ten-minute walk into the forest had Kaitlin lagging at the back of the group behind Meredith, who'd often turned around to face her as the two of them exchanged sympathetic smiles. "Everyone gather around for a picture!"

"Not an easy path, Kaitlin," Meredith whispered.

"Yeah, I really need to go the gym more!" *Now, how many times have I been repeating that phrase lately?* Kaitlin thought, chuckling to herself, though she noticed that Meredith's serious glare into her eyes had continued despite her little joke.

"It's starting to get dark," Kaitlin said, staring up at the sky. "I hope I didn't forget to bring my little flashlight with me for my walk back…" Rummaging through her bag, Kaitlin was glad to have located the golden-plated brass metal flashlight she'd often carry around in the winter time upon Paul's advice. She placed it in one of the large pockets of her coat, and hugged herself to ward off the briskly gusts of wind that had just begun to blow in their direction.

Tan and Finn had been walking speedier than all of them. At one point, Kaitlin could swear they were saying something about her from the serious glances they threw over their shoulders in her direction.

Why isn't Finn coming to join us? Kaitlin thought, taking her place in the picture on the other side of Anja. Finn was leaning on a tall tree opposite them, watching them with an intent yet blank stare.

"Finn?" Kaitlin called out, "come join us. It's apparently picture time."

"Nah, you guys go ahead," Finn said. "I'm not into pictures as much as Tan," he attempted a chuckle.

"But it's for your friend Anja's birthday," Kaitlin insisted, looking around for support. "Right?"

To her surprise no one muttered a word.

"Someone needs to take the bloody picture," Anja deadpanned, snuggling her head into Bjorn's shoulder and striking a sulky pose.

"I have many poses with them, don't worry Ms. Kaitlin." Finn tried to reassure her. "But, alright…alright…." Finn finally got into the frame, kneeling down on one knee in front of Bjorn. *Away from me*, Kaitlin thought with a surprising feeling of disappointment.

"Everyone, smile," Tan requested, clicking the button.

"And now, Tan, you get in the picture…" Finn said, taking the plastic-looking disposable camera from Tan and then taking his place by the tall evergreen beauty. "Smile everyone…perfect".

"We'll take another one of just the two of you by that tree, Finn…" Anja said in a slightly evocative tone that gave Kaitlin the chills. Was she trying to take a picture of herself with Finn alone? As if they were some sort of couple? Now, *that* was really not necessary—as far as she was concerned.

"Anja, let's mind our own business, shall we, my sexy one?" Bjorn said harshly, grabbing Anja's hand abruptly.

"It's Ok, Anja, really," Kaitlin interrupted something Finn was apparently going to say. She really wasn't liking the way these guys seemed to exert power over their girlfriends.

"Guys, Lar's going to love these shots," Anja said.

Lar. There's that name again, Kaitlin thought. "Guys, look, I really need to get going, so… "

"Hey, not so fast! We didn't dance to celebrate my big day yet!" Anja said, as she took Kaitlin's hand and pranced closer to the deep-orange flames like a little girl. Kaitlin found herself being twirled beyond her control not once but twice (once in each direction) to some tune that only Anja seemed to be able to hear in her own, shut-eyed world.

"Alright! We need some music for you, girls," Bjorn said, taking out his phone. "Tan, where's that playlist?"

"Right… here," Tan put down a can of Hoegaarden beer he'd just popped open and grabbed Bjorn's smartphone, hitting the screen twice for a Norwegian pop track to begin pumping.

"Karpe Diem!" Bjorn raised his eyebrows excitedly at his girlfriend, taking a can of beer from the cooler himself. "Baby, show Kaitlin some of our moves."

"Kaitlin, this is one of our favorite music groups," Anja ran her other hand through her hair and touched her hips, which had now begun to sway to the soft hip-hop sounds. "Come on! It's warm by the fire… Do you like this style?"

"I have to admit I do," Kaitlin said honestly, as she found herself moving to the beat along with Anja. She'd had some good times dancing with her girlfriends in Toronto when she was a student. She recalled back to those times, and decided not to let it bother her that Anja's right hand was still holding her left one while they danced. It was definitely a purer form of entertainment than being coupled with Finn in photographs, she decided.

For a moment, Kaitlin lost track of time, but as the song came to an end, she turned to see what everyone else was doing. Finn was strangely still on his own, leaning against the same tree with his eyes fixed on his phone. He didn't seem to catch her eyes. That was good, but Finn was definitely acting weird. *Why isn't he conversing with the guys?* Kaitlin wondered. Tan and Bjorn were apparently laughing at something incredibly funny next to the fire they'd set up, oblivious to both Finn and Meredith too.

"Meredith?" Kaitlin called out, looking at the sad-faced young woman sitting on the edge of a big rock, playing with her nails. "Come dance with us!"

"Thanks," Meredith smiled. 'But I'm not good like you, guys."

"Oh, don't do the downplaying-thing, Mer," Anja said, still dancing to the beat as Kaitlin went to join Meredith to sit on the rock. "You're just more into KISS and that Guns N'Roses stuff, aren't you?"

"Yeah, yeah," Meredith said. "I'm more of a rocker. You got me, birthday girl."

Kaitlin got the feeling the two ladies weren't particularly fond of each other.

"Look at her still doing her thing," Kaitlin turned to Meredith. "What a burst of energy!"

"You can say that," Meredith chuckled. "But hey, you're not a bad dancer yourself!"

"Aw, well I tried to get into it," Kaitlin blushed. "Is this what you guys always do when you come out here to hang out?"

"Sometimes," Meredith said in a somber tone, staring blankly into space now. The young men had now joined Anja in moving to the music, and were calling out to Finn now to join in. "You don't regret coming, do you, Kaitlin?"

"Umm, no, I don't think so," Kaitlin spoke, taking in a deep breath through her nostrils. The music had come to a stop and Kaitlin felt eyes on her again. She turned to face the others, who had now all walked closer to them. This time her eyes made full contact with Finn's serious gaze. *Damn.*

"I mean, I must admit this clean air has been refreshing. I'll probably sleep like a baby tonight… Speaking of which, I really should…"

"We're sleeping in Finn's big fancy bed again tonight, right baby?" Bjorn asked Anja, sending chills down Kaitlin's spine.

Was she hearing correctly? Finn's bed? Why would a couple want to sleep in someone else's 'big fancy bed'? Did these people use each other's rooms interchangeably, like a hotel? Did different people use cabins, too? Is that why each home lacked personal touches from the housemates? A million thoughts were suddenly dispersing through Kaitlin's head in all directions.

"Well, where would Finn sleep, then?" Kaitlin asked. The look that she received immediately told her perhaps she was being naïve.

Oh my God, she thought to herself soon after, just as an image popped up in her head. Maybe Finn would be in his own bed as well after all.

"Aww, she's a sweetie, Finn," Bjorn smirked. "Our bed isn't too shabby either, you two. Don't worry… Just something to keep in mind Kaitlin if you can ever stay over…."

Had she dreamed it? Nope. There they were. Crisp and clear. The words had truly left Bjorn's mouth, confirming her suspicions of some freaky practices these folks were apparently used to conducting in their bedrooms and God knew where else. Kaitlin straightened out her coat, looking around to try to find the direction back toward town. She found herself unable to think anymore. All she could feel was an innate instinct that she had to get out of there as fast as possible.

"Guys, thanks for today, but I'm going to be leaving now, so…"

"Kaitlin!" Anja called out with a pout. "Bjorn just meant you should stay with us at the cabin since, you know, it's getting dark."

"Happy birthday, Anja," Kaitlin tried her best to look as calm as possible while she put on her coat and took out the flashlight from inside her right pocket. "But I have to go. You're right. It *is* late."

"What's going on?" Tan asked nonchalantly, opening a can of beer and taking a sip.

"It seems I was never going to get a contract today, was I, Finn?" Kaitlin brought herself to look at the shocked man now in front of her straight in the eye. Bjorn's words had strangely given her courage. She was hoping she sounded less scared than she truly was inside. She tried to assure herself that, despite being away from civilization, the men around her wouldn't exactly rape or kill her or anything with Anja and Meredith present, would they?

Without giving Finn, who was still uncharacteristically standing very far from her, a chance to respond, Kaitlin took long steps to get away from the Group as fast as possible, without looking like she was running scared.

"What? She's leaving?" Bjorn was asking someone behind her, audible enough for Kaitlin to make it out despite the sound of cracking twigs underneath her feet. "You failures..."

Chapter 11

"**W**ait! Kaitlin!" Finn ran after her. "Bjorn was just kidding, Kaitlin!"

Kaitlin walked faster and faster until she was sure she'd lost him. She looked ahead over some low-lying bushes and was relieved to see the lights from some of the buildings in town—already lit in the early winter twilight. *He said my name*, she thought just then, as her heart began to pound slower with the vision of familiarity. *He finally just said 'Kaitlin'.*

Why should I care? Kaitlin pondered. These people were obviously more than just colleagues or even roommates. Whatever they did, or didn't do, it instinctively felt too *wild* for her to be around; and she thought *she* was liberal-minded! Next to people like Bjorn and Anja, and probably even Tan and Meredith, she felt conservative—and, dare she say it, more like Paul.

"There you are!" Finn suddenly jumped straight in front of her. Kaitlin let out a loud scream and dropped the flashlight from her hand. "Let me get that… please…" she said.

"Wait, stop!" Finn interjected. "Forget the damn flashlight… Why are you… Relax…" Finn first placed a strong grip on her mouth then quickly placed both his hands in a softer, more comforting way around her shoulders. "I hope… your… little misunderstanding back there… doesn't mean that… you won't be coming back or anything… does it?"

"Misunderstanding? Right. And I should *come back* to do what, exactly, Finn?" Kaitlin realized she was yelling, yet immediately knew it was most likely that no one could hear her, except for the rest of the gang themselves. Attempting to wrestle her arms out of Finn's firm grip was a futile effort. Where were those daily Norwegian joggers when you needed them? Why did they prefer to circle lakes? Didn't they ever come out here? Some of the more adventurous ones, at least?

"Please, let go of my arms."

"Okay. Okay," Finn chuckled nervously, holding his palms out in retreat. "Come back, to just hang out with us. I mean, forget what Bjorn said. You seem to get along with Meredith… and… me?" He actually smiled at her, and in *that* way, too! The nerve of him: face lowered, eyes opened-wide and looking up with a pout. *Her* favorite puppy-eye look!

You barely even spoke to me out there with everyone else around, she was going to say, but then quickly stopped herself. Kaitlin took a deep breath and gulped.

"I came again today with the sincere wish that this was something serious: more serious than Tan's casualness had let on last time. I'd chosen to look past all that." Pleased to see that Finn wasn't interrupting her and actually listening, Kaitlin took a deep breath and continued to speak. "You gave me an actual task. Translation. I told myself you guys must follow some sort of nature-living philosophy or whatever—along with a genuine business. And I came today to sign a project-based contract, like you promised. But, everyone's attitude, and Bjorn's implications… I just can't… That's not something I can handle, I'm sorry!"

"I *have* your contract, *and* your pay," Finn continued begging her with his eyes as he reached into the back pocket of his form-fitting dark denim and took out two bills of 500 Kroner from his leather wallet. The bills had been placed between a folded white sheet of paper. "Here is the payment, as promised. Kaitlin, we *are* genuine. I hope you can see that. Please don't be judgmental like this without knowing everything or without meeting Lar."

"Look, I appreciate I could be of some use," Kaitlin said, taking the cash hesitantly and throwing it randomly into her purse—she would place it in her wallet later. The 'too-little-too-late', yet still professional gesture eased her nerves a little bit.

"Thank you for your payment, like you promised. I… I'll be in touch. Right now, I really can't think… I'm sorry… I've got to go…"

"You're *judging*, Ms. Kaitlin," Finn said with more ease now. He must have caught her looking at him more softly.

Cocky bastard, Kaitlin thought, sensing her blood begin to boil once again. "No. If I had, I wouldn't have come all the way out into the woods again. So, no judgment, just, disagreement, let's say. Please, just, let me go home and process everything. I'll be in touch!" Kaitlin managed an ever-slight smile and turned to walk back toward town.

"You never signed the contract!" Finn exclaimed somewhere now far behind her. "So you obviously have no serious intention of considering... translating for us again."

"That's not true," Kaitlin stopped to turn around slowly in her tracks, grateful she was no longer being followed, since Finn's voice had sounded as if it were coming from a longer distance now. "Look, this has been a strange experience for me. Please, understand. And allow me time to just, think. Okay? I'll be in touch, I promise."

Finn was already gone. The only thing remaining in his place was the golden-colored torch she had dropped, which Kaitlin desperately wished could somehow magically shed a light on her situation.

Chapter 12

Kaitlin fixed her curl-ironed ringlets in the mirror one last time before heading to the living room to join Paul for a dinner he'd volunteered to prepare all by himself. She'd asked what the occasion was (especially feeling as guilty as she did), yet hadn't persisted any further since Paul told her to "…just stop asking and enjoy it."

I'll try, she thought with a shrug. She'd been avoiding Finn's phone calls for an entire week now. It had strangely become a routine. She would receive precisely three rings on her cellphone from him: one in the morning, another one in the afternoon and one around dinner time each evening for over a week now. Just one ring. It was like he knew she wouldn't be picking up, but wanted to be annoying or just be a reminder to her of his presence. At first she'd thought he had dialed her number by mistake then hung up, but the pattern had made it clear that wasn't the situation.

Each time was enough to make her heart jump. The weekend and evening calls when Paul was with her were the most troubling for her. It'd forced her to keep her phone on silent mode. *After all*, she thought, *with Paul with me, who else would call me, really?* The thought of blocking his number had crossed her mind, of course; yet she couldn't exactly bring herself to do that either. How long would he keep up this childish, bordering on obsessive, behavior? She'd been flattered (indeed) and had to also admit that the excitement of trying to keep a call hidden from Paul had proved to be simultaneously both terrifying and titillating for her.

"Mmmm." The smell of oven-baked salmon made Kaitlin immediately run up behind her husband (who'd actually brought himself to wear one of the several girly aprons her mother had bought for her after her marriage) and place her arms around his neck. "Thank you, honey! I've missed getting my Omega 3's."

Paul leaned down and kissed her forehead. "You're welcome, babe. But just wait! Look! There's more than the usual."

Kaitlin leaned over to her right to feast her eyes on two of their finest guest-plates adorned with a variety of vegetables accompanying the sesame-sprinkled boneless and juicy-pink salmon, alongside steaming white rice and… some sort of, cake?

"Babe? Did you actually make dessert? All by yourself?"

"Of course!" Paul said with a mockingly-confident smile that soon turned into a sheepish grin. "Nah! I wanted to, but I figured I wouldn't be able to fix it in time. This was your favorite from that bakery *Scholade-Pikken,* from what I remember…"

How could she forget? The all-chocolate cake with multi-colored sprinkles *had* looked familiar. But they hadn't eaten it since they were still dating, from what she could remember. "But, honey," Kaitlin started to say, taking her seat as Paul followed suit, "we haven't gone to Scholade since… since…."

"Yes?" Paul's encouraging smile suddenly turned into a frown. "You don't remember, do you?"

Remember? Kaitlin was truly taken aback. It sure wasn't any of their birthdays nor their anniversary; and normally she was the one adamant about this stuff. In fact, she'd even insisted on celebrating every anniversary they possibly could think of to celebrate: from their first time holding hands, to their first kiss, their first… *Oh my God!* Kaitlin thought.

"Baby! Oh my God! Today's the 27th, isn't it? Anniversary of the night we first made love! After that night out at the café. What did we call the cake? Our 'aphrodisiac', right? Aww, we haven't gone there since…"

"Good, girl. See? I told you I could be more than romantic when you are *not* expecting it!" Paul winked at her. "Bon appetit."

Kaitlin was at a loss for words as they began eating. It was too beautiful. So beautiful that she was afraid the moment would be fleeting and something would soon happen to upset her again, as she often found to be the case.

As if on cue, her phone began to vibrate on the living room coffee table. *Crap!* She thought. *Best to ignore it.*

"Babe?" Paul asked.

"Mmm, the fish is especially delicious tonight, sweety! We *forgot* the mood music! Let me get the remote..." Kaitlin tried to change the subject.

"Umm, yeah, and your phone too while you're at it. It's pulsating like crazy!" Paul spoke in a firm voice, while Kaitlin stood up to turn on their favorite 'Slow Jam' music station on their television set. "And why exactly *is* it on vibration-mode, may I ask?"

"I don't know, honey," Kaitlin said honestly, finally reaching for her phone. That's what she was asking herself, too! She had apparently mistakenly pressed 'Vibration' rather than 'Silent' before Paul had come home. *Damn it.*

"Sibel!" Kaitlin let out a sigh of relief, seeing the name flash on her screen as she pressed the button to answer her phone call. Her new friend had saved the day like an angel.

***

Kaitlin woke up the following morning to the sounds of seagulls. She smiled. Not only had she and her husband managed to make rather satisfying love the previous night, but she was looking forward to meeting a real friend –honestly, this time– and perhaps telling her everything again. She needed her conscience to also unload, despite her body having been satisfied.

She stretched her arms over the top of her head as far as she could. "Mmm, what time is it?"

"Good morning, sunshine," Paul snuggled up to his wife and planted a sleepy, breathy kiss on the back of her neck. "I'm going to work a little late today. They'll be easy on me since I've worked so hard for tomorrow's party."

"Oh you've been working *real* hard, haven't you?" Kaitlin teased turning over and laying her head on his white tank-top. *God, why does he have to insist on wearing that cheesy, school-boy thing, for 'warmth'?* He looked so much sexier to her topless—despite his flabbiness as of late due to one or two office-sweets too many.

"Yes, I have," Paul pouted, right before giving Kaitlin another kiss on her cheeks and getting up to head to the shower. "You should get going, too, babe. When are you meeting your friend, again?"

"At one o 'clock," Kailin replied groggily, still holding on tight to their duvet. She'd been looking forward to the company and conversation –yes– but not the exercise that was apparently to come with it. *Argh*, she thought, *why does the only girl friend I seem to have made in Norway have to be an Olympic-runner wannabe?* "Do you have enough time for breakfast together?"

"I think I'll grab a croissant at work, babe," she heard Paul respond just before the sound of rushing water filled her ears.

"Alright..." Kaitlin said to herself, disappointed. "Eat breakfast alone and go sweat it out just for the sake of friendly companionship, I shall."

***

"You.... are... extremely... slow this week!" Sibel yelled over her shoulder to Kaitlin, who wasn't able to score an empty treadmill next to her this time. "Have you gotten *any* work out over the past week at all? I finally manage going on *one* business trip with the husband and apparently no one else steps in to keep whipping you into shape!"

"Yeah, well, I don't want to be too worn out, you know," Kaitlin chuckled, walking it off at a more comfortable pace. She'd missed her new friend over the last few days and had had to resort back to visiting the H&Ms in town to pass the time. She was also grateful that the new money in her pocket had given her a self-made mission to spend time shopping away for a new outfit for herself, rather than dealing with Finn and the gang's craziness. "Tomorrow *is* the big Ball. I'm so glad to hear you'll be there, too, right?"

"Oh yeah, Engin gets tickets to... stuff like this all the time," Sibel panted, running speedily with both arms angled perfectly high next to her torso. "Many of his colleagues get jealous of his Statoil contacts. We didn't go last year, but I convinced him this year!"

"We couldn't go last year, either," Kaitlin added, panting now too, despite only doing speed-walking. "I'm glad to hear there'll be a familiar face there."

"That's right! In all my classic black-gown glory," Sibel chuckled. "You're sure to outshine everyone with your red number. Can you show me that amazing picture again? If you're almost done as well, that is."

Sibel slowed down her speed and Kaitlin gladly accepted an excuse to slow down as well. My *God*, she thought with frustration. How exercise or rather her inability to quite master it yet had made her feel older and worse about herself, despite many compliments from various people on her 'youthful looks' over the years pointing to the contrary.

:05… :04… :03… :02… :01… LAP COMPLETED.

Just as she held on to the rail to step off the apparatus, Kaitlin felt the strongest sensation to look straight ahead of her—despite seeing nothing but the white wall with a flat-screen TV airing music video clips.

"Kaitlin?" Sibel called out softly, wiping the back of her neck with a white towel. "What is it? What's wrong?"

"Huh?" Kaitlin whimpered. She could have sworn she felt eyes gazing at her again, piercing through her skin like an accidentally-touched flame from a candle, and giving her the chills like no creepy glance from a random pervert back in Toronto she'd ever experienced before. But she could not see anything. No sign of *him*. Nothing. "Oh, I'm fine," Kaitlin laughed nervously. "I just felt a little light-headed for a moment there, I think."

"Do you want to sit down?" Sibel asked with concern. "Why don't you kneel down for a bit? You're obviously still stressed out over that creepy bonfire-dancing ordeal!"

Walking to the gym from their meeting point in town, Kaitlin had gotten the events of the prior week off her chest—leaving out the last detail about Bjorn's bed comment, which she still felt a little ashamed about for some reason. She figured sharing the part about the Group trying to take a photo of her and Finn alone was enough to give Sibel the picture of the situation that was still giving her the creeps.

"Thanks, I'm good," Kaitlin took in a deep breath. "Let's go upstairs and get dressed in the Ladies room. I'll show you the photo. I left my cell in the locker. You know, I've been saving that picture for over a year now… Hey, what are you looking at?"

Sibel's attention had become fixated on a Bulletin Board hung up next to the staircase. "Have you checked these out before, Kaitlin? I try to look if there are any interesting concerts or comedy shows in town. Engin and I went to a one-man comedy sketch last summer at this little club right near *Timbuktu*. It was hilarious! I actually thanked my lucky stars that my mother-in-law was on a visit and at home to look after the kids!"

"Oh yeah? I see," Kaitlin chuckled. "No, I never looked at these things, actually. I'm such a bad Stavangerian, or, whatever."

"Stavangerian?" Sibel laughed. "What, like Hungarian? You're too funny, lady... Hey, look, Norsk classes. The weekly prices for this one don't look too bad."

"Yeah, well, we don't really need it, do we?" Kaitlin dismissed the sheet of paper Sibel was pointing at. "Luckily everyone speaks English here, so we get by."

"True," Sibel insisted, "but we *do* need it if we're going to be living here for a while, and want to *work*, remember?"

"Oh, yeah, that," Kaitlin muttered. How could she forget? "If I were you, I would definitely try to find some *real* work to do before having kids. It's a rich place and they pay workers well here—even secretaries and saleswomen! If I didn't have the kids, I would totally do it!"

"You *do* have a point," Kaitlin stated right as a perky blonde in a high-ponytail said "excuse me" to her with a smile. "Oh, sorry, here you are."

"We're blocking the way," Sibel snickered. "Let's go change already before our sweat really sinks into our skin and we stink up the café. Are you coming?"

Kaitlin had taken out her cell phone and written the number provided in the ad. "First name: Norsk. Second name: Classes. Got it. Saved. Let's go!"

"You're going to call?" Sibel asked with a smile as they were entered the Ladies changing room. "I'm impressed."

"I think so," Kaitlin said in a sure voice that surprised even herself. "I mean, even like, basic knowledge, mastered over several months should be enough for a job, right?"

"Yeah, I think basic knowledge is fine," Sibel responded, her voice suddenly taking a serious tone. "I take it you're no longer considering those strange people in the forest 'work', right?"

"No," Kaitlin said, thinking about the phone calls and the burning sensation she experienced on her skin earlier. "Definitely not."

She was not going to lose her mind (or her dignity) in this town.

Chapter 13

The circle of tiny mirrors on the futuristic wall-decors enhanced the power of the dim-yellow lights of the dangling crystal chandelier. Planet-replicas and tiny model-spaceships were abundant throughout the ballroom. Jeanette Johnson had made sure Venus and Mars were the most visible in size, standing for 'women' and 'men', in accord with one of her favorite books. With the addition of the silver balloons now covering the ceiling like a cloud of metal, and the matching covers culminating in a bow placed over the backs of ten chairs for each table, the decorations were all set. She had never been more excited in her life. Or at least from what she could remember of life before she'd met Tim.

She had never believed in love at first sight until she first heard his voice: that low-pitched, masculine voice which had penetrated into her soul much earlier than his boyish-looks-for-a-man-of-his-age had.

She would often picture the two of them married. In her mind there was a vision of her wearing her favorite silk apron, the one she'd bought but never really worn, cooking his favorite dish of steak and gravy-soaked potatoes. It was a date, in her mind at least, since he had proposed to 'discuss their ball project' at the chicest Italian restaurant in town. They were having ravioli (yet the man's mind was on steak, which he'd just said he regretted not having ordered instead). His cliché, masculine predictability was one of the things Jeanette found most charming about him. Steak, football, beer with the guys, barbeques—she was ready to accompany him through it all, as long as she could be an appreciated woman in her man's world.

She had refused to settle for the countless number of rather attractive men who'd come up to her to 'order her a drink' at the seaside bars in town: flirting in ways that suggested to her she was not the only recipient. If she was going to get married, or live with someone at least, it was going to be for keeps: all or nothing. Jeanette looked at her reflection on the glass doors and opened them with a heavy sigh. Annoyed, she tugged at her dress pulling it up over her heavy bosom one last time before allowing the first guests in. *Tim better make a move tonight*, she thought, or she sure was going to. No one was getting any younger.

***

Kaitlin glanced at her reflection over her left shoulder in the wooden-framed mirror hanging in the Ladies lounge. The satin mermaid-gown was hugging her curves a little tighter than she knew Paul would like. His look of simultaneous attraction and jealousy when he'd first seen her try it on was still fresh in her head, but she also knew that he would have to just deal with it for this special night. She had to admit she was looking pretty damn good and felt even better. Had she actually managed to lose a kilo or two at the gym? Or even walking to the cabin and back? Perhaps it was the stress of having led a mini double-life lately that had dampened her appetite. Either way, she was definitely looking slimmer. The deep crimson color of the hot number covering her pear-shaped body also helped.

Looking at her smiling reflection, Kaitlin realized she was feeling more excited to be spending this fancy evening with her husband than she had been hanging out with Finn and the Gang or Group or Nature Bang or whatever they wanted to call themselves. *What a relief*, she thought.

"Kaitlin!" an instantly recognizable, almost squeaky voice called out to her just then. Kaitlin took a deep breath before turning around to meet the 'nemesis' for her husband's affections she knew she had created in her head: her and that mysterious dead girl. The woman who was now standing a couple of inches away from her face, leaning in to give her a kiss on the cheek, was attractive alright, yet there was also something slightly homey and unthreatening about her in person that instantly calmed the feeling of dread in her stomach.

"Jeanette! Right? Nice to meet you in person!" Kaitlin said as she kissed her cheek back, thanking her lucky stars this woman wasn't kissing both cheeks like the Turks apparently did, the way she'd seen from Sibel during their latest coffee date.

"I know, right! Finally! Look at you, darlin'! You look amazing! Even prettier than the wedding photo Paul's got taped in his cubicle!"

Kaitlin didn't know whether to be flattered or obsess over which photo she was talking about. Could it be the photo where her husband was looking good but her close-mouthed smile, which Paul claimed to find endearing, made her look as puffy-faced as a preteen with too many Oreos in her mouth? She decided it didn't really matter, but secretly cursed herself for not taking Paul up on his offer of visiting him at his office yet. What kind of wife was she? She had honestly feared appearing like some 'jealous housewife', 'monitoring' her husband's every move, but she was beginning to realize more and more how backward her own perhaps unfair stereotypes had set her own self.

Jeanette's body was curvy alright, and her fair, Scandinavian-like features were delicate; yet Kaitlin could see her love-handles bulging from the side of her grayish dress that was too tight on her (hadn't the woman heard of a corset?) alongside her extremely-tired looking complexion. Perhaps she should be more thankful she's finally been having time off to take care of herself, Kaitlin thought, something she definitely had less time for working in Toronto. "Thank you. You look lovely yourself. I just came from the Ballroom. You guys did a brilliant job with the place!"

"Aww, thank you, sweetheart," Jeanette stretched out the words slightly longer than regular-accented speech.

Has this woman been drinking already? Kaitlin thought.

"Oh you have no idea how hard it was to fit it all in with all the work we already have. Tim and I have been in-over-our-heads for the past ten days trying to squeeze this thing in before New Year's Eve! I left him by the door. Oh I hope he's alright. He's been stressin' about this whole thing. We all have. I mean the caterers gave us the most trouble. Can you *believe* they had the *audacity* to say they could only promise a dish with steelhead trout fish rather than salmon since they didn't have enough time to ship in new salmon before re-opening in January? I mean, yes, trout tastes fine and just like salmon but this is *Norway* for friggin's sake. I mean…"

Kaitlin proceeded to nod and smile politely as she zoned Jeanette's rambling out in her head. "Tim and I," she'd said, not mentioning Paul. She knew her husband had been involved with some phone calls himself, but Kaitlin was glad to hear they apparently didn't spend as much one-on-one time together as her and this Tim guy did.

"I'm sure the food's going to be great. Everything's going to be great. Don't you worry. Come, let's go inside, shall we?" Kaitlin nudged Jeanette lightly on the back of her left shoulder in the direction of the ball room where she was surprised to see tens of people had already begun to arrive. Many of them were older than she was: in their 40's and 50's, but still dressed ravishingly.

"Oh my, it's gettin' crowded! I'm super nervous! Where *is* that darn girl who's supposed to be takin' care of our Welcome refreshments? She's become a ghost today. And speaking of ghosts, where's Paulie?" Jeanette asked, pressing one of the rather loose-looking planetary decorations behind the drinks table tighter against the wall. Kaitlin guessed they must have been scotch-taped.

"Oh, Paul had to get something from the car," she grinned. "I came before him in order to use the Ladies Room right away…"

"…I see," Jeanette winked at her. What in the world? Kaitlin was beginning to get a strange feeling about the woman once again, just as a tall, rather good-looking man with piercing brown eyes behind elegant black-rimmed glasses came over to them. "Oh, Tim! You have to find that Laura girl. Where *is* she? The guests have begun to arrive!"

"Jeannie, relax!" Tim said, placing a calming yet firm hand on her slightly jiggling upper arm. The dark-grey tuxedo he'd chosen for the event stood out from the sea of black-white, penguin men in the room. "I just passed Laura, she was helping Carlos at the door. I told her to come start the service soon."

Kaitlin leaned over their heads to see who they were talking about, wondering when Sibel and Engin would arrive. She was just about to send her friend a text message when she saw Paul rushing in, looking more dashing than the other penguins in the room, if she did say so herself. His eyes locked on hers across the gathering crowd in between them, right before a mutually-traded mischievous smile. In accordance with the space theme, they were on Cloud 9.

154

"Oh! Where are my manners? Tim, this is Kaitlin. Kaitlin is Paul's wife…" Jeanette interrupted Kaitlin's moment.

"…I know who Kaitlin is," Tim cut her off softly. "Has Paul ever *stopped* somehow always bringing the topic of his lovely wife over the past year? It's time we finally met!"

Kaitlin blushed as Tim reached out his hand and she returned the gesture.

"I see you guys have all met and started the party without me already," Paul exclaimed as he put an arm around Kaitlin's waist, giving her a kiss on the cheek. "Sorry I took longer than expected, darling."

"No problem, babe," Kaitlin snuggled up against him, while the others said their hellos back. It had been over a year and she still couldn't get enough of his intoxicating, signature cologne. "Did you find what you were looking for?"

"I think I did," Paul said slyly, looking at her like a five-year-old hiding a secret. *What is going on?* The nervous tension coming off her husband was so strong it reminded Kaitlin of the way he had been in the moments leading up to his marriage proposal to her. Strange? Yes. But perhaps he had bought her a necklace or something? Kaitlin didn't exactly get a *bad* feeling, so she let it go for the moment—just as the guitar player in the band started strumming several chords at the left corner of the room.

"They've got the finalized playlist, right Paul?" Tim asked. Kaitlin noticed Jeanette looking at Tim like he was Justin Bieber—the American pop singer she'd been surprised to see was idolized here so much more than he seemed to be back in North America. Maybe her suspicious intuition wasn't as dead-on as she thought. Who did she think she was anyway? Nostradamus?

"They're good to go, Tim. Don't worry. Everything's under control," Paul assured his colleague, giving a thumbs-up sign with his right hand.

"Shouldn't we be by the door for when the boss and his old lady arrive?" Jeannette asked.

"They're late and they know it, no need," Tim said as they all took a seat at the same round table, covered by a delicate Belgian-lace number. "Besides, they're sitting too far away."

"Let's still say hi when they come…" Paul started, just as the 'it' couple saw all four of them and nodded hello from across the room.

"Wow… great timing. See? No need to stress anymore, babe," Kaitlin similarly nodded and smiled at Lars' wife Lesley, dressed in a classic beige dress with long sleeves. "I'll have the red, thank you," she immediately responded when the waiter asked her preference before handing her a glass from the exquisitely-bright tray he'd been carrying around.

"Ahem," Lars was now clicking on the microphone, having been able to sit for less than a minute. The music stopped as if one cue. Kaitlin would have to curb her husband's panicky need to be punctual all the time from now on: his own boss wasn't exactly a good example this evening!

"Ladies and gentlemen, welcome to our New Year's Ball!"

Kaitlin turned to glance at her husband as everyone began to give Lars a round of applause. How proud the man looked: as if he were delivering the graduation speech at Oxford University.

"I know all of you are eager to get to your delicious dinners straight away, but we'd like to start the evening with a special request. Feel free to dance to our opening dance, all you lovebirds! Orchestra, let's hit it!"

Lars is certainly a fun-loving guy. Kaitlin smiled at Paul as she clapped along with everyone else, noticing Paul staring at her funny. And just like that, it started. A Lee Ann Rimes sound-alike but not so much look-alike, dark-featured curvaceous woman in a green mermaid-gown appeared on stage with the microphone in her hand, singing a familiar tune.

"How do I… get through a night without you? If I had to live without you… what kind of life would that be?"

"Oh my God, Paul! This… it's our wedding song!" Kaitlin exclaimed in a high-pitched whisper.

"Yes, yes it is, my beautiful darling," Paul stated proudly, reaching out to kiss her left hand, which was twinkling with the three-karat diamond engagement ring she saved for special occasions along with her every-day wedding band.

"I made sure it was the first song tonight. I don't ever want you to think that I don't appreciate you being here with me," Paul's warm hazel eyes were staring straight into hers. Her husband, who hated dancing, reached out his hand. "May I have this dance?"

Kaitlin felt a teardrop graze upon her right cheek. Cloud 9 had proved to be absolutely breathtaking.

***

Just as they had finished dancing to the second song, upon insistence by Jeanette and Tim to 'keep them company' since pretty much everyone else had begun to sit down and started eating their hors-d-oeuvres, Kaitlin felt a horrible pit at the bottom of her stomach. She had certainly grown to rely on her instincts and sixth-sense more and more lately, and there was no mistaking it now. Psychic or not, she could definitely feel a pair of eyes with familiar energy, watching her and Paul from somewhere to the left of the room.

She quickly turned her head toward the door. And there he was. Her now nightmare. Standing with his arms crossed around his chest. Wearing a suit himself, like one of the guests. A most handsome yet most spooky penguin.

***

"Was that Kaitlin runnin' out like that? Is she crying?" Jeanette's tipsy voice squeaked in a higher-pitch than usual.

"Oh I don't know," Tim responded. "Oh my dear, I *do* know you shouldn't have had that gin to relax before dinner—you can barely stand now!"

The rush of Tim's strong arms against her bare skin proved too much for Jeanette to handle without a reaction. She was feeling like Scarlet O'Hara. "Oh, kiss me, you fool!"

"Wh… What?" Tim blurted out, sporting a shocked yet smiling expression.

"Oh my manners… I'm so sorry… It's a line from this movie… like you said, I think it's this gin and my empty ole stomach, I…"

Jeanette's words were cut off with the firm and needy kiss planted on her lips, simultaneous with her hips being grabbed and drawn closer to Tim's body. He didn't need to know his American movies. As far as

Jeanette was concerned, his deep kiss and firm grip confirmed Tim to be the cowboy of her dreams.

***

"Please, Paul, I just want to go home, OK?" Kaitlin turned her face toward a small nearby mirror and wiped the tears that had finally broken loose. "I'm sorry. I'm *so* sorry."

"Baby?" Paul spoke softly, caressing Kaitlin's left cheek at the entrance doors, which were empty aside from the concerned concierge staring at them. "Look at me. I'm not mad. You don't have to apologize. You wouldn't just leave like that. I know you! *Obviously* something happened. Just, please, *share* with me!"

"Look, Paul, this evening has been lovely, so lovely, thanks to your special touch. I love you so much for that... for..." Kaitlin finally managed to look at her husband's concerned eyes, and erupted further in heavier tears.

"Whoa, whoa. Easy there. What happened? Did someone say or do something to you? Is it Jeanette or someone? I mean, I don't understand. And don't think I haven't noticed you acting weird and distant lately in general, either!" Paul's voice began to grow more upset than worried. "Look we have to go back inside eventually. So just tell me. I'm really *trying* here!"

Kaitlin decided then and there that there was only one way to get her husband off her back, just until she had enough time to develop a permanent exit-strategy with The Group and get Finn to stop following her. "Baby... Yes. There *has* been something I've been meaning to tell you... I didn't get my period this month..." Oh God. There it went. She was *truly* blurting out the cliché lie she'd seen from soap operas, wasn't she? "...and being that I'm usually spot-on every month and regular..."

"Darling?" Paul cut in excitedly, staring at her with eyes as wide as saucepans now. "Are you saying you think we might be... well, you might be... I mean, is that why you've been so... moody?"

Kaitlin nodded, relieved he seemed to have taken the bait. "I think so, yes." She managed to add a half-hearted smile for effect as well.

"Oh, wow. But, baby, why did you run out of the dance like that…" Paul asked, concerned.

"I… I just realized… I shouldn't have drunk anything. I mean, luckily it wasn't much, but what if I hurt the embryo or something already… I suddenly felt so guilty… I just had to get out of there… Please, let's just go home. You can tell Lars, or I can call Lesley and apologize…" Kaitlin realized she was rambling on.

"You said *embryo*. Oh my God… *baby*…" Paul hugged her and Kaitlin let out a sigh of relief, grateful to have a moment in his arms where she could avoid his eyes.

***

What in the world was Kaitlin staring at before she ran off like that? Sibel thought out loud, later that evening in the comfort of her home. *It was as if she'd seen a ghost!* She and Engin had been one of the last ones to arrive – thanks to their teenage-babysitter running late again– yet they'd made it just in time for Sibel to see her friend dancing romantically with her husband. It had made her happy to see the two of them like that—and she had been waiting for them to be seated so she could introduce their husbands to each other. That is, until she saw Kaitlin suddenly starting to stare blankly at the empty area near the doors… horrified! Had her friend suddenly remembered something important? Was that why she had run off? What else could it have been?

She was waiting to give it a day to call Kaitlin and find out. She told herself to mind her own business, and stop letting both curiosity and her imagination get the best of her. But she was genuinely worried about Kaitlin and her husband (a man she hadn't even officially been introduced to) for some reason. It wasn't like Kaitlin had committed adultery or anything—as far as she knew, anyway. But lying like that was never a good thing. Sibel remembered her own guilt over lying to Engin about how much she liked spending time with his sister back in Turkey, when in reality she sometimes wanted to claw the nosy and jealous woman's hair out!

But meeting strangers in the woods under 'work' pretenses… Trying to lure her into a secret, cult-like circle that didn't seem to be up to any good... Being coupled with a socially-strange man who didn't want to take pictures when Kaitlin had her coat on with her metal flashlight ... A man who seemingly appeared and disappeared into thin air, surprising Kaitlin often...

Wait a minute. Could Kaitlin have seen *that* man at the ball, though Sibel was sure no one else could? She could have sworn Kaitlin had had a similar expression staring at the wall when they were at the gym as well, now that she thought about it. Either her new friend was schizophrenic, or there was a religion-based word for such creatures in her native country, Sibel suddenly recalled, since she didn't exactly believe in what Western society labeled as *ghosts*. Creatures made of fire, unlike light (like angels) or clay (like humans), according to the holy Quran in Islam. Entities that could take on forms of other beings, yet uncomfortable near metal objects...Beings that could be good but also evil...

No. Not a ghost. But there was certainly another word for what she was sensing this man might be, a word which was also the root word for the word 'genie'. *Can this Finn person Kaitlin told me about be a jinn?*

Chapter 14

Paul was feeling excited and terrified at once, and it was creeping him out. They'd had such a good time the previous night, hadn't they? He was sure he hadn't seen his wife that much into him in a while. Darn his coconut-flavored vodka shot and Kaitlin's glass of merlot before their dance had started! He'd always hated to drink, and even more so now.

"…I didn't get my period…"

Paul couldn't get her words out of his head. Her words had been repeatedly echoing in his mind, lying next to his still sleeping wife. He turned his head and watched her crimson-chocolate mane cover the half of her face adorably as she breathed heavily.

Any hint of nervousness Paul had been feeling disappeared as soon as he heard those words. Could their luck as a couple finally be turning around?

***

Kaitlin was feeling smaller than the dust particles she was staring at on the bathroom sink, realizing she still had yet to wipe and sweep the place clean this week. As if things weren't rough enough for her with Finn now apparently full-on harassing her, she was taken aback by the pinkish spot on her crispy white underwear (something she would usually welcome) with disgust. *Why did my period have to come today of all days?* she pondered in frustration. *The morning right after I tell my husband I may be pregnant? Just to get him distracted while I sort things out…*

She decided she had to hide it. The bleeding. But first she absolutely had to talk to someone. *Was* Finn stalking her? Did he have some sort of supernatural powers? Did she even believe in such things? What was going on?

She couldn't talk to Sibel, who probably now thought her to be crazy. Kaitlin caught a glimpse of the way her friend had stared at her before seeing her run out the doors at the ball—with a look of utter shock. Sibel would have more questions than Kaitlin could handle right now. She decided to call Sandy, who was luckily physically far-removed from it all. And she would call directly from her phone, too. The bill would just have to be taken care of. But Paul was home. Darn it.

"Hon, I'm going out to pick up milk, do you want anything?"

"Baby, let me go get it," Paul offered. "You should relax today. You've had a rough night!"

"No, no, I'm Ok now. Thanks babe, but I really could use some air. Besides, it's not a long walk…"

"Nonsense," Paul waved his right hand in the air, walking to the door to put on his favorite blue pair of Converse sneakers.

As Paul closed the door behind him to pick up some groceries from one of the only markets open in Stavanger on Sundays, Kaitlin decided that maybe it would have been easier for her to make that call to Sandy from inside her home anyway.

"Girl, I don't know what's wrong with me," she said as soon as Sandy picked up. "I just lied to Paul again. And about being pregnant, none-theless! Am I, like, turning *evil*?"

"Hmm… Maybe you *are* preggers, hun," Sandy chimed humorously, munching on something. "It could be the hormones."

"What? No, Sandy! Didn't you hear the word *lie*? I *got* my period! I have to hide it! I made the baby thing up, to avoid confessing I saw Finn… again".

"Umm, Kaitlin excuse me for my slowness but it *is* 2:00 a.m. back here! You're lucky I got back late from dancing with Lisa and the gang. My head's still pounding and I can't fall asleep. I've got the munchies. Oh by the way, guess who I saw…"

"Oh my God, I'm so sorry!" Kaitlin stopped herself. "Sandy I forgot! You see, that's how messed up my mind is right now! I totally forgot our time difference… I mean, how am I going to hide this? Throw my pads out the window so he doesn't see them in the trash? But, I digress. Sorry, who did you see?"

As Sandy went on and on about running into her ex at their local supermarket, Kaitlin stared out the window at the cloudy sky. *Sigh*. Sandy wouldn't be much comfort to her this morning.

***

"I'm *so* glad you invited me out Sibel," Kaitlin said, taking a big sip of the foam layering the top of her warm coffee. She was feeling very grateful her new friend in town wasn't avoiding her after her strange actions from the Ball, and that she had called her out to have a drink later that afternoon.

"It's funny because I really *was* thinking about you, and how I needed to call to apologize for not saying hi at the Ball, and…"

"Calm down, calm down…" Sibel said, concerned. "Even when you're thanking me you look absolutely nervous. Look, I actually called you out here because I wanted to *share* something with you. Something I thought of last night when I got home. I've got to get back to the kids with my neighbor back home, actually, so I'm just going to cut to the chase… I'm not exactly sure how you'll receive it, how open-minded you'll be about it, but I've been having this feeling about these forest folks. The Group, or whatever…"

"A feeling…" Kaitlin repeated. "I see. Well, please, do share. I've been running my mind so *much* about the recent events, as well, to no logical conclusion. So, I believe I'll be open to just about anything right now!"

"Right," Sibel started to say, tugging several fallen strands of her piled-up hair behind her ears. "Well. You say 'logical', but I'm guessing what I'm about to say kind of depends on your belief system. I mean, the other night I had a sudden revelation, based on what I've been told and experienced in my own culture… It's hard to explain, but my thoughts kept going back to how I think that a friend of mine, Merve, went through something similar to what you're going through actually…"

"Belief system?" Kaitlin was hoping this wasn't going to be too much of an awkward conversation at least. "Well, though I'm technically a Christian, I come from a pretty liberal home. But I do believe in God, and being good and all that, if that's what you mean."

"Well, sure, there are many religions and various possible explanations, I suppose," Sibel continued. "But, just hear me out for a second. I think... I think Finn and maybe some of the other people you told me about, not sure about them, but Finn in particular, may be a *jinn*."

Kaitlin almost spilled the gulp of latte she had just swallowed from out of her mouth. "A *what?*"

"A jinn. They're creatures Islam tells us were also created by Allah, or God. They're like humans, except they were created from fire whereas we were created from the earth. They're uncomfortable being near metal, like your flashlight, and can move very rapidly with no notion of human time. And many times, they're invisible to us, unless they choose to appear, for they exist on another plane although still on the same planet like us. I mean, I suppose you could say they're similar to angels, but of course on a much lower plane, since they could be good or bad, whereas angels are always good..."

"Whoa... Okay, so... so, let me get this straight..." Kaitlin said, feeling a most-scared sensation at the pit of her stomach, though still not fully convinced. "You're saying Finn really *could* be something other than human...," Kaitlin interrupted eagerly. "And not just because I've been describing him as such... as a figment of my imagination?"

"Kaitlin, I really want the best for you. You know that. Now it may sound strange to you, trust me, I understand. But let me tell you what my friend Merve went through..."

"...Oh please do," Kaitlin cut in again, gulping down the remaining portion of her latte. She definitely had just become thirstier with her mouth drying up. She could also feel her increased heartbeat through her chest. "I mean, I have indeed been thinking that my entire situation is *strange*, already. And if you say this is part of a major world religion, who am I to judge? Heck, I want to know more. Well, oh, you were just going to tell me about your friend, I'm sorry..."

"...That's alright," Sibel said in a relieved tone. "I'm glad you feel that way because I'd really want you to be open to it so that you can protect yourself if necessary, if need be. I mean, there isn't exactly garlic or something to ward them off, like vampires, as superstition describes, you know. This is serious stuff. Some people believe it's just some pagan, pre-Islamic mythology, but a lot of Turkish people really believe in them. And, like I've said, I've read there are good Jinns also: those who serve the purpose of God instead of Satan. There's even an Arabic prayer, 'Ayet-Al-Kursi', from what I know, to ward off the bad ones when you fear them around you… I don't know if you would try it, since it's not your religion, but keep it in mind if your ever need… I mean, I don't want to automatically conclude that Finn and maybe the others you've met are any of the bad ones or anything, but…"

"…Well, I doubt they'd all be particularly *good* ones, either," Kaitlin deadpanned, flashbacks of Finn's sultry gazes at her, as well as Tan and Bjorn's double innuendos crossing her mind.

"Well, let's just hope that regardless of which type they are, that is if they even *are* jinns, since, again, I'm just speculating here; let's just hope you're not in any danger."

"…You were saying…" Kaitlin continued solemnly. "… about your friend…"

"…Merve! My friend back in Istanbul, right," Sibel exclaimed. "I digress. Sorry. Yes. So there she was, fresh out of college and, oh boy,' what a completely *lost* girl she was at the time…"

"…Lost," Kaitlin cut in solemnly, thinking naturally of herself when she heard that word. She inherently felt that there may be a pattern in regards to whom may get targeted by these creatures. Sibel's words were filling every empty box of unanswered questions in her soul with magical words, like some ancient wisdom that she began to wish her own late grandparents or someone warm and protective like them could have been able to bestow upon her.

"Oh yes," Sibel continued, her eyes fixated on a spot just behind Kaitlin's head as she attempted to recall the story with full concentration. "This girl's father was the owner of a major factory in the surrounding suburbs of Istanbul. Her mom was the daughter of a prominent lawyer who worked with politicians. Merve was definitely someone in the spotlight when I met her during our internship at *Sabancı Holding*. We'd both studied Business Administration, you see. But anyway, to make a long story short, despite everything going for her, Merve would tell me how she was crumbling under the pressure of so-called 'high society' around her. She was still crazy in love with her high school boyfriend. He was some musician kid who didn't pass the exams to get into college and her parents had deemed him to be a 'loser', forbidding them to see each other. But, of course…"

"…I'm sure she continued seeing him anyway, am I right?" Kaitlin was wishing Sibel would just get to the good stuff already.

"Of course. That's how it always goes, doesn't it?" Sibel continued. "Well, lo and behold, her father found out and became so furious that things accelerated to paying the kid off enough money for him to study abroad in the US!"

'What? That's crazy!' Kaitlin exclaimed, most intrigued.

"Yeah, he was *that* serious… and rich. So with the guy gone and completely out of touch with her after about a month into her internship, Merve could barely concentrate on the tasks they would give us. I mean she was *desperate* to find him: apparently he'd left her with just some short note saying he had to leave for the States and for her to move on since it was for the best, blah blah blah. But she was using the office internet and phone lines daily, *determined* to find out which city he had gone off to. She was especially keen on fantasies of running away to be with him after she found out what her father did. She even began to spike her morning coffee with liquor: she was *that* deep down in the dumps…"

"Did you try telling her that running away wasn't the solution and that maybe she really *should* have used the opportunity to move on as well? To advance professionally?" Kaitlin asked, feeling sympathy for this girl already—like a younger sister she never had. "I mean, you were very young then yourself, but, surely she had to have been told the guy wouldn't have taken the money if he was worth it and genuinely loved her, no matter what!"

"That's *exactly* what I told her!" Sibel exclaimed, shaking her head side to side as she took a deep breath and drank the last of her coffee. "But, yeah. She was in that sort of state. So she comes to work one morning, I can never forget that crazy-smiling expression on her face, and she goes, 'He came to me'. Of course I asked her to explain and basically during our lunch break, when it's just the two of us at the local *simit*[7] shop, she

---

[7] Simit: a Turkish breakfast staple, similar to the bagel

goes into this whole tale of how this guy came to her room while she was sleeping and made love to her!"

"What!?" Kaitlin shouted. She was expecting to hear about some Finn-like person introducing himself to Sibel's friend, but nothing this personal! This Merve person was sure more open-mouthed than even herself! Kaitlin found that to be, strangely, a little reassuring.

"Yeah," Sibel continued. "I didn't know what to quite make of it, to be honest, until she told me the next day that he'd sneaked out toward the morning, without giving her any new contact information. She then went on to say that she'd seen him at least twice on her morning commutes since the three or four day-old sexual incident, just watching her from afar, and then seemingly disappearing into thin air when she tried to get closer to him. Apparently, she didn't say anything at the time since she felt she could have been mistaken, or hallucinating with longing. Anyway, so that day she drops this crazy bombshell on me, then she skips work for the next three days after that! A whole weekend goes by and, come Monday, she's still not back. Our supervisor's asking *me* what happened. I call her house and her mom answers, starting to sob when I introduce myself and ask about where Merve is. She says Merve left a note saying that the kid, Emir or whatever his name was, came for her and that they were going to fly back to New Jersey together and she was going to study with him and so on and so forth. 'Your plan backfired, but in a way that's actually going to keep us together, and far from everyone. Thanks a lot, mom and dad!' She apparently wrote..."

Kaitlin took Sibel's pause as a cue to whet her still unsatiated curiosity. "That's so very unfortunate. Wow. But, Sibel, how does this story relate to *my* situation? What does this have to do with *jinns* like you've said?"

"Kaitlin, it wasn't her boyfriend!" Sibel exclaimed. "That is, according to her mother, it couldn't have been. The *real* Emir had apparently long returned to Turkey by then due to some visa issues and was apparently continuing his education at some private university near another city, Ankara, aided by Merve's father for his upheld promise to stay away. Don't you see? Poor Merve, the *real* Emir truly *had* long forgotten about her. After Merve disappeared, her parents questioned him *in person* about her note, and he swore he had already moved on and had nothing to do with it. He told them that she must have lied and that this New Jersey guy must be someone else." Sibel was looking Kaitlin straight in the eyes now, begging her to put two and two together since she seemed tired of talking.

"Are you saying this Romeo, the guy who made love to her and apparently took her away to the US or wherever, was a *jinn disguised* as her ex-boyfriend to lure her?" Kaitlin asked in horror.

"Merve would have told me if it was someone else," Sibel spoke solemnly as she nodded her head. "She *truly* must have believed it to be Emir. And my family and I definitely believed it was a jinn. Why a jinn might have targeted her I'm not really sure. But I *do* know, like I said, she'd just been feeling so… so… vulnerable."

Chapter 15

Advertisements for *New Year's Eve* were scattered all over town in various media, as if the Pope were to arrive in Stavanger for a stop on some sort of world tour.

Despite the candlelight dinner plans Paul had made for the two of them to celebrate two occasions: the new year *and* the 'baby', Kaitlin wasn't spending the day pampering her nails and hair to prepare for the evening, like she usually would have while her husband wrapped up several loose ends at work. No. She had spent the past ten minutes walking from the center of town into the woods, determined to get some answers.

Her absolute frustration, and anger as to why *she* was targeted for the latest harassments (by *jinns* or whoever these beings were), also managed to give her perhaps a foolish yet strong sense of courage. That and, of course, she had also placed a sturdy iron-cast kitchen knife in her large purse this time. She didn't exactly think she could have it in her to stab someone with it, but figured it would be a larger piece of metal to potentially scare off a jinn than her flashlight. Just in case.

Inching closer to the red cabin, Kaitlin took in a deep cold breath of air and reached for the doorbell. Before she could, Tan had already opened the doors. They must have seen her walking hesitantly from the window, she thought.

"Kaitlin," Tan said casually, wearing green boxer shorts and little else once again. "What a lovely surprise to see you here. After last time…"

"…Hey, Tan," Kaitlin cut in. "Is Finn here?"

"I'm afraid he's out of town: a meeting he had to attend… you know the drill…" Tan still sounded out of breath. Kaitlin decided he must either have run down the stairs very fast or have been knocking the boots with his girlfriend again. *Oh boy.*

"A meeting. Ok. When will he back?" Kaitlin insisted. "Say hi to Meredith for me, too, by the way."

"She's not here either right now," Tan said. "But will do. Thanks."

"Oh," Kaitlin said, starting to get that alarming feeling in the pit of her stomach once again. "Is she okay? Where is she?"

"God, Kaitlin," Tan spoke stoically with a half-smile. "Why on earth are you so concerned?"

"Hey, Kaitlin," Anja called out from the living room just then, holding a fruity drink in her hand. "Is everything alright? Come inside, it's just us."

Kaitlin was taken aback once again. Just as she thought these people couldn't surprise her any more than they already had, here were these two: apparently alone in the house and comfortable with their significant others not present. She didn't exactly want to assume anything, but then again, from her experience with them so far, one could never be sure.

"Thanks. Umm… I just wanted to ask something to Finn," Kaitlin stammered. "I couldn't tell him on the phone. I… wanted to see his face when I asked him why in the world he's been… following me."

"Oh, boy," Tan let out a laugh. "Our boy Finn has gotten in deep, huh."

"Shut up, dufus," Anja hit Tan's arm playfully. "Kaitlin, oh, come on! Isn't it flattering, though? By the way, Tan, did you e-mail Kaitlin that cute group photo of all of us?"

"Hmm, not yet," Tan said, staring at Kaitlin with a serious face. "I will."

"*Flattering?*" Kaitlin asked angrily. "Maybe if we'd been teenagers, and maybe if it were welcomed, like if I were single or interested. Which I'm not…"

"Yeah, we know Kaitlin," Tan interrupted coldly this time. "You're married. Good for you."

"Tan!" Anja warned him, raising an eyebrow.

"I… I just meant… oh come on, Kaitlin, isn't your marriage… a little… dull?" Tan continued.

"How would *you* know?" Kaitlin was growing angrier by the minute. She also knew she had to take advantage of the fact that Finn wasn't there, and get back safely to her house fast. Yet she couldn't help the words from coming out of her mouth. "You guys *just* met me. You don't even know my husband. There's no need to be *offensive*. Now, if you'll excuse me..."

"Kaitlin, don't be so defensive," Anja called out as soon as Kaitlin had begun to walk away back to town.

"Let her go," Kaitlin heard Tan say somewhere farther behind her now, loud enough so she could still hear him.

***

"These... stupid keys..." Kaitlin mumbled, fumbling through her red leather hobo bag. "I can never find them in these big bags."

"Oh it's not the keys, sweeeeeetie," Paul slurred, smiling back at their place after a lovely dinner of curry chicken and rice at the local Indian restaurant they'd both loved. "You're always finding ways to put *way* too many things in your bags, you disorganized thang you!"

"I got it!" Kaitlin exclaimed, taking out the sparking Norwegian-flag keychain. "Hey, that hurt!"

"I've gotten used to it though," Paul yawned. "Always waiting.... waiting for you."

"Oh my God, I'm not used to seeing you drunk like this," Kaitlin couldn't help but laugh once she finally managed to open the door and the two of them had come in. "I thought you said you could handle two glasses!"

"Well yeah, with many drinks, but you know I'm not a wine-guy, dahling," Paul said as he took off his black loafers and slipped his feet into the house-slippers placed by their door. "I just wanted to drink for my lady too, since her... fancy highness... wanted to celebrate the Big New Year with a Bang! Yeah! Woohoo!"

"Ok, now you're just being mean," Kaitlin purred, secretly glad she had the pregnancy-excuse not to drink: alcohol tended to mess her stomach up whenever she had her period.

"Oh, come on baby, lighten up," Paul grabbed Kaitlin by the waist with a sudden pull, giving her a slobbery kiss on the neck. "New year is just another day."

171

"That's not what you said earlier, Paul," Kaitlin pushed her husband away playfully. She wasn't liking where his passionate embrace was going: surely he'd see she was on her period if they were to get intimate. *Damn it.* "You wanted to celebrate tonight as a, and I quote, 'new beginning for us as a family', didn't you? But I guess drinking has made you more honest…"

"…Shut your lovely mouth and come inside …" Paul called from somewhere inside their bedroom while Kaitlin was still stalling for time in the bathroom now.

"Come here, before I fall asleep…" Paul continued.

"…And holidays are just *commercial hoaxes*, aren't they, Paul?" Kaitlin knew she had no choice but to keep it up. Even the slightest little tenseness between them was usually enough to dampen Paul's interest, yet Kaitlin couldn't believe she was exactly bringing the negativity on purpose this time. "You would have probably even insisted on staying in, if it hadn't been for the baby…"

Silence.

Was Paul still awake? He couldn't have fallen asleep that fast. He would surely normally be coming up with a retort to her attitude before doing so, at least. "Babe?" Kaitlin whispered, creeping quietly into their bedroom.

"Goodnight," Paul said flatly under the covers. "I've got a major headache."

Mission accomplished.

***

"Happy new year, handsome," Kaitlin kissed her sleeping husband on the cheek. Outside, the first day of the new year was slowly bringing on flurries of long-awaited snow. The chilling temperatures tended to increase when the sky was able to release its miraculous specks. Just for a moment, Kaitlin's thoughts went back to a time in her childhood back in Toronto: a peaceful time when her mom would make her favorite drink of hot chocolate with marshmallows.

"It's still early, isn't it?" Paul managed to mumble with his face buried in his pillow, and his back turned to his wife. "I've got the alarm clock. Go back to sleep."

Ouch. Paul still sounded angry with her, and Kaitlin did not want to start their special day on a sour note. She had woken up exactly fifteen minutes before waking him, daydreaming of playing in the snow together.

"Don't be angry, Paulie," she whispered softly, inching her body closer to his. *Sigh.* Her menstrual pad was filled up to the max. She couldn't lie anymore nor did she want to, she then realized, though it sure had felt good to be pampered like she was an expecting mom. "I think I was just upset… because I… I got my period."

Silence.

"Paulie?" Kaitlin asked.

"Is that why you were giving me all that attitude out of nowhere last night? PMS?" Paul said finally, without turning his body to face her.

"Babe! Don't you see?" Kaitlin asked as she vigorously shook his arms, forcing him to finally look at her. "I was upset because I realized this means I'm *not* pregnant after all!"

"I know…"

"You… what!?" Kaitlin felt genuine tears nearing the corners of her eyes, ready to splash themselves across her face.

"I mean, I figured you had to be mistaken," Paul started to say, sitting on the bed and leaning against the wall now. "We've been using protection each time, upon *your* insistence, little lady. I doubted that one of the condoms could have just gotten torn like that! I mean, that's such a small possibility… but I guess a part of me wanted to believe it was all true…. that we were finally going to be a family."

"We *are* a family!" Kaitlin placed her head on her husband's shoulder, unable to hold on to the tears any longer. "Why can't you see that, Paul? We already *are*…

Chapter 16

"Kaitlin?"

"Meredith?" Kaitlin asked, pleasantly surprised she recognized the voice at the other end of the line. At first, she'd naturally been nervous to receive a phone call from an unknown number. "One... second, please." She quickly put on a knit-cable sweater from her closet and headed out of the bedroom toward the balcony. Paul had headed straight into the shower after waking up, but could indeed still overhear her if she was to speak from anywhere else in the house. "How are you?"

"I heard that you..." Meredith said softly, "...that you asked for me, that is. I just wanted to say, thanks."

"Of course. Look, I don't know if I'm wrong..." Kaitlin took the opportunity to say exactly what had been on her mind. She was determined to get at least *someone* from that house to give her some answers, and for some reason Meredith seemed to be the only person there who had always appeared to be disturbed enough by her surroundings to do just that. She pulled open the sliding door to the snow-covered balcony, which had proved to be more difficult than she thought, as the temperature made it stuck. She placed the phone between her cheek and shoulder to use both hands. *Got it.* It was freezing, especially with the gusts of wind that managed to blow all of her hair in her face. "...but I just got a sense that you were not exactly welcoming this whole *sexual* arrangement the Group seems to have. You didn't come across to me as, I don't know, 'free-spirited', shall we say, as Anja or whatever, alright? So, I just... wanted to make sure you weren't being taken advantage of in a way that you didn't welcome. That's all. Other than that, of course, in the bigger picture, at least, none of this is my business."

"Oh, but it is," Meredith exclaimed, to Kaitlin's surprise once more. "It *is* your business, Kaitlin. I mean... there's much more to everything than I can really say. But, just know that Finn didn't exactly 'run into' you in the woods. He... They... sought you out."

"What!?" Kaitlin screamed in shock, peering inside through the glass to make sure Paul hadn't stepped out of the shower yet to hear her. "But why... *why*?" Kaitlin paced around the small balcony. Her suspicions of something being 'off' with her current situation, more than just running across some 'sexualized forest cult', were finally being confirmed. And yet, she was more confused than ever.

"Look, I've got to go," Meredith was almost whispering now. "I'm not entirely sure I haven't gotten myself into big trouble already by calling you. I wouldn't be surprised if Lar has our phone lines tapped..."

"No, don't you *dare* be scared, honey," Kaitlin said firmly. "You hear me? We live in Norway, in a civilized society. If need be, pretend you need to buy something from town and escape them! Go to the police or come meet me... or go back to Trondheim... But first, please, just tell me why me... why...?"

"Your husband, Kaitlin!" Meredith interrupted her with a louder whisper now. "They didn't exactly tell me. But I know... I heard them... And their thoughts... He's, done *something*; I'm not exactly sure what he did, but... oh and I'm not sure if you saw, but, there was a girl on the news, the one discovered dead. They all knew her... Oh shit, I've *really* gotta go..."

"Their *thoughts*? *Paul*? What did *he* do? Meredith? Mer..." Kaitlin attempted to get more answers, but Meredith had already hit the off button on their conversation.

***

"You *still* shouldn't have gone out into the balcony with just slippers on, babe," Paul said over his second cup of tea. "If you're going to *insist* on not wearing socks, then please at least start wearing the furry reindeer-slips we bought you... You have to take care of your ovaries."

Kaitlin drew in a deep breath, rolling her eyes at the word 'ovaries'. "Don't worry. I think the cold did good, actually. It got me thinking."

"About that snow trip out to the mountains, right?" Paul asked in a hopeful tone of voice. "You know, I think we need something like that now more than ever actually… to get away and…"

"…Did you *do* her?" Kaitlin interrupted sternly.

Paul sulked lower in the chair and took a very audible gulp, placing down his fork on his plate of cake. "What the…?"

"You heard me," Kaitlin stood her ground, albeit with her voice quivering almost as much as her still-shivering body. She realized her dream of a fun snow-day out wasn't exactly going to happen now, but after Meredith's phone call she could no longer hold it in. "Did you screw her? Or have a relationship with her or something? And then get rid of her? And then… I don't know…"

"Me? *Me*, Kaitlin?" Paul asked angrily. Kaitlin noticed that his hazel eyes literally looked extra big and puppy-like at that moment. "And, umm… Who, Kaitlin? Who? *Jeanette*? The poor woman's been nothing but nice to you, and you saw her with Tim. Are you *serious*? I mean …"

"Not bloody Jeanette: the *dead* girl! The dead girl, Paul!" Kaitlin ran her hands deep through her hair, grabbing her scalp wildly, avoiding Paul's burning gaze on her. She didn't want to face his eyes just yet—not before she finished what she had to say. She had to get to the bottom of at least one of the many troublesome questions in her mind. Lin or Linette or whatever her name was, Kaitlin decided she had to find out the deal about her. *What is with all these "-ette" named women suddenly in my life through some connection with my husband anyway?*

***

Watching his wife pace back and forth, occupying a space of only around a meter or so in their kitchen, Paul had gone into absolute shock. He knew this day would come and he knew he had to spill the truth, but he was taken so aback by how far out of left field Kaitlin's particular timing and interpretation was that he couldn't utter any sound.

"I mean, I've been going out of my *mind*, thinking about why you've been acting the way you have since you watched the news that evening," Kaitlin continued, holding on the kitchen counter for support, to be able to stay in place, it seemed. "I mean… I'm sorry, but you *do* have to admit

176

it was a little strange the way you overreacted quite a bit when we watched the news…"

"I knew her, Kaitlin!" Paul interrupted. "Yes, you got me! Okay? I *knew* her. And… *No*. I did not have any sort of relation with her whatsoever. We were barely even friends at the office where I worked with her in Canada years ago, alright?"

Kaitlin felt dumbfounded. "You… *knew* her? You *worked* with her? Ok. So, why not just tell me that, then? If you guys weren't somehow *involved*, then why not?"

"…And what if we *had* been involved, Kaitlin? Hmm?" Paul asked with steam seemingly coming out of both his nostrils. "It was years before you and I got together, so I'd have no reason to hide it from you." Kaitlin knew he was being logical, but it sure hurt her feelings the way he seemed to disregard her potential jealousy.

Paul got up from the chair and kicked it softly to the side. "Anyway, so that's *not* why I felt so *bad* for seeing she was killed," he continued, placing his arms on his hipbones. "I mean, first of all, I was frankly surprised at the coincidence that she'd even been in *Norway* now, like I was… 'What a small world,' I thought… And soon after that, the fact that she was *killed* registered in my brain, and I remembered… that day when… her boyfriend had come in to the office all in a rage and I… oh man, what if I was responsible…"

Kaitlin couldn't believe what she was hearing. Where in the world was her husband going with this? It sure didn't sound like anything she thought it could be. "Responsible?" she asked calmly. "Paul, what are you saying?"

"Do you want to hear this or not? Let me get this out, Kaitlin," Paul's stern tone meant business. Kaitlin nodded in both obedience and curiosity as she took a sit on the chair Paul had kicked. "So there I was, with four years behind me of having worked hard at that damn company, and I mean *hard,* trying to climb the damn proverbial 'corporate ladder'. My sisters were making fun of me for still being single while the two of them had already gotten married and the youngest engaged. 'You're all work and no play…' they'd tease me…"

Kaitlin held on to the sides of the chair's cushion as if she'd be falling overboard into a cold, deep sea if she didn't.

"Linette..." Paul continued, dreamily. "Linette Jensen or Petersen or something, I believe her last name was, started with us as an intern fresh out of college. This was right around the start of my last year in Canada before coming here... I have to admit I'd never noticed her much at first: she always appeared to be this shy, modest girl. But *then* she became John Walker's assistant, he was the Company president. And, oh boy, suddenly she started wearing these new outfits, started getting this air about her... well..."

Kaitlin got the picture and didn't want to hear any further detail about how her husband had obviously become smitten with this woman. "Ok Paul, yes, I got it... she *did* look very pretty in her picture, and you were a single guy, blah blah blah. But, what *happened?* You mentioned something about her boyfriend coming in...?"

"I was getting there, babe," Paul's voice had calmed down. The words definitely flowed more smoothly than he thought they would now that he was getting his secret off his chest. "So this tall, dark, rough but good-looking guy comes in one day around Christmas time. I even remember he spoke with an accent. He must have been Greek, Persian, or something, not really sure. Anyway, he barges right past our receptionist asking to speak to Mr. Walker, rather rudely and loudly. The poor old lady at the front desk couldn't take him on, if it came to that, you know, so I wanted to help. My office was close to the entrance and my door had been open. Anyway, I called him into my office to speak 'man-to-man', I believe I'd called it then, thinking that speaking this tough guy's language would yield a better result. Mostly everyone else at the office was out having lunch, including Mr. Walker and Linette..."

Was it just she or did Kaitlin sense a negative connotation each time her husband spoke her name? Was he somehow still slightly angry with this late woman? Did she not give him the time of day? *Well, she had a boyfriend, duh, earth to Paul!* Kaitlin thought.

"She'd never mentioned her boyfriend during our several chats over coffee," Paul stated as if he'd read her mind, staring straight into her eyes, as if seeking understanding. "If she had, maybe I wouldn't have been upset with her for being so damn flirty! It's like she was so *needy* for male attention! Not just with me, but with several other guys at the office and especially John, whom she would often have lunch with, just the two of them. She was like this little kitten with him! Well... anyway... so when this tough guy started asking questions, I sympathized with him. I asked him what coming face to face with Walker would accomplish. I said that surely they'd deny having anything going on, and he'd get in trouble for nothing... that Walker could even sue him if he wanted to, with all his money, and that he'd just look like a jealous freak in his girlfriend's eyes..."

Kaitlin pulled her chair closer to him, placed her hand on his arm and took a deep breath, licking her now-dried lips. "Let me try to get this straight," she said, attempting to offer comfort. "You implied to this tough guy that you *also* indeed believed she was having an affair? When all you had as *proof* was frequent lunches and her *flirty* personality?"

She was feeling bad for her husband, but a part of her was upset at this machismo coming from the man she'd married—especially since Kaitlin was sure her own friendliness must have been assessed wrongly a couple of times too, judging by the stares and coldness from women she received throughout her life. Had she been similarly misjudged by Finn and the Group? Yes, she had to admit she had indeed been enjoying the attention, and lying to her husband about her new group of friends, but still...

"I didn't really think too much, Kaitlin," Paul interrupted her thoughts. "Alright? It began as just me trying to calm this guy down to get him to leave the office with his dignity still intact before anyone came and saw him. But in the process, I only realized much later that I'd also unwillingly told this guy I agreed his girl was most likely cheating on him with her rich boss..."

"...*Was* she? But you know what, it almost doesn't matter, Paul. That was so... so *presumptuous* of you... Was it really even about Linette? Did you really develop such a bitter attitude towards women, after... Sarah?" Kaitlin spoke Paul's ex fiancée's name only in a whisper. The name of the college sweetheart who broke his heart when she left him for his best friend on the football team had become taboo for them, along with the name of *her* own first heartbreaker, Shawn, back when she'd been a teenager.

"*What* in the...? Kaitlin? You're making it seem as if... if I *killed* Linette!" Paul burst out, banging his fist on the table. "As if it isn't enough that I felt for months and months that I may have… *indirectly*, of course, after she stopped coming to the office and that guy was nowhere to be found…"

"Indirectly?" Kaitlin cut in, touching his arm again to calm him down. She was still torn between feeling sympathy and being angry for his way of thinking. "You mean, you suspected that her boyfriend felt your word was enough confirmation and, like, did something to her out of jealousy or whatever?"

"Well, yes," Paul continued. A glimmer of sun suddenly peeked through the clouds for the first time that day, lightening up the entire living room. They both looked out the window together. The green in his hazel eyes took over and Kaitlin sighed. What was going on inside the mind of that man of hers? She also had the thought right there and then that she actually preferred his brownish eye color to Finn's enticing yet creepily powerful light-green ones. She cursed herself. *Why the hell am I thinking about Finn now?* She had to concentrate on the matter at hand.

"Babe, you didn't do anything wrong," Kaitlin offered. "I mean, how were you to know the guy was a psycho, that is, if it was even *he* who caused her disappearance in the first place! The police haven't exactly discovered her killer, right? It could just be your suspicion since the guy acted shady, as you say. I mean, what did that *Walker* guy say? What was *his* explanation for his favorite little office employee suddenly not coming in anymore? Firing her?"

"I think I see where you're going with this: John, he couldn't have," Paul went on as he grabbed an apple from the turquoise ceramic fruit bowl near him and bit into it hard. "He told everyone at the office that the two of them had a disagreement over her working conditions and that she'd quit. He later confessed the truth to me over a couple of drinks at the local place where we all hung out. Yeah, John was cool and close to everyone like that, I suppose, in retrospect. He told me that she hadn't actually quit, but had moved back in with her mom here in Norway. He said she was scared, but couldn't be bothered to share by whom. John said he assumed it must have been her father who'd come to Canada to find her; said that Linette and her mom had spent most of her life without him in the picture, though he didn't really share any details…"

"Wow…" Kaitlin muttered as Paul continued to speak with his eyes locked to the view from their window.

"John confessed to me that night that he'd tried to take care of Linette like the daughter his wife and him were never able to conceive. She didn't come from a lot of money. The only way she was able to come to Canada, apparently, was as a transfer student on some scholarship. John said she had regretted leaving her mother behind in Trondheim, but that she'd had big ambitions: she was going to 'make it big in Canada' and help with their housing debt. Apparently she sent her mom a check every month for the house bills, a check that John said he continued to send to Trondheim himself, even though Linette gradually lost touch with him…"

As Paul digressed about how he himself related to Linette's ambitions to rise socio-economically, Kaitlin felt herself zoning out and shifted her thoughts to focus on her own dilemma with The Group. Something about what Paul was telling her (about Linette, and her own feelings of victimization from the Group) was nagging at the back of her mind, but for the life of her she couldn't put her finger on it. *What on earth could it be?* She realized she did indeed feel scared of Finn's power over her and his mysterious appearances, like a stalker at the very least, if not as the *jinn* creature Sibel had mentioned, but how in the world were her instincts urging her to combine the murder of some girl from Trondheim with some shady forest hippies she'd befriended? Then again, Meredith *had* just pointed her in a connective direction. 'We knew her,' she'd said. Perhaps Linette had been a part of the Group?

Maybe I'm just being silly, Kaitlin thought. *I'm no psychic.* Yet she'd had enough experiences in her life to not believe in coincidences, and not just because Finn and his weird buddies said so. It was also a part of her Christian faith—one of the several fundamentally spiritual points from it she held dear, regardless of her non-religious upbringing.

"…It's such a horrible thing for me to live with now, this thought of *What if?* You know?" Paul continued to talk as he walked to and from the dinner table, his left hand comforting his right elbow, with his right hand placed pensively on his jaw. He threw the remaining pit from the juicy-sounding crispy red apple he'd been munching on, and turned to face Kaitlin.

"I mean, yes, her murderer hasn't exactly been discovered, though the news says that her unnamed ex-lover is still being sought out, high on the suspect list," Paul said with a whimper. "But, what *if* it was *he* who did this to her? That guy I talked to. And he wouldn't have done it otherwise if I hadn't told him about her closeness with John, as if I had proof it was anything other than platonic? What if…"

"Honey, stop and take a deep breath," Kaitlin said softly. "I believe you. Okay? And I understand you better now. Just calm down," Kaitlin pushed her husband gently toward the nearest chair and pulled out the one to its left for herself. "Did you ever think about going to the police with any details you remember about that guy? I mean, I'm sure the *Politi* here ought to have some sort of connection with the ones up in… Trondheim, was it? Or maybe the killer really *was* her dad or whatever, as your boss said Linette told him she was afraid of her father for whatever reason?"

Kaitlin stopped to catch her breath. "Trondheim," she repeated out loud as Paul nodded, suddenly remembering Meredith had said she had gone to university there. And wasn't their precious mysterious Lar a professor there? "Paul… did Linette go to Trondheim University before moving to Montreal? Or wait, I'm sorry, it's officially the Norwegian University of Science or something or other that's there?"

Paul looked genuinely befuddled, raising his right eyebrow at his wife. "I don't really remember, babe… Could be, now that I think about it. Sounds familiar, yeah. But, why? What gives?"

"Oh, nothing," Kaitlin shrugged, trying to keep a cool tone, though her stomach felt like it had been punched. "I recalled reading about that school somewhere and it crossed my mind again when you mentioned Trondheim, that's all."

"Can we move beyond this?" Paul cooed, looking at his wife pleadingly. "This whole thing has been hard enough on me already. I'm sorry I didn't share it with you sooner… I should have."

Kaitlin wasn't exactly feeling like she had the right to be judgmental at the moment. "I just hope her case and everything can be resolved, babe," she smiled. And she really meant it.

***

Kaitlin glided the mint-scented soap softly across her arms aimlessly, staring blankly at the droplets forming on the walls from the heat of the bathtub water. She didn't feel bothered by the sting of the heat. In fact, she relished the way it touched her senses and made her *feel*.

"God?" she called out, turning her eyes to the ceiling.

"What am I going through here? Why is all this happening to me… and now? If I'm not doing anything wrong, why am I keeping things from my husband? He's good to me, isn't he? But then again he has been keeping things, too, hasn't he? What if there's more that I don't know?"

Kaitlin stared across at the picture frame with her and Paul's wedding photo hanging on top of the hand towel hangers next to the sink. She smiled at the happy pose they'd struck in each other's arms. 'We have enough pictures in the living room. Do we really need to adorn the bathroom too, babe?' he had asked. 'People will think we're showing off…'

Her smile faded. "So what if we *are* showing off a little, Paul?" she whispered softly to the picture. "It's only been a year. People constantly tell us we're in our supposed 'honeymoon' phase anyway, so they'd only find it natural, wouldn't they? Don't *you* want to show off our happiness, Paul, if only a little? You used to post pictures of us all over your social site when we were dating, right before you shut it off after our marriage to preserve its *'sanctity'*. Is our excitement over for you now, Paul? *Am I* no longer relevant as a love interest? Just your 'good ole wife' like another family member or relative?"

A tear rolled down Kaitlin's right eye. Another one from her left eye was wiped off as soon as she felt it coming. Soap bubbles stung her eyes but she didn't care. Maybe Paul was right. Maybe they weren't as happy as they were when they'd finally begun dating after years of attempt on his part. Now that he had gotten what he wanted, maybe she wasn't the only one whose expectations of romanticism weren't met. Perhaps domesticity for him was as important as romanticism was for her, and he wasn't happy either.

Happy.

"*Am* I happy or not? Would I be feeling like this if I truly were? But then again, how is one supposed to feel once they're 'happy'? Content? Satisfied? If so, if all feels well, why feel motivated to continue living...?"

Speaking out loud to herself, Kaitlin stopped with a smile. In her mind, she was beginning to sound like a drunk person. Perhaps she should have indeed poured herself a glass of something bubbly. *Maybe a baby really would have been good for us,* she thought.

She smirked. *What the hell am I thinking? I can barely even keep the orchids by our windows alive.* She glanced at the cell phone she had brought with her into the bathroom with the intention of calling Sandy or her mom or someone to feel like she was cared for, to vent off steam or at least just chitchat to get her mind off her confusion. Holding onto to the edge of the bathtub with her left hand, she reached out and grabbed the phone after wiping some of the soap bubbles off on the nearest towel.

"Mom?" Kaitlin asked after the phone picked up on the second ring.

"My baby!" her mom answered with genuine warmness in her voice. Despite hanging up the phone after only around five minutes of conversation, it felt good to hear the familiar voice of someone from back home: away from all of the craziness going around her in Stavanger.

***

"Hello?"

"Girl, are you alright?" Sandy's panicked voice asked amidst sounds of blaring car horns and sirens.

"Sandy? Is that you? What number are you calling from?" Kaitlin put down the linen towel she'd been using to dry her damp hair. It was interesting to her that she'd be called by Sandy right after she'd talked to her mom: two people she missed from her life back in the Western Hemisphere. *Perhaps this is God's way of answering my questions to Him,* she thought as she smiled. "I'm fine. Are *you* alright? Where are you?"

"Oh, thank goodness!" Sandy exclaimed, "I'm just crossing this crazy busy street downtown, hon. They've got this crazy road construction going on and I counted exactly three ambulances and two fire trucks trying to get through, something must be up somewhere. But anyway, your mom called me and said you were in the bathtub, sounding like you're about to cut your wrists, and well naturally, I…"

"My *mom* called you?" Kaitlin smiled. Although she'd barely remembered her father, she definitely must have gotten her flair for the dramatic from good old Linda Ramsay. "Oh, man, I can't believe her. Cut my wrists? I wonder why she'd call *you* and not Paul?" she continued, chuckling. "And, umm, once again, why are you calling from a blocked number?"

"It's this trick I use when I need to, let's say, deal with some boy situations, alright?" Sandy exclaimed. From the sudden echoing of her voice and audible clicking of her heels, Kaitlin could tell her friend had entered some building. "I didn't exactly want you to avoid known phone calls in case you were, you know. I know you enough to figure you'd at least be curious to pick up an unknown number —even if you were about to, *you know*! And besides, I think your mom was saying something about her thinking Paul may have done something to you and that you didn't want to share it with her. So maybe she thought I could get you to open up!"

Oh brother. "Well, no, Paul and I are fine, babe: for the most part anyway. Don't worry. I'm just having one of those days. I wanted to hear my mom's voice. That's all! But *argh,* I swear that woman makes me regret calling her sometimes. It's nuts!"

Sandy chuckled. "God bless her! She's a funny lady, Mrs. Ramsay, that's for sure. It's interesting *she* told me *you* don't like the phone unless it's a birthday or a holiday; and that's why you keep in touch with her mostly through e-mail. So that's why she was *so* convinced you were beaten up or cheated on or…"

"Sandy! Thank you! But I'm fine! Really!" As soon as she'd interrupted her friend, Kaitlin realized how harsh she must have sounded to someone who called her from all the way across the Atlantic (and not even on their usual free Wi-Fi line, either) just because she was concerned. "Look, I know you just got worried and I love you for that. But… I don't know. I think I just need a good distraction; you know? Get out of my head a little? So talk to me. Where are you? Are you good? What's going on?"

"Yeah, I just got to the Starbucks on the corner of the building where I'm about to, get this, go on a job interview!" Sandy said excitedly. "Now, don't say it! Don't say you're disappointed since it means I must have given up on this *Acting* thing, or anything..."

"Hey, I'm not saying anything, hon!" Kaitlin said with a giggle. "I mean, I know how much you hate temping work so if you're actually excited about an interview, it must be interesting."

"Can I have a Tall Mocha Latte, please?" Sandy ordered.

"You there?" Kaitlin asked impatiently. She still needed to dry and style her hair.

"Sorry. So get this..." Sandy started to explain after an audible sip of her drink. "You'll never guess how I landed this interview. It kind of reminded me of your forest story, actually. Maybe it's some astrological period of us meeting strangers as professional contacts, hon".

"Oh, yeah?" Kaitlin was intrigued. "Do tell".

"So this tall guy comes up to me the other day when I'm at this very same Starbucks, actually, going through some new headshots," Sandy continued. "He says his name's Matt Evans...Handsome as hell...He says he likes the creative way I've styled my folders and that they've been looking for someone like that at this Marketing firm where apparently he's a recruiter...When I ask for more details, he keeps saying they work with *paper*, and not much else, and I think: how weird it is for a guy with such excitement in his green eyes to talk about a mysterious job which sounds so... so... *plain*... I mean... *paper*?"

"Wait, wait, wait... something sounds fishy, Sandy..." Kaitlin interrupted. *No details except 'paper'?* she thought. It took hearing it being told from someone else's mouth for Kaitlin to realize just *how* dangerous, and perhaps even foolishly brave, what she herself had done was. "Now, I know you're going to call me crazy if I blurt it out on the phone. So please don't ask any questions, just answer me after I e-mail you something..."

"Umm, ok," Sandy said, confused. "Kaitlin? What are you talking about? What's wrong? I don't..."

"Just tell me whether or not you can receive emails while on the phone, ok?' Kaitlin interrupted. "I'll be forwarding you a picture attachment. I'll explain, I promise."

"Well, I don't know, I never tried," Sandy explained. "With a picture attachment, I mean. I can see e-mail but… well, you can try…"

She didn't have to tell her twice. Kaitlin was already on it. "Hold on…" she said into the receiver, throwing her hanging white fluffy bathrobe over a purple thong she'd grabbed from the back of her underwear drawer. She realized she had gotten the floor between the bathroom and their bedroom wet with bubbly water and that Paul would make a fuss, but she didn't care. She'd deal with the clean-up later. Right now she had something more important to find out, something that hadn't left her mind ever since Sibel shared the story of her friend's experience with her, and Kaitlin herself followed up on the subject matter with some online research. No theory sounded too paranoid to her any longer.

Wiping her hands on her bathrobe for one last drying operation before searching for Tan's last e-mail to her with the photo from the birthday celebration in the woods, she typed in Sandy's email address before clicking on the button to forward it to her.

"Ooh I got it! I pressed the link in my notification… it's loading…" Sandy called out.

"Great. I'm waiting." Kaitlin said, tapping her fingernails on the wall.

"…Oh my God! Kaitlin!" Sandy exclaimed. "This is you in this picture… and I'm guessing these are those forest buddies you've been hanging out with. But… Mr. Evans, my Marketing recruiter… what's *he* doing in this picture?"

Chapter 17

Kaitlin put on her rubber-soled boots by the door as she prepared to walk out to confront Finn once again. "He's not going to be able to hide this time. Not in New York. Not even all the way in friggin' China or Australia or wherever. Not anywhere!" She told herself out loud for motivation.

Despite her occasional temper tantrums with Paul from time to time (which she increasingly realized to have been childish), she didn't remember feeling *this* angry in a long time. And the recognition itself was an actual welcome feeling over her recent phase of confusion and self-pity.

What would she do if these people reacted to her violently? What if Sibel's suggestion was true? What if these people really *were* jinns? Could they use special powers over her? Had they used any (and she suddenly physically shuddered at the thought) against Meredith after overhearing her on the phone that day?

Approaching the red doors that had now been revealers of both enticing intrigue *and* regret, she didn't even need to knock. She instinctively knew that *he* knew she was coming.

"Hey, Finn?" Kaitlin called out as calmly as possible, though her palms had long started to feel sticky and sweaty inside her leather gloves. As the door surely began to inch open and revealed Finn's blond head sticking out to peer at her, she added, "I suppose you're going to tell me that it's a misunderstanding, or a *coincidence,* seeing you wherever I go, and now hearing that my friend Sandy all the way across the Atlantic has done so, as well...?"

"It's not a coincidence," Finn retorted with his smile in its standard slick form. "I figured it wouldn't be too long for you to come back here to interrogate further. And I told you: *nothing* is coincidence, Ms. Kaitlin.

I can read your imagination… your thoughts… but only mostly the darkest ones. You mustn't be afraid of those: for, you see, this is how you can get the most joy out of your life. Our most daring thoughts are our true nature…"

"Cut the bull crap, please, Finn. Where's Meredith? I want to see Meredith!" The part of her that had once shivered with a pleasurable, exciting feeling looking into his eyes now only hurt her stomach and spine and whole being with discomfort and disgust. Kaitlin had no idea how she could be so brave to stand in front of this instant, transatlantic-traveling man.

"I wasn't aware… that you had taken a particular liking to our Meredith. You're… a woman of interesting tastes, Ms. Kaitlin." The wink Finn gave her as he spoke her name, the same one which would have excited her before, now only gave her chills.

"I want to speak to her, *Mr. Finn*!" she retorted, ignoring his comment suggesting she had alternate sexual preferences. "She's just a young woman. What are you so scared she's going to tell me, huh? I've become a friend to her and I want to make sure she's alright…"

"I thought *I* was your most special friend here," Finn said with a pout, later adding a smile. "Why wouldn't she be alright? Believe me, you don't need to worry about Meredith. She's… a tough one. She's not some vulnerable kitty cat as you apparently think. But, look, it's cold. Come inside…"

"I'm not going to do *anything* until I finally get some answers from you!" Kaitlin spoke softly but firmly.

Finn tilted his head to the side and looked saddened like a little boy for an instant, right before regaining a firm composure and looking angry. He grabbed her left arm and yanked her inside the house, closing and locking the door behind them—so fast that Kaitlin couldn't help but let out a scream.

"Shh, shh, shh," Finn jumped toward her and clasped her mouth with a firm hand, which smelled to Kaitlin like a curious cross between rubbing alcohol and something burned by fire. "Relax, just relax," he now whispered to her as he led her toward the main living room couch and pushed her down, sitting down next to her with his hand still on her mouth. "Why wouldn't she be alright? Everyone is bloody *fine*. See, I don't know why you're acting so upset. Somewhere deep down you must have wanted something like this, or at least needed it. Subconsciously…"

"Let… go," Kaitlin *managed* to muffle through his fingers.

"Hush," Finn said with a whisper. "I will, I will. Just, no need to scream. There's no one in to hear you anyway. Let's just, discuss what's bothering you like two civilized adults, okay?"

Kaitlin turned her head to give him a look of genuine disgust. It was also then that she noticed he'd been playing some classical music in the house. Could anyone even hear her scream? Would any potential Group members even help *her*? Did she have any choice other than complying with Finn's demands?

"*Okay?*" Finn asked more emphatically this time, smiling softly now.

Kaitlin nodded. He let his grab on her go as promised. She looked toward the door and considered for a second to try and escape, yet deep in her heart she knew this man would almost *fly* or do something else unearthly to stop her. *Damn it.* She'd even settle for seeing Anja again now, anyone, just as long as it meant the two of them weren't alone.

"Yes, maybe 'subconsciously' I needed to be awakened from my stupid fantasies!" Kaitlin confessed calmly. quoting the word with her fingers in the air. Tears of anger rolled down her cheeks. "But now I just want to go home… please… please, Finn," she lowered her voice to a soft whimper she was sure would win over with Finn easier.

"Kaitlin, I don't know what got you this upset. I really liked you, you know that?" Finn fixed his green gaze on her eyes once again like he had first done that day in the woods where they'd first met. To her disappointed surprise, Kaitlin was able to once again feel excited in the same way she had back then.

He leaned in to give her right cheek a soft kiss. "Your life could become so much better than it is now. And I know you must know this. You're a logical woman who knows deep down what she wants, and deserves. Things could be so *good* if you were here with us. With *me*…"

"Please," Kaitlin continued, lowering her gaze onto the ground and taking a deep breath. "I wish we could have maybe met in another life, another time, under different circumstances. Are you happy? So yes, yes… I was attracted to you. Ok. And you know it. Ok. But… not like this. Don't you see this isn't my idea of 'good'?"

"What *is* your idea of *good* then, Ms. Maverick?" Was that a little tang of hurt in Finn's eyes she was seeing? "A life of boredom wrapped around one man's wishes?"

"Is that all that the concept of marriage *is* to you?" Kaitlin asked defensively. "A life of boring servitude? Now, you know very well what I meant! What about your gang's 'wishes'? Huh? Sexual adventures? I mean how in the world can you possibly try to convince me that those things are…"

"*Good* girls don't exactly come out to the woods to play behind their husbands' backs, do they?" Finn's interruption was stern in tone and took Kaitlin by surprise.

That was it, as far as she was concerned. The evil she felt behind his last comment erased any small feeling of regret at possibly hurting his feelings. *If he even really has any*, she thought. How dare he? It's not like she was having an affair with him. Yes, lying to her husband about where she went was wrong. And she was guilty of some unsuitable thoughts, she had to admit, but it could hardly be considered something exquisitely shameful, could it?

Besides, *she* was the one misled into thinking this had been an innocent gathering in nature, kind of like that Book Group or Babysitting Group the Women's Club tried to get its members to join over e-mail requests. She had only kept her coming there a secret because it could easily be taken out of context and misunderstood; that was all, wasn't it?

Kaitlin sighed out loud, still eyeing the door as well as the huge porcelain vase on the television counter she decided she would use if things came to her life becoming endangered. *Damn it, why didn't I bring that knife with me this time, too?* She cursed herself. She had left the house abruptly without really coming up with a plan. Sandy's recognition of Finn in the picture had unnerved her senseless.

She *did* technically mislead her husband and she just had to face up to these repercussions. Albeit in her peculiar case those repercussions apparently meant having gotten herself involved in some sexualized forest cult with potential jinn-creatures as members!

"Good girls know when enough is enough, and want to repent," she muttered under her breath. She felt a tear drop from the corner of her right eye. More audibly, all she could manage was a weak "I'm sorry, Finn.

You do have a point, I'll admit. I should have never come here after that, well, let's just call it: 'birthday party incident'. I should have never gone to strangers' homes, regardless of how *fooled* I was that there were professional circumstances. I…"

"That was *not* trickery, sweetheart," Finn interrupted, using a soft tone. "We are who we say we are. You can call our clients, you can…"

"Oh I'm sure. Yeah and why do those 'clients' work with *your* company, with your unconventional offices, may I ask? Do you promise them certain favors?" Kaitlin asked, yet as soon as she had, she placed her hands on the corners of the couch in case she needed to run after another potential unwelcomed reaction from Finn for her courage.

Finn placed his right forefinger on his lips. "You watch it. You can choose not to approve of the enlightened way we've all chosen to live our lives. But you have no right trying to insult our genuine business."

Oh this guy is good. Shit. Kaitlin knew she had to bite back her tongue. This wasn't exactly like confronting a pervert in the metro where tens of by-standers could help her. This was confronting a fast-traveling jinn and possibly even a sicko alone in a wood cabin.

"Ok. I'm sorry," Kaitlin said calmly. "You're right. It's none of my business how you lead your personal lives. I just genuinely didn't think too much in coming here. It's not okay, especially for a married woman like me to do so. And believe me, even if I weren't married, it simply isn't. I believe in a committed, romantic relationship between two people, that's all. And look… I… I won't tell anyone where you guys are… believe me, I just want out… I…. can't handle this…"

"Kaitlin," Finn interrupted, sighing impatiently. "What in the world are you going on about? You're talking as if you just discovered we were some sort of Norwegian Mafia!"

As Finn started to laugh like a crazy person (lasting for a lot longer than a normal laugh should), all Kaitlin could do was smile and nod for sympathy. It was all she had left to do to save herself out of the situation, she felt. "No, of course not. You guys are just lovers of nature, as you've put it. I understand. Though I don't really get why you didn't even allow me to take a picture, but, anyway. It's just, not for me. I just… I just want things to be the way they were before you met me. But while I'm here, I just wanted to make sure Meredith is alright… And…" Kaitlin was just about to bring up Sandy again when Finn interrupted.

"Romantic love and relationships, you say?" Finn asked mockingly. "Huh! Do you know how much that leads to *destruction*? Don't you follow the news? What kind of world do you live in? Do you know how lives become ruined for what people mistake as 'love'? The only real love is familial love. And we here are family: we are daughters and sons of the Earth. Alright? Not everyone can get that. If you take a picture of the beauty surrounding us, you'll share it, and we don't need any unsuitable people finding out about us. The most strangers do is pass by our cabin, thinking it's just a random one they simply came across during their morning jogs. You were supposed to be *special*. Do you know…"

"Finn," Kaitlin interrupted this time, unable to hold it in any longer. Come hell or high water she was going to be brave and speak her mind. Perhaps one last time for a long time if she managed to make it out of this situation alright. She stood up. "Ok, so you guys live by some… some *philosophy* that this Lar person bestows. Fine. My respects. But let's cut to the chase, ok? Why are you following me? Why were you at the Ball? And I thought I was mistaken at the time but now I'm more certain than ever: why were you watching my husband and I jog? And, putting me aside, because, let's say, it's my punishment or something for coming here. Fine. But why on earth are you following *Sandy*!? My friend in New York? What does *she* have to do with anything? How did you even *know* she was my friend? And I'm not even going to *begin* facing myself to ask how in the world did you, like, friggin' teleport yourself there and back in a manner of just an hour or so!"

Realizing she'd just gone on for a while without a peep or much of a reaction from Finn, Kaitlin just stood there, frozen in further confusion.

Finally, Finn spoke in a relaxed and sly tone, back in his element strangely enough. "Are you finished with your little monologue, Ms. Kaitlin? You and your questions amuse me."

"Does it matter, Finn?" Kaitlin asked, encouraged by his considerably well-tempered reaction to all her questions. "Because I don't believe you've answered any of them. And, no, I'm not finished. Not really. Isn't *honesty* a part of you guys' famous life-philosophy? You haven't been completely *honest* with me, and yet you expect me to *trust* you guys and let down my guard and so on and so forth." Kaitlin felt her nerves relax a bit the more Finn appeared less angry and more teasing, like he usually was, and so she sat down back on the couch—though a bit farther away from him. "I mean, come on, who *are* you, exactly? And, more important for me at the moment, what do you want from *me* and *my friends?* Don't think I forgot how Tan was interested in finding out about Sibel the minute I mentioned her name, either."

"Kaitlin, Kaitlin," Finn said melodically, smiling. "We always want new, quality friends and if people are friends of *our* friends, well, then we just believe it means that more similar-minded people can mingle. That's all. Is that so hard to understand? As I'm sure I've told you, we have similar brotherhoods everywhere. I mean Sibel's quite pretty too, though you are more my type, but I must admit, I was a bit disappointed by Sandy. I mean, no offense, she's cute, but *way* too average to be friends with a woman of *your* caliber. And she thinks *she's* going to make it as an actress? It's almost tragic how funny it is…"

"Whoa, there. So let me get this straight, wise-ass," Kaitlin started with a stern face. "You met me and liked me, or whatever, and then wanted to see how many 'caliber' 'lady' friends I could introduce to you guys for your… activities? Oh I'm sorry but I'm thinking *you're* the tragically-comical one now. I'm sure you could fool, and probably have fooled, many gorgeous ladies right here in Norway… like Anja!"

Finn just smirked. "You don't know anything. And I asked you to watch your insults: this is not a brothel. The real brothels are the clubs and bars 'regular' people go to on weekends, alright? So watch what you're saying in our home…"

He shot Kaitlin a look that made Kaitlin's skin crawl. She took a deep breath, albeit inhaling with difficulty due to the deep lump that had developed in her throat, and wrapped her arms around her body protectively.

"I had some other business to attend to in New York, and wanted to check out your little friend, out of pure curiosity, since she is *your* friend," Finn continued more softly now. "I then chatted her up to amuse myself, that's all. No harm done. Why are you all worked up?"

"Just… tell me why? Why me?" Kaitlin pleaded, deciding to ease up on her tone of voice again. After all, she didn't exactly want to let out any deeper-rooted anger in Finn that was obvious from his eyes he was trying his best to contain, as it would likely end in disaster for her. "Finn could you please come straight with *that* at least? Why me and *my* friends, then? Do you, like, I don't know: follow Anja's friends too? Or Meredith's?"

"As a matter of fact, we've gained a lot of sisters through their circle in our other networks, sure. I mean if you were smart and could have been patient enough to work your way up to meet Lar, you would have met them in our many cabins. It would have been a *much* more exciting and quality environment for you than your *Women's Club*," Finn chuckled again his Dr. Jekyll & Hyde laugh, looking crazier to her by the minute.

Poor girls, Kaitlin thought. Then she realized *she* was still possibly such a victim 'girl' herself, on the cusp of a similar situation. What was it that they'd always promoted on airplanes right before a flight, about placing the oxygen mask on *yourself* before attempting to help anyone else in case of an emergency situation?

Heading to the door in a medium-paced walk, Finn ran after her and stood in front of her. With neither contact nor force this time. "Come on, where are you going? You don't have to like our ways, but we're friends, aren't we? No harm done. Let me boil some water for some coffee and I'll walk to town with you. It's the least I could do…. And the least *you* could do for coming in with your boots still on." He winked. And Kaitlin melted, again, hating herself. After everything, all the craziness and creepiness, he could still affect her. *Oh well.* She just had to face up to her feelings. *Denial helps no one*, she thought.

"You're not answering my questions," Kaitlin stared down at her boots, realizing she was slightly pouting. This would have to be her one last attempt. It also would have to be slightly flirty in order to try to get Finn to be nice and understanding with her, and leave her alone once and for all. "*And* you rather *impolitely* dragged me in, if you recall. So I haven't exactly been welcomed as a 'colleague', 'friend' or even guest, for that matter. So, thanks, but no need for coffee. I can walk myself out." Kaitlin headed slowly to the door, peeking backwards from the corner of her left eye for him to follow.

"Ok. I know when to apologize, as well," Finn came after her, sure enough. "Don't worry, Ms. Kaitlin. It won't happen again. Just please sit down… or at least allow me to walk back with you. I'll answer you… I promise... I just felt some things are better unsaid, that's all. Purely to avoid judgement. But, if you *must* know... Isn't it rather simple? What ill-intent could I possibly have for wanting to simply *see* you? Jogging and sweating heavily...looking absolutely gorgeous at a Ball, in the arms of a man who doesn't deserve you...Coming out of the gym with your hair in a cute ponytail..."

"...So you *were* always watching me in the gym as well? Whoa!" Kaitlin began panting now, her heart beating faster. *This guy has followed me more often than I could have even imagined.*

"Well no, no, no!" Finn held his palms out defensively again. "It was just that one other time when Sibel got picked up by her husband. I swear. That's the only time I didn't show myself to you. Other times, I wanted you to see me, to see how *much* I wanted you... simply to see you. Think about it: if I had meant harm (and had you been in any danger) don't you think I would have come up to you? Said something? Caused a scene?"

Kaitlin was flattered, turned on and yet slightly scared again all at the same time. Finn proved to be annoyingly adept at accomplishing all three simultaneously.

"Thank you, for saying all that, I guess," Kaitlin stated, crossing her arms together in exasperation. "But, Finn, like I said, it can't be. I mean, since we'd become, I don't know, *friendly*, you could have seen me anytime. Given me a call to hang out in town, or, I don't know, given me another document to translate or something! I mean, why did you have to appear so... so... *mysteriously* all over the place? Finn, you had me thinking I was going crazy!"

Taking a deep breath, Kaitlin took the final jump into the big, cold pool of bravery she'd been circling and dipping her big toe in. "Look, I promise I won't judge if you're honest with me. So, out with it. Are you a..."

Finn smiled and she knew. She knew that *he* knew what she was going to ask. So she chose to just leave the question hanging in the air: giving him the proverbial ball.

Finn nodded. "That's why Tan was actually nervous about you befriending a Turk like him. We're more common knowledge in their culture and religion for the most part. But I'm sure you've learned all of that by now, since I'm sure it was your little friend Sibel who must have shared with you all of her suspicions, for you to even ask me. *He* is all human, by the way: Tan, I mean. We live mixed. I mean, I wouldn't have 'turned you' like a vampire or something had you chosen to be with us...." He added, laughing.

"I see..." was all Kaitlin could manage. "I mean, I'm not really sure how much of this I believe in or understand. All I know is some otherworldliness definitely went on that I still can't explain. I cannot get it out of my head! And I've been raised to respect all religions, and folks from all walks of life, let's just say. I guess..."

"The only thing *otherworldly* for me is your beauty, Ms. Kaitlin," Finn started to say, staring intensely into her eyes once again. "And your fiery spirit. Believe me, if I come across your mind at any point throughout the day, it is because of the law of attraction. It is only because I'm thinking of you at that point too... It's our connection and I know you feel it, too."

"Finn... I appreciate the things you're saying," Kaitlin remarked, surprisingly feeling that she was indeed telling the truth. "I just want us all to forget everything... forget I ever came here... and I promise I will never say anything to anyone and will remember you guys fondly, alright? I mean, thank you, but you're wrong. My husband's actually a good guy. I'll be fine."

Finn smiled and looked at his shoes, and back up at her in his deep gaze. "Well, he's a *lucky* one too. I can tell you that. But 'good' is a subjective and relative term, I suppose."

"And just what do you mean by that?" Kaitlin asked angrily.

"Well, he's in an exploitive business for one," Finn said. "Do you truly ever know what they do? Whose lives they affect? What tragedies may happen because of their cockiness? Their disregard for other people's lives?"

"Wait, *what?*" Kaitlin had finally had enough of hearing her poor husband dragged into all of this over and over again. "You know what, since you opened up the subject, just what *exactly* do you have against my husband? And *please* don't bullshit me about some vendetta against the petroleum business or this and that, ok? There are *lots* of other people in the business here in Stavanger you could have targeted, or their spouses or girlfriends or whatever it is that you've done with me, which I'm still not sure of, by the way. But, anyway! I mean, don't think I haven't noticed

Tan's constant questions about my husband, either! Out with it!" She couldn't remember ever acting out so bravely —or perhaps, so foolishly— ever in her life!

Finn gazed at her for a good twenty seconds or so: no smirk, no smile. He looked like a cross between angry and sad. "You're right, Kaitlin. See, I knew there was another reason I liked you, besides having to. You're a smart one. You're literally both smart and beautiful, which is a rare thing in a woman, in my experience."

"You *had* to like me? Just what is *that* supposed to mean?" Kaitlin's patience was running low. "But, you know what? I almost don't even care right now. I was a target apparently, for whatever reason. But, as you were saying? Paul? My husband? What's your issue with him? Do you *know* him or something?"

Finn paced back and forth in front of the furnace, covering his body with his arms and taking a deep breath, as if preparing to give a speech or tell a story. Tilting his head toward Kaitlin and looking her straight in the eyes, he spoke. "Let's just say, your husband was involved in some poor decision-making in his past, before you guys were together. And, let's just say, his stupidity led to some bad things. Please. I don't want to say anymore."

"Oh, no, you don't," Kaitlin said, standing up to face him. "You don't just lay all this on me and get to get away that easy without any further detail. I mean, come on, Finn, just tell me. I already found out you're a genie, a Jinn, or whatever, and look, I'm standing right here!" Kaitlin opened her arms wide and found the courage to stare straight into Finn's eyes. "There's no other logical way for you to have done the things you have done: to have learned the things about me that you have. Yet, look. I'm not afraid, or the one to judge. So, please. Why did you target *me*? To get back at Paul? For whatever bad thing he may or may not have done?"

"I appreciate your understanding, Ms. Kaitlin," Finn said, smiling again at her now. Just then he reached out and placed a strand of hair that had fallen in front of Kaitlin's face behind her left ear, causing her to jerk back slightly. "You're an open-minded, fun-loving girl: another reason why you deserve more than that boring guy, in my opinion. But, what was I saying? Oh yes. Look, let's just say: *an eye for an eye*, alright? And leave it at that?"

"What did Paul do, Finn?" Kaitlin asked. "Take your woman? Or Lar's? Or whatever? I mean, what else could it be? Wait a minute... does it have anything to do with that... *Linette* girl?"

Finns eyes suddenly popped open. Kaitlin had just then remembered Meredith mentioning that the Group knew her. She immediately knew that a nerve had been hit, and that her suspicions were likely correct.

"I don't know what you think, Finn. But Paul didn't hurt her. He never confirmed to her boyfriend back in Canada that she was a cheater or whatever. It was all a big misunderstanding. If that boyfriend then went on to kill that girl, then it was *his* stupidity, not to mention criminal character. It was not my husband's fault! *He* would never purposely mislead or hurt anyone... But *you*? I mean, I don't even want to begin to think you could hurt me. Yet the way you behaved at the door, pushing me in like that..."

"Kaitlin, no!" Finn went near her and touched her arm gently. "Of course not. It's not like that. And of course I would never hurt you. It may have begun as... well, what it began as. But as I got to know you, I really began to like you for *you*..."

"I... I just want to go home and clear my head, alright?" Kaitlin said, feeling extremely lightheaded all of a sudden.

"Kaitlin..." Finn inched closer to her, with his eyes staring intensely into hers.

"Please... stop" Kaitlin begged softly.

"Kaitlin... I cannot," were the last words spoken, right before Finn's hands fully cusped her face in his palms and they embraced each other's flaming skin tingling with both fear and excitement, soft and wet lips locked passionately in the hungriest and most devouring and lingering kiss Kaitlin had ever experienced in her life.

Chapter 18

The stray branches sliced stingier across her skin the more she tried to sway them away with her hands.

Kaitlin didn't flinch. *I deserve the pain as punishment,* she thought.

She'd run as fast as she could after the surprise embrace with Finn, and was completely out of breath by the time she'd reached *sentrum.*

The unique and pleasantly tangy taste of his lips and tongue entwined with hers was still fresh in her mind.

Oh, no.

A vibration coming from her crossbody bag told her she still had to hurry back home to Paul, and act like everything was alright.

{Someone's waiting for you…} the message read.

She could visualize Paul's puppy-eyed look opening the door for her. *Sigh.*

Picking up a roll of paper towels she knew they'd run out of, Kaitlin popped a chewing gum into her mouth and took a deep breath in front of their apartment door twenty minutes later.

She had to ring the bell a second time when Paul didn't answer the door. *That's odd,* she thought. *I could have just gone in myself, but this guy did message that he'd been waiting for me, so what gives?*

Placing her head on the door to listen for any sounds from the inside, Kaitlin was just beginning to get worried when she was startled by a series of playful barks of someone's dog coming from the direction of the elevator on the other side of their building.

Just as she was beginning to think how rare it was that they'd been living in a Norwegian apartment building which actually allowed pets, she saw Paul's familiar face turn the corner into her direction. He was holding the most adorable Golden Retriever puppy she believed she'd ever seen.

"Oh… my… Gosh!" Kaitlin exclaimed, rushing next to her husband to pet the dog. "Whose is this, Paulie?"

"Yours, my lady… well… ours." Paul said, beaming.

"What!?" Kaitlin asked as she met his eyes. She'd been expecting a puppy-eyed look from her husband, not from an actual canine.

"That's right, babe," Paul explained proudly. "One of my colleagues, Stephan; his family dog had just given birth to four more just like this one, and his wife told him they could only keep one… so… I'd been planning to surprise you with him…"

"*Him*… it's a boy? Aww… how old is he… does he have his shots… what's his… oh, Paulie!" Kaitlin hugged her husband as tightly as she could. She'd instinctively reached for his lips as well, but decided she couldn't yet bring herself to do that after the cabin incident, and settled for his neck instead.

"Thank you. I truly do not have the words…" she continued, nuzzling the Lab in her own arms now. "Hello… hello, handsome… what's your name?"

"No name yet. I didn't really want to think about it before asking you. Stephan brought his mama from France. Well, let's go in, babe," Paul gently pushed her back into the direction of their apartment, unlocking the door. "We've made too much noise for the neighbors already. I'll fill you in on all the details."

"Tu es un chien français?" Kaitlin playfully asked the puppy, back inside the house as she took of her shoes. "Oh, la la… tu es très beau."

"He really is a handsome little fellow, isn't he?" Paul agreed. She'd forgotten he had picked up a little bit of French back in Canada as well. "Très beau, oui,"

"Beau… should we just call him that, Paulie? *Beau*… or like B-O-more international?" Kaitlin smiled while the puppy started to bark three times in a row excitedly.

"Sounds good to me!" Paul chuckled. "Bo seems to agree... What's that sound?"

Oh, shoot. The phone inside her bag was vibrating again, this time more than two seconds. Kaitlin knew it was a phone call rather than a text message.

'Sibel must have forgotten something… one second, babe." Kaitlin fumbled through her hand, pretending she was still looking for it, although she had recognized the same 'unknown' number calling her immediately, and pressed silent. "Oh shoot, I couldn't reach her call in time... whatever, I'll call her later... Bo is more important now!"

"Are you sure?" Paul insisted, wiping the puppy's paws clean with a cloth towel from the kitchen. "You don't want to be rude to your new buddy..."

Kaitlin pretended not to notice the hint of suspicion in his tone of voice, as she picked up her grocery bag and placed the paper towels inside their kitchen cabinet for storage. "No, no... we were just together... I don't need to be *that* available... I'll call her back..."

A change of tactic suddenly felt pressing and Kaitlin went into survival mode. Inching closer to her husband and grabbing him closer to her by his buttocks (Finn-kissing guilt or no Finn-kissing guilt), she planted a deep one on her husband. "I could be busy, too, she has to realize... mmm."

"Oh yeah...?" Paul seemed to take the bait.

"Oh, yeah..." Kaitlin teased, just as Bo barked and hopped in between their legs, causing them to almost fall.
They laughed instead.

"Whoa..." Paul suddenly exclaimed, crouching down to observe the right leg of his jeans. "What the... Bo... did you just...?"

"Oh yeah... he just peed," Kaitlin finished. She was thanking her lucky stars more and more each minute with her new puppy. *Our new puppy.*

"Do you know how to house train...?" Paul annoyedly walked over to the kitchen sink. "No, boy, no!"

"Go easy on him," Kaitlin pleaded as she picked Bo up and walked with him to the bathroom. "I'll get all the dog supplies we need, and I'll break him in soon enough."

"It needs to be sooner than later, Kaitlin," Paul continued in a serious tone, putting his shoes back on by the door. "I'd been so excited to surprise you that I didn't even think about these things. We can't have a smelly house. I'm going to the pet shop. Do you want to come with me for a ride?"

"I think I'll just play with the poor pooch a little more before his daddy goes all military discipline on him soon enough, babe," Kaitlin called out from their bedroom now.

***

As soon as she heard the door close, Kaitlin gently placed her new friend down on the floor and reached back for her cellphone in her bag.

"Sit... good boy... here, you can play with this pillow right here...." Just as Kaitlin was feeling her blood beginning to boil again, she recognized that the last missed call was from a similar but different number. For some reason the number looked familiar to her as well, but she knew it hadn't been Finn's.

"Meredith!" she suddenly remembered. *Let me call her back. If Finn picks up, I'm just going to hang up on that chauvinistic bastard. Who does he think he is? Kissing me like that... and someone could have seen us.* "Hello?"

"Kaitlin?" A soft voice whimpered on the other line. "Thanks for calling me back," Meredith continued. "I'm lucky I'm still alone to talk... how are you?"

"I'm fine, Meredith," Kaitlin replied. "Well, as fine as I could be, anyway. But the real question is you: I was worried, I didn't see you with Tan at the Cabin, and he was acting kind of strange..."

"I was in the hospital, Kaitlin," Meredith continued. "I still am, in fact... Tan forced me to have an abortion."

Kaitlin felt stunned, in complete silence for a moment. "Oh, wow, honey."

"Yeah, I was pregnant," Meredith explained. "Can you believe it? I mean, babies aren't exactly welcome in the Group. I still love Tan, I can't help it. He's not an asshole *all* the time. And besides, I have no one else now I can turn to... Oh, you found out about Finn, huh?"

"Finn?" Kaitlin asked, intrigued.

"Yeah..." Meredith continued. "I can hear what you're thinking too when I want to.... You see, Finn and I are the same. We're not *all* bad Kaitlin..."

"You? Oh," Kaitlin stated, astounded. "You are... a *jinn*, too?"

"Yeah," Meredith managed a soft chuckle. "This must all sound so crazy and random to you... a whole other world..."

"Right... It's ok," Kaitlin continued, despite her double shock. "And Tan?"

"He's actually not," Meredith said. "You'd think so, right? The way he's got *me* wrapped around *his* finger... I know I'm crazy to take his controlling ways sometimes, but around him I'm not myself. I've never felt this way about anyone, Kaitlin... I guess love makes you do crazy things..."

"I can imagine, yeah..." Kaitlin offered, glad to see that at least Meredith was aware of Tan's seemingly mental abuse over her.

"Sometimes I wonder if he's got us fooled, actually..." Meredith continued. "...but then he says something so ludicrous I actually smile to myself, since it then becomes so obvious he's a regular human being. Besides, aren't there many humans that are also capable of controlling behavior even without any extra powers? I mean, forgive me, I don't mean to be offensive to your kind, and I know I've been living in the woods for a while now, but..."

"No, I get you," Kaitlin cut in, thinking back on some mentally abusive people she could definitely say she unfortunately encountered in her life. She was pretty certain they were humans. "Absolutely... I suppose we cannot generalize ... Every carton can have a rotten egg now and then, eh?"

"I appreciate your impartialness and sympathetic concern, Kaitlin," Meredith said softly.

"Look, I told Finn as well," Kaitlin said, "I'm not judging. I just don't want to be judged myself, alright? Nor do I want to be lured under false pretenses and be asked to do things I don't want to do...But what's more important here is your health... and the baby... well... the fetus... and, oh, what am I saying? I'm so sorry you had to go through something like this..."

"Just don't become like me. Ok, Kaitlin? Fight as hard as you can," Meredith interrupted. "Fight for a pure form of love before you ever enslave yourself to something you know isn't ultimately good for you. Be good and safe with your loved ones. Throw yourself into your faith when you're feeling lost. Life is really too short to live on the edge, when we're all on its edge to begin with, as dull as things may sometimes seem."

"Thanks Meredith, for opening up to me, for your bravery... everything," Kaitlin spoke, still astonished by the confession. "As you can imagine, I won't have anything to do with the Group anymore, but I wish you well. You can call me whenever you want."

"I believe you," Meredith insisted. "And believe me, I can meet you at lightning speed if you ever want to meet somewhere and I can carve out some time. But, don't think Finn and Tan will give up that easily on you…"

"Finn? Well, I can understand his interest, I suppose… but Tan?" Kaitlin asked, confused. "What could possibly be *his* deal with me? Meredith, can you finish telling me about the link with that dead girl? And my husband? Please?"

"I've got to go now… Bye, Kaitlin," Meredith said hurriedly.

"Meredith… Mer…?"

"Just trust your instincts… about Tan and the Trondheim girl," Meredith whispered right before clicking off.

***

"Whoa… down, buddy," Kaitlin heard Paul call out from the kitchen.

Oh, shoot. He had come in already. *Too fast.* Had he heard her? "Babe, you're back," Kaitlin walked over and reached nervously for the refrigerator. "What happened? And what's this poor thing going to eat?"

"The pet shop was closed today," Paul complained. "Can you believe it? And the guy at the market said pet food had run out of stock and the new shipment hadn't come in yet. Luckily, I'd already been feeding him these bags his owner gave me… I just picked these up from the trunk, at least…"

"Hmm. Let's put some more in a bowl then…" Kaitlin said as she closed the refrigerator. "What should *we* eat?"

"I'm not hungry. I already took a couple of bites off a sandwich I got while at the market," Paul said, distracted.

"You? Non-home-made food? The horror, Paulie, why?" Kaitlin teased, ruffling his hair.

"Yeah… I have been uncharacteristically compromising, haven't I?" Paul threw himself on their leather couch and turned on the TV. Kaitlin was grateful for the sudden sound of wild animals blasting from some documentary.

"Bo is more appreciated than you know, babe," Kaitlin came over to sit next to him. "Aren't you, boy?"

The dog didn't bother to turn his face away from the food he was now ravaging from his bowl.

"Who's Meredith, Kaitlin?" Paul asked, not taking his eyes off the television.

"I'm... sorry... what?" Kaitlin asked, in shock. *Oh, shoot.*

"I heard you hanging up the phone with someone as I was coming in," Paul explained, turning his head to face her. "I've only heard of Sibel. So that name wasn't particularly familiar..."

"Oh..." Kaitlin started to say. She knew her husband's bullshit detector was always on, so she couldn't stray too far from the truth. "Meredith... well, you've never heard of her, yet, because honestly I only saw her like once or twice, and we didn't really talk long. She's an acquaintance of Sibel's, and we ran into her at the gym... A fit young woman, she is!"

"Why would she call you then?" Paul asked, still not convinced. "Or you call her? If you're not particularly close?"

That did it. Kaitlin knew she had to delve straight into her spontaneous bullshit file and pull one out. The timing of all this wasn't good. Not good at all. And she felt completely unprepared. "It's... well, to be honest, silly womanly gossip, Paulie," Kaitlin stammered. "Sad, really. I think the woman must be more of a frenemy than a friend! To actually have the audacity to call me to complain about Sibel; I mean, I remember I'd given my number to her at the gym to be polite, but still...."

"Hmm..." Paul muttered. "Well, you women are all indeed... full of strange surprises, that is for sure." He was still watching roaring male lions looking greedily at some animal leftovers the lionesses in the herd had apparently hunted and brought back.

"Oh, hush, Paulie. Don't let me start one of my, as you call them, *feminist rants* now," Kaitlin said as she forced a smile. "I'll be right back... ooph, I've been holding it in for too long..."

As Kaitlin closed the bathroom door behind her, she immediately turned on the faucet and massaged some water onto her forehead before letting out a big sigh. *Breathe, Kaitlin, breathe... it's just a woman he heard me talk to... he'll get over it.*

A bark at the door reminded her of her new additional source of responsibility. *Oh boy.* Timing indeed truly was everything, wasn't it?

"Oh, hi Bo… do you have to go Pee Pee again, too?" Kaitlin had just opened the door and kneeled down to pet him when she saw Paul from the corner of her eye playing with his… no… wait… *her* cell phone. *Oh, crap.*

"This must be where you've been… working out, huh Kaitlin? Who are these? Your gym buddies?!" Paul asked in a calm but stern voice.

"I guess we started looking through each other's phones now, very nice," Kaitlin said, crossing her arms.

"Don't change the subject, Kaitlin," Paul insisted.

"Paul… I can explain," Kaitlin stammered, holding her palms out toward her husband. "I had *nothing* but professional intentions with those people; and, yes, Meredith is one of them. I was to be translating some documents but I knew it would sound weird to you that they worked from a home office located in the woods…"

"Oh, they work from the woods, do they?" Paul asked mockingly. "Where do they work from? Their summer *hyttes*[8]? Or winter ones? I mean… oh… what's next? I suppose you're going to tell me they feel the need to live like out in nature because they farm and raise herds of sheep, or log or do yoga or something like that…"

"Well they *do* log actually. It's for a paper production business they run from there," Kaitlin explained, as calmly as she could muster, despite her rapid heartbeat and the painfully-nervous knot inside her stomach. "But, really, Paul, I *was* going to tell you. You didn't need to go through my messages and e-mails, I mean…"

"Oh they *do log*, do they?" Paul interrupted. "So it's some *timber production* business. Oh, I see," Paul's nostrils flared as if steam were coming off of them, just like a cartoon bull. "No wonder they're dressed more like Brad Pitt than friggin' Paul Bunyan, because they actually run a home *business.* Fancy, Kaitlin. Real fancy. How old are these kids? Where did you meet them? Online? The Women's Club was too 'dull' for you so

---

[8] hyttes: 'cottage' in Norwegian

you joined some kind of what, Cool Kids Club? What the heck have you been up to while I was at work? I mean, I cannot believe this…"

Kaitlin jumped on the opportunity she saw in Paul's abrupt stoppage as he continued to stare at the photograph, and she held on to her words for dear life. "Baby, they introduced themselves to me about two weeks ago when I was in town, asking if I knew any languages other than English for translation services they needed, so on and so forth. I mean, you see those people trying to sell magazines in town all the time. I just assumed it was some unique Norwegian thing. I mean, I'm not an idiot. When I was told their main location was in a cabin in the woods nearby, you know, where I'd have to drop off my CV and get my trial-document to be translated… and so and so forth, I was creeped out, of course. But there was this nice young lady there. Meredith. It eased my discomfort. And another one, Anja. They… you know… talked about the way nature heals the soul and stuff like that and I, I just became mesmerized, okay! I knew it would sound *fishy* to you. I know how you even mock Yoga practitioners. I knew you'd call them some New Age hoax…"

"Wait… Kaitlin, wait…" Paul said suddenly. Kaitlin could see that Paul had his finger on a particular spot on the photograph, but she was on a roll. She knew she was giving her husband partial bits of the truth but she didn't need to make it sound any more suspicious than it really was. It wasn't like she'd broken her marriage vows or anything. She'd just used some white lies about the company she had been keeping recently, hadn't she?

"Look, I didn't do anything wrong, ok? I swear, baby!" Kaitlin exclaimed. "I know I told you I was with Sibel more times than I actually was, but I *had* to for a while—and I *was* getting paid. And it felt good to know I could contribute to our income. Be a working woman as I was before. And… I'm so sorry! I was *going* to tell you if it had become something more permanent, but you're right. You're right. It turned out they're too crazy for me, not as professional as I thought. So I stopped working with them or talking to them, I swear!"

"Kaitlin…." Paul said as soon as she stopped to breathe for one second. His eyes were still fixated on the photograph on her phone.

"By the way, they're not exactly kids," Kaitlin went on. "I mean, Lord knows they still act as if they were teenagers, but they're all in their 20's or early 30's, which, don't forget babe, I still am as well. I know it's not an excuse to lie, but it was just…"

"Just stop it! Kaitlin, stop talking for a second!" Paul blurted out angrily. "This woman with the straight hair here. Is *that* the Meredith girl you mentioned? Because, I mean, that tall, buff guy with the dark hair with his arms around her…"

"…Yes. That's her! How'd you guess, babe?" Kaitlin was genuinely intrigued.

"I'll be God damned. I guess the douchebag has a type…" Paul muttered under his breath, shaking his head. Kaitlin's jaw dropped as her next choice of words remained in the air, unable to escape her mouth.

"This Meredith looks so much like Linette!" Paul finally continued after a moment of silence, surprisingly in a level-tone of voice. His eyes appeared to stare straight off into space over Kaitlin's head now, nostalgic. "The same face almost! Just with a lighter shade of brown hair. But that's *definitely* Linette's boyfriend next to her!"

"Oh my God…" Kaitlin whispered, covering her mouth with her palm.

"Yeah. *My God*, Kaitlin! Indeed!" Paul mocked, tossing her phone to the corner of the couch. "And you say these people just *randomly* approached you as you were walking? This can*not* have been a friggin' coincidence!"

Now it was Kaitlin's turn to be shocked. She stood up and held on to the edge of the nearest dining chair with both hands, feeling her feet about to give way. All her blood felt as if it'd just flushed away from her head. "Whoa. Paul. You mean, that guy who came storming into your office? Asking about his girlfriend? You think that's him? In the photograph? Are you sure? *Tan?*"

"I *know* it's him. Is *he* the one who came up to you, Kaitlin? Tan… Is that his name? It *does* ring a bell… I guess I'm not the only one who blamed myself for fueling his fire with fire. This guy must have had it in for me after Linette's death, which, God knows, he must have done himself! Why else would they come after you… after *me* through *you*? Oh my God…" Paul now pulled up the chair next to the one Kaitlin was holding on to and sat down, placing his head on the table with his arms covering his head.

"An eye for an eye…" Kaitlin whispered to herself, recalling Finn's only explanation offered to her after she'd questioned him in regards to their choice of targeting her.

"The body was discovered in her hometown: Trondheim," Paul continued. Kaitlin wasn't sure whether or not he'd heard her. "The jerk-off must have followed her there, after Canada. Oh, I should have known when she never responded her e-mails. That was not like her. Even if she were to shut me down, she would have said *something*…"

Kaitlin was taken by surprise. "You still couldn't get her out of your mind even after she left your old company, huh? You kept on e-mailing her?"

"Kaitlin, please!" Paul interjected, waving his right hand dismissively. "Let's not change the topic, okay? This was years ago; we weren't dating and you were still giving me the cold shoulder romantically. I just wanted to contact her for answers. I mean, she left so abruptly! And of course my mind went wild at the time, especially since I'd had that talk with her man… this *Tan* guy."

"And I cannot believe you became work buddies with him?" Paul continued, his voice taking on an increasingly derisive tone. "A potential murderer? Oh, you not only get an 'A' for honesty, but an 'A' for street smarts too, sweetheart."

"And how honest do you think *you* were with *me*, exactly, Paul?" Kaitlin asked angrily. "If *I'm* guilty of being dishonest for withholding information, don't you see that *you've* done the same thing?"

"It's not the same thing!" Paul said calmly.

I hate this passive-aggressive thing he's doing, Kaitlin thought. "Yes, it is!"

"This is about danger, Kaitlin. You're being a child!" Paul continued loudly, with the sternest look in his eyes Kaitlin had seen in a long time, causing Bo to whimper closer behind her right leg.

"Then don't treat me like one!" Kaitlin exclaimed, surprising even herself. She stormed into their bedroom and shut the door loudly behind her.

"Way to go, teenager!" Paul shouted.

Chapter 19

A mere twenty-four hours had gone by with her and Paul not speaking to each other, yet it felt like twenty-four days, a whole month even. Kaitlin had never quite realized how much she valued his usual annoying updates on football match results and other simple daily news, until she didn't hear them anymore.

She was lucky, she supposed just then, when compared with the fate of some other women around the world who constantly got cheated on and abused mercilessly. Or maybe she'd just been watching too much television. This silence could have been the calm before the storm, for all she knew.

The only thing she was certain of at the moment was that she'd been wrong to lie to her husband. As annoying as he could be, that was the one thing Paul was definitely right about. She couldn't lie to herself about that.

Taking baby steps to walk into the kitchen so as not to alert her husband of her presence more than she had to, she reached into the cupboard for Paul's favorite cup to have his afternoon coffee: the one she'd bought him for his last birthday.

Kaitlin thought she could literally feel her stomach tie itself into a cherry-pit knot—the same one she used to do with her tongue during cocktails to impress her friends back in the day. Paul's lingering silence, even as he took a sip of the coffee she'd prepared for him, let her know the Cold War between them was apparently still going to continue.

She took Bo in her hands and gave his neck extra loud kisses, hoping Paul would notice.

"You appreciate me, don't you, boy?" she asked the puppy. Bo began to wag his tail happily after having had a full meal from his bowl in the morning.

"Oh yes, you do... oh yes, you do…"

Paul let out a loud smirk in response to her remark and broke the Arctic chill in the air. "I'm going to go out to the corner store and pick up the paper…"

"All right," Kaitlin managed to mutter. Paul had already put on his shoes and was on his way out the door.

"He's so mean to me, Bo," Kaitlin said after the door had been shut. "Without even trying to understand. Thank God, I have you now…"

"And speaking of mean guys…" she continued. Bo barked and picked up the rubber yellow ball they'd used to try to teach him to fetch. "Maybe I should call Mr. Finn-the-Jinn himself and let him know I know their dirty little secret… that Tan obviously killed Linette and blamed Paul for making him suspect her…"

"Woof," Bo barked and tilted his head to the side with curiosity.

"But, what if Tan hurts Meredith? His Linette-replacement, Bo," Kaitlin asked, staring off into the distance. "Because of *me*, this time. I mean, these people apparently love scapegoats to blame for their evils… You're right, Bo. Maybe I should just keep everything to myself. No need to stir up further trouble…."

[Ringggggg]

Trouble through technology apparently was not going to let her go.

***

"Ms. Kaitlin?"

Kaitlin had to admit Finn's voice sounded uncharacteristically soft.

"It's not anybody's fault but *Tan's* that he didn't believe his girlfriend," she started to say straight away on the phone, without saying her hellos. She instinctively felt she knew why he was calling her, and she was too angry to allow Finn to get so much as a word in before she was able to get some things off her chest. "The woman he was apparently *so* into that he's now dating a look-alike. Besides, even if she *had* been cheating on him, it's no excuse to *kill* her, Finn! How can you guys be friends with a murderer? Are there any more like him that you guys are hiding?" She almost could not bring herself to ask what she then decided to ask anyway (all hell had already broken loose, as far as she was concerned): "Have *you* killed anyone?"

"Kaitlin! No!" Finn protested. "You've got it all wrong! Relax! Good afternoon to you, too? Sheesh…"

"Ok, I'm listening…" Kaitlin said with a loud sigh. "I will give you the chance to talk, just this one time, Finn… Ouch!"

Bo had apparently given up on Kaitlin playing fetch with him, throwing the ball toward the balcony window, which in turn had bounced off the glass and straight onto the side of Kaitlin's head.

"Are you OK?" Finn asked.

"Don't change the subject," Kaitlin answered. "I have to take care of Bo- my new puppy- please, just make it quick…"

"Puppy…" Finn began after a moment of silence. "The husband likes to buy gifts to buy your love, does he? How… innovative of him."

"Finn… I'm warning you…" Kaitlin felt more adamant than ever not to fall into his verbal and emotional entrapments again.

"…Ok, Ms. Kaitlin. Ok!" Finn said with a serious tone of voice. "Look, if you must know: a lot of our friends are people Lar helps. Either people whose families have hurt them, usually emotionally but sometimes even physically, or life in general has hurt them in some way. Tan has been trying to repent for the longest time now for his perhaps unfair and hurtful accusations against his ex. But he's not some murderer! His ex's case is an ongoing mystery. We feel she must have committed suicide. But Tan, meanwhile, has vowed to control his anger… and we trust him…"

"Yeah, okay," Kaitlin mocked. "Some angel he's become, right? Oh, sure. That's why he had Meredith have an *abortion*!" For the life of her, Kaitlin could not fathom how anyone (with jinn powers or not) could trust their lives living with a potential murderer, proven or not.

"The child would have had half his blood, Kaitlin!" Finn exclaimed. "You see, Tan is *so* afraid of his violent nature, which he says he got from his own father, that he simply doesn't want any offspring, that's all… For one thing, I actually wanted to see a little half-Jinn, half-human cutie running around the cabin. The pregnancy news actually made me dream of you and I maybe one day having…"

"Don't even!" Kaitlin said, her voice shaking. "Not a chance! You very well know that! Look, I won't go to the police if you promise to leave me and my family and friends alone from now on. Here, in New York City, in Toronto, everywhere. Please!"

213

"Police, huh?" Finn asked softly. "Oh, Ms. Kaitlin, Ms. Kaitlin. So you've actually thought about something like that. Without any evidence or any harm done unto anyone. I'm hurt…"

After letting out a long sigh, Finn added. "Anyway, I wish it were that simple. Too much has been revealed…"

"I'm trusting *you* here, Finn," Kaitlin continued, hearing Bo still barking for attention from the living room. She had come into her bedroom to take the phone call in private, just in case Paul came home earlier than expected again. She promised herself to take the poor dog out for a walk as soon as she hung up. "You don't trust *me?*"

"I don't trust Paul!" Finn shouted. "He'll somehow catch you slipping in a lie and do some digging and then go to the cops. He'll stir up needless trouble once again in his life…"

"He doesn't know anything!" Kaitlin half-lied. After all, his husband only had a theory about Tan, didn't he? "I mean Paul just told me he knew the dead girl from the news, that's all. *I* came up with the theory that Tan must have killed her, due to the Trondheim connection, and the sixth-sense alert I felt when I realized Meredith looked a lot like the picture of Linette on the news…"

"I see," Finn finally spoke after a long pause. *She's ignoring that I can read her bloody mind,* he thought. "I hope you're right, Ms. Kaitlin. You know what you guys… have a nice life, alright?"

What the…? "Th… thanks," Kaitlin muttered. But Finn had already hung up. *This is so not like him,* Kaitlin thought, still unable to let go of the phone from her hand, as she started getting chills down both of her arms. *To just give in and hang up the phone.*

Walking into the living room, Kaitlin's eyes searched for her new best friend. "Bo? Come here boy!"

A sudden breeze coming from the balcony took Kaitlin by surprise.

"That's weird…" she said out loud, wrapping her arms tightly around her body. "I didn't leave this door open! A dog couldn't have… Oh… no…"

The sight in front her was one she could never get off her mind for as long as she lived. "Bo…" Kaitlin gasped with a low whimper as she placed both her palms around her mouth. She tried to stifle a scream she knew should be coming for release, but couldn't to any avail.

With the exception of two plastic chairs and a small wooden coffee table, the balcony stood completely empty. There were no traces of blood or body hair, and yet Kaitlin couldn't shake off the eeriest feeling she'd felt in a long time travel throughout her entire body.

"Bo…" she called out, holding on to the rail of the balcony to look down in the garden and ground area around the apartment for any signs that he may have jumped off… or been thrown off. "Bo!" *You poor thing,* she thought. *Did you… actually jump off… but you couldn't have… the balcony door handle… it's too… no… no.*

With slumped shoulders, Kaitlin was just about to return to the living room when she noticed a yellow post-it note sticking out from underneath one of the table legs.

As a falling teardrop almost froze between her eyelashes and her left cheek, Kaitlin's shaking hand reached out and quickly grabbed it to read.

"I haven't hurt the dog. This is just insurance to keep the cops out. If you don't want Paul to disappear next, don't tell anyone else about The Group."

Evil had officially let itself into her home.

***

Back inside the living room and with the balcony door shut behind her, Kaitlin slumped on the leather couch and closed her eyes. She allowed tears to fall without wiping away a single one. Could she really trust what Finn's note said? Would he really not harm Bo? Did Finn just grab him somehow with his powers and let him go off into the woods somewhere to fend for itself? Would someone be able to then somehow identify the dog? A million questions were whizzing by inside Kaitlin's head, but she could not answer any one of them.

I have no idea what in the world I'm going to tell Paul, she thought.

Kaitlin was glad her husband still hadn't come home. "Some newspaper…" she muttered out loud, while additional thoughts, as if she could handle any more at that moment, started coming to her mind, like where Paul could be just then.

Could he have been so upset with her that he'd decided to have a drink at the local seaside pub? She never exactly liked the type of scantily-clad women who tended to frequent that place which Paul and his friends went to every now and then.

But, then again, did she have any right to get jealous? Perhaps she deserved it if he got drunk and kissed someone as well.

What the hell am I thinking? Kaitlin stopped herself. *I don't deserve anything but just some peace. I didn't do anything to purposely hurt anyone… my God… my God.*

Just then, the sound of keys opening the door had Kaitlin instinctively reach up to her face to wipe her tears. She took one final peek outside the balcony doors to make sure there had been no trace left or anything that would give Paul a clue as to what had truly happened to Bo.

She'd already crumbled the post-it note and tossed it inside one of her rarely-used handbags. She decided she couldn't dare tell him the truth. *How exactly can I tell Paul that Finn-the-jinn used his powers apparently to speedily just make his way into our balcony, likely enter our living room to grab the dog, and then manage to run off with it somehow? Or perhaps Finn just opened the balcony door and lured Bo into the balcony, so as not to make too much of a sound in the living room that would alert me?*

Kaitlin couldn't bring herself to face her husband just yet. *He'd first look at me as if I were crazy or, worse, lying. He may even suspect me of allowing him into our house and could go to their cabin and try to confront them about the dog and everything else, for sure.* Now that she'd actually witnessed firsthand the lengths that Finn and the Group's evil could actually reach, she'd decided she wouldn't dare ever be so foolishly brave as to confront them for as long as she could avoid it.

"Kaitlin…? Earth to Kaitlin…?" Paul asked impatiently.

"Oh, hey… you're back," Kaitlin turned to face her husband, who'd now inched closer to her near the balcony, still holding a plastic bag with the daily newspaper and a couple of magazines.

"Have you… been crying?" Paul asked.

Kaitlin broke down again as Paul inched closer. "I apparently can't take care of anything, Paulie…" She whimpered. "Bo… ran away… He… I…"

"Wh… what? Where's Bo…? Kaitlin, calm down," Paul was holding on firmly to both of her shoulders now. "What happened? Take a deep breath and tell me what happened."

"I can barely even look after our plants…" Kaitlin started to say. She'd decided that telling him the dog had run away was the best lie she could come up with. "And now our Bo… even our Bo apparently didn't warm up to me enough to remain in the house. I left the door open… I was going to go out for a walk, too, but I walked back to our bedroom to grab something to put my hair up… and… and…"

"Baby, baby, oh no…" Paul hugged her. "How could you just leave the door open like that, Kaitlin?"

"I know… I'm an idiot," Kaitlin whimpered. "Paulie, I'm an idiot…"

Paul let go of his grasp on her and grabbed his own hair instead, pacing speedily back and forth between the kitchen refrigerator and Kaitlin, who had still been unable to move too far away from the scene of the event.

Scene of the crime. Crime is more like it, she thought. *Animal theft certainly is a crime.*

The word echoed in her mind and brought additional chokes down her throat.

Paul stopped pacing and let out a big sigh. "Anyway… hey… look at me… hey…" Paul grabbed Kaitlin softly by the chin and lifter her face up to meet his eyes.

"It's Ok," he muttered. "Babe… he's just a puppy. He hasn't been trained yet. I'm sure he must have chased after a little fly or something in the hallway and gotten lost… Did you check the other floors?"

"I checked everywhere I could," Kaitlin said, feeling a little more relaxed. "I looked around the yard and then back here on all of the floors in the building. You… you're not mad?"

"Animals run away all the time…" Paul reasoned. "I should have been more attentive in training him, too. Oh, the poor thing. But, hey, look. Maybe someone will find him and bring him back to us. We'll put out some posters around the building and our neighborhood. But in the meantime, we've got each other, okay?"

"And that's enough? For you?" Kaitlin looked up at him with sad eyes.

"Yes, my darling," Paul replied, kissing the top of her head affectionately. "It's enough."

Kaitlin couldn't believe her ears. Was this the same man who had been hounding her to start a big family so soon?

"I know for sure now," Paul continued. "Look, I've been thinking. You mean so much to me, more than I ever thought was possible. And a baby? Well, I suppose a baby should happen when the time is right... Like the icing on top of the cake, and that *cake* should be our happiness together. Oh, I don't know what I'm saying... I've just... Really been thinking... Despite the whole forest group ordeal... or maybe *because* of them, even... Maybe I haven't been fair to you... You're still young, and..."

His words were interrupted as Kaitlin grabbed his face and planted a long one on his lips.

***

Snuggling on the leather couch after a haphazardly-prepared, ready-to-eat soup meal Kaitlin had concocted from some powder in their kitchen cabinet, Paul's eyes got glued on the news again.

"Whoa..." he exclaimed, getting up to inch closer to the television set.

"What is it?" Kaitlin asked eagerly, though the feeling of déjà vu almost already had confirmed the answer in her gut, based on her husband's interest in the news.

As Paul turned up the volume, Kaitlin was surprised to discover she could hear the speaker in English this time.

"...Officials are now able to confirm that the typed note discovered in the victim's handbag, discovered over the skeletal remains of 25-year-old Linette Peterson, was indeed *suicidal* in nature..."

"Oh, come on, suicide? Really, lady? Now, this is truly getting even *rarer* for Norway," Paul responded angrily to the female newscaster. "I mean the newspapers here usually never disclose the countless suicides that happen daily... And the note was *typed*? So they can't even check for a handwriting confirmation? Brilliant play by the murderer. Just brilliant! And the police are just so eager to be satisfied with this 'suicide' explanation and close this case... Damn!"

"Oh wow… strange… yeah," was all Kaitlin could mutter in response. She could not even dare think about what she now suspected even more greatly: that Tan was behind all of this, and somehow The Group, Inc. was aiding him cover it up. She could feel somehow that this was the secret that poor Bo was most likely taken for, in order to hide. She couldn't bring herself to believe Finn's explanation fully. *Suicide,* she thought. *Yeah, right. How convenient.*

"Wow… did you hear that?" Paul went on to say, his eyes still glued to the screen. "*Romantic love isn't real. It's destruction…* read the note, apparently. It sounds like she may have killed herself over unrequited love. If this really was suicide, that is. I wonder if it was John…" Paul went on.

Kaitlin now felt more certain than ever. She didn't need to be a police detective to recognize at once that this note was obviously planted by Tan or one of his buddies to make it look like Linette had suffered unrequited love and killed herself. Those words about 'romantic love' were familiar to her: after all, she had heard them almost verbatim.

It all came full circle to her, just then. *Tan, or Lar, if he indeed advises these people, is one smart son of a gun. By making it look like suicide, they now even managed to get Paul to think off the track of the truth.*

"But, no, no, something still just isn't right," Paul continued, shaking his head. "If she killed herself, that still doesn't explain why Tan would have it in for me, and have his cult-mates target *you* for some sort of sick and twisted revenge, though," Paul continued, as if reading her mind.

"Well, they *did* just confirm the note now, didn't they?" Kaitlin reminded him. "Maybe Tan didn't know it was suicide. *Or,* he may have thought she'd killed herself because of his relentless, harsh accusations. Something he may be blaming you for—for solidifying his suspicions or something." She purposely misled her husband. Kaitlin knew she had to play dumb. "Oh I don't know, babe. You can never expect these types of people to think rationally…"

"Hmm," Paul interrupted, taking a loud bite of the red apple that'd been lying solo in the fruit bowl in front of him now on the kitchen table. "I suppose I *can* totally see that macho dude accusing her relentlessly to the point of madness; though I never saw Linette as a depressed girl or anything of that sort. But a suicide still doesn't explain why she was found buried in a coffin in the ground, babe. I mean, a dead body that just died by suicide isn't going to be able to bury itself, for God's sake! So the alternative theory is that someone otherwise innocent saw a dead body and buried it with a coffin, without calling the police? I don't know. It's still beyond suspicious to me. And I don't think I'm the only one... I was wrong about them trying to close the case up. Did you hear that last part? Apparently it's still an ongoing investigation, regardless of the discovery of that eerie note...."

"The world is a crazy place, babe," Kaitlin muttered. "People are indeed full of surprises..."

Chapter 20

The Revelation
(December 11, 2011)

"I had to see her again, Finn," Tan started to say that afternoon over lunch. Finn couldn't believe the words coming out of his most recent housemate's mouth.

"I had to apologize for my anger," Tan continued. "So I spent the following month desperately trying to find a way to get to her. I had come to Norway on a student visa, and had already overstayed my limit after my program ended. The only option left for me was to continue being a student. So I managed that in Trondheim, and soon found work at a Japanese restaurant. I worked so hard and moved up so much that they made me manager, yet I could see this was still nothing to Linette... I remember meeting that boss of hers, her precious John. The guy had some advanced degree from Oxford, and Linette would often quote him on pseudo-intellectual things he'd apparently said..."

"...Right," Finn said as he nodded. "Ladies dig those intellectual conversations, man. Bullshit or not...."

"Yeah, I guess," Tan said with a hint of sadness in his voice. "So I was now enrolled in the Master's program at Trondheim University where Linette had immediately found work as a Student Advisor upon her return from Canada. This way I was both closer to her, where I could keep an eye on any men trying to hit on her, and I could continue dating her, too. Not that she minded. She couldn't ever deny that. Our chemistry was still palpable and electric as ever, and I knew she still couldn't get enough of me physically despite being scared of me: we had become each other's addiction. Nonetheless, romantically, I could still feel her emotions were elsewhere. It seemed to me she still had her mind on that John guy..."

"I get it, man, I get it," Finn attempted to ease his friend's troubles. "Please, stop pacing back and forth. Come, sit next to me here. I'll get you some wine. Red, was it?"

"Red is fine," Tan replied, sitting down with a loud flop on the couch. "She told me she'd come back to Trondheim since she was worried about her lonely mother, but I knew better... I realized her coming here was only a disguise, since her and John had been caught... I knew... I had hacked her computer. Found her mother's address in Trondheim, and showed up one day on her doorstep when I saw that her mother had gone out of the house. How childlike she'd looked: so scared at first. Yet she gradually relaxed and saw how genuinely sorry I was for yelling at her... But in time, like I said, my suspicions were confirmed as I saw she was still corresponding with John... Mostly they were mundane comments about the crazy weather in Norway, the social life she missed back in Canada, etc. But no mention of *me*... No mention of her having a man in her life who did everything for her... Why would she hide me if she didn't plan on reuniting with her former boss? I knew then that Paul guy was right...."

"Paul?" Finn asked.

"Yeah. Paul Maverick was the guy's name," Tan continued. "The one responsible for my accusations that apparently drove her to the point of running away from me. I'll show you the bastard's photograph. He's here in Norway now, too, apparently. I found him online. Anyway... Then one day I saw that article that changed my life, about Lar's lecture. And the rest is history, as you know. It was meant to be... I was meant to meet you, guys. Thank you, by the way, for listening to my story, without judgments, I mean..."

"Hey, we have no judgements here," Finn said, offering him the glass of wine. "Remember? I'm always here... I'm listening."

"So, last year, on this exact day, actually, I did it," Tan continued, taking a large gulp of his Merlot. "Thank you," he added, tilting the glass toward Finn in appreciation.

"You did... *what* exactly?" Finn asked.

Killed Linette and then buried her, of course, Tan thought. *The fake suicide note... planted in the latest Burberry bag I was now able to afford first-hand...It's all behind me… It's all in the past…It's a shame, though… She would have liked this new, richer me. It's all too bad…*

"…Tan?" Finn interrupted his thoughts.

"Oh, I'm sorry," Tan said. "Well, I just stormed right into her house and just said the worst things you can imagine, you know… About how she was a whore and… and… how she couldn't keep her legs closed when faced with money, and how she was a really bad liar on top of it all… and… I then stormed out and left her in tears. I never saw her again…"

As tears fell from Tan's face and boyish whimpers escaped his mouth, Finn actually found himself feeling sorry for the guy, despite trying his best to hide the shock over the guy's thoughts. He'd temporarily decided to ignore the fact that this guy was apparently his ex's killer.

"You, crazy human. Have another sip… It's Ok… It's Ok. You couldn't have known…" Finn told Tan. *You couldn't have known we can read minds when we really focus on someone*, he thought. *You couldn't have known I sure as hell intend to call Lar tonight and confront him about accepting a damn murderer in the Cabin.* "We all lose our temper sometimes… But you said it's been a year since you saw her last, man. Where's all of this coming from *now*?"

"You don't understand, Finn," Tan said, taking a deep breath and wiping his tears off with the sleeves of his shirt. "I was feeling nostalgic this morning… because, like you said, it had indeed been a while. *But it's been exactly* one year, to this day, actually, since I last saw her. So, this morning I finally read her diary…"

"Her *what*?" Finn asked with surprise, almost spilling the wine inside his mouth he hadn't yet swallowed. "Dude, you go around carrying the diary of your dead ex-girlfriend? When did you even take it?"

"Yeah, I kept it and some of our old photo albums together, too," Tan explained. "Well, like I said, I was suspicious of her and that John guy," Tan continued, intertwining his fingers and moving them nervously. "Before the big fight, when she'd been in the bathroom, I was sort of trying to quietly look around her room and drawers for some more evidence of the guy, I suppose. I found her diary. I later just threw it in a box of my stuff but never read it. I guess I was angry at her for disappearing without a trace. With all that happened, I just forgot all about it…"

223

"Right…" Finn said, nodding. *No, I'm sure you were angry at yourself for messing everything up, dude.*

"But, hey, when I woke up and realized the date this morning, I guess I began to feel nostalgic that it'd been a year exactly today," Tan went on. "So I began looking through her writings. And, well, as luck would have it, the wind blew open to those two damn pages in particular… and I had to look. What I saw, nearly killed me. I had to look, Finn," Tan repeated as he broke down in tears.

"Shh, it's all in the past now," Finn said, placing Tan's glass back on the wooden table in front of them. "Remember what Lar always says, Tan: everything happens for a reason. Now, calmly, tell me. Tell me what the diary said…"

"Here…" Tan said with a heavy sigh, taking out the folded sheets from his pocket. "I ripped out those pages. *You* read it…"

"Are you sure?" Finn asked with a raised eyebrow.

Tan's nod allowed Finn to start reading the letter, first out-loud, and then gradually to himself, as he saw that Tan had gotten up and continued pacing around the cabin living room in tears.

"My Tan is crazy…" Finn began to read.

"…but I guess I love him anyway. He's the reason I came back to Trondheim, yet he's followed me here and I'm still with him. I guess that means I must be crazy as well? Or maybe it just means that we have this passionate love, and that we're meant to be? Oh, who knows. All I know is I feel terrible he still suspects John Walker and I of having an affair… I've been too embarrassed to tell him the truth, that John's my father and has been sending my poor mother monthly checks to help her out, or we would have been out on the streets already! Her life's been practically ruined because of my father. Yet he is my father and I guess it would be equally immoral of me to write off half of my own DNA completely as well.

Yeah, he left my mom for his now wife … But, still… I'm glad John finally felt the guilt, and came to his senses. It's been so nice to talk to him like the child he's never been able to have again, you know… and in turn be able to have a father figure finally in my life… He's actually really been a blessing. I mean, I suppose God punished him enough for how he left mother and me: his rich wife has apparently been unable to carry out a healthy child to full term. But if I tell Tan about the truth of my father, of what he'd done to me and my mother… and… oh I don't know. I don't want him to feel sorry for me. And I don't want him to misunderstand John's help.

Besides, what if Tan reacts too emotionally to the secret? If word gets out that I'm John's daughter out of wedlock from his former lover, oh the horror that would cause! Surely his wife would divorce him and he'd lose his job. Secretly I always thought she was too good for him anyway. But, even then I'm sure he'd be especially nice to me and I would forgive him. I guess that's my weakness: probably why I always forgive Tan, too.

Argh! Diary! I hope I did the right thing! I mean, being together in the same environment with John in Canada was already drawing too much attention and Tan's questioning only raised the bar. I knew it was only a matter of time our blood-bond would be discovered, and if he lost his power and prestige because of his decision to finally make amends with us… I just couldn't bear it…"

"Wow," was all that Finn could mutter. He couldn't bring himself to look at Tan in the eyes.

"Finn, she was innocent!" Tan cried. "My Linette was innocent! She'd lied to me, yes, but not to cover up any sort of affair. She was the guy's daughter, not his lover! My baby was innocent. And that Paul, the asshole at her office who encouraged my suspicions… he is to blame!"

"He said, 'Calm down, there are always other fish in the sea! Women are like this: they may care for you all good and well but it ends the minute someone they could show-off more comes along…' Finn, I can still hear his words in my head."

"That Paul Maverick dude said that?" Finn had begun to feel angry too. *It doesn't excuse the girl's murder, but still, this Paul guy should have minded his own damn business,* he thought. "Let me see that photograph you mentioned. Maybe we can find the bastard…"

"Yeah, I got his address and numbers, too," Tan continued, sounding stronger with Finn's moral support as he clicked on a website on his smart phone. "Here he is… Works at Statoil… Right here, in Stavanger…"

He then proceeded to show Finn the picture which wouldn't be leaving Finn's mind throughout the entire year before gradually tracking down and 'running into' Kaitlin. "The Board of Trustees congratulates Computer Specialist Paul Maverick and his wife, Kaitlin Maverick, on their recent nuptials." Finn read without even as much as a glance at Paul. His eyes glued to the screen at exactly the precise spot where Kaitlin's smile was. *Her eyes. Her wavy auburn hair. Her bridal gown hugging her womanly curves. Her legs. Her…*

"Finn?" Tan interrupted his thoughts with a wave of his hands.

Maybe I'll hold off on complaining about Tan to Lar for a little longer, Finn thought just then. *This could actually become rather interesting.* "Does Lar know about your suspicions? The diary?" Finn asked, without a need to ask about whether or not Lar knew that Tan had been his ex's actual murderer. Lar, a human, was always looking for spiritually-lost but attractive new potential members to recruit, just like Tan. Still, Finn knew that he was a kind man who just wanted all of his Group members to be happy and love and support one another. *If he had been a jinn and read Tan's thoughts of his murderous truth, or even if Tan had straight-out confessed it to him, Lar would have never allowed a killer in our midst, would he?* Finn could never be too sure of humans.

"No, umm, no not the diary, but my guilty feelings over what I believe may have led to her suicide, yeah… yes," Tan stammered. "That much he knows, yes, of course."

He's lying, Finn thought. But by that point his intrigue in Paul Maverick's wife had become too strong for him to ignore or risk losing the opportunity to grow closer to her. Lar didn't exactly condone random meetings of strange young men or women to join the group, Finn knew. He believed in meaning and purpose. *I'll play along in helping Tan get his supposed revenge on Paul,* Finn thought. *I'll do whatever I have to do in order to have an excuse to study and later approach this exquisite woman. Let's see how she is in person.*

"You know… I think God is speaking to me, Tan," Finn started to speak in a monotone voice, as if in a trance. "I'll talk to Lar about using Paul or his wife in the picture as new recruits, but either way, you *will* get your revenge. Paul will taste what it's like to lose his loved one, too… One way or the other."

"Finn…" Tan had stopped crying already. "Thank you… but I hope you're not suggesting… *murder.* Believe me, you don't want to go that route… I mean, the poor woman has nothing to do with this, you know…"

"I'm not going to *kill* her, Tan," Finn cut in, rolling his eyes. *I'm not a murderer, and a pathetic human, like you.* "That would be a shame… and a waste. No, don't you worry. There are better ways to get revenge on a man. Keep your mind at ease. You'll see. All in due time."

Chapter 21

"Are you ready to do this, babe?" Kaitlin asked, taking a sip of her warm cappuccino. "Mmm, is it just me or does the coffee taste even better in this city?"

"I think I am, babe, "Paul nodded. "And yeah, it's delicious, indeed. But come on, let's go."

Ever since learning the details of the cemetery for Linette's remains from an online newspaper article, Kaitlin had decided she had to help Paul get some sort of closure.

"You need this." She'd told her husband back home, a week prior to their Trondheim weekend getaway, trying to convince him to visit Linette's grave. "And maybe, maybe *we* need this."

"I suppose we could also just view it as a weekend trip out there," Paul had nodded in acceptance. "I mean, we never visited Trondheim together before." He could always be counted on with the logical reasonings behind decision-making, in contrast with Kaitlin's more romantic and symbolic ones.

"Look, there's a police car," Kaitlin pointed out, slightly tilting her head in the direction where she'd spotted the vehicle. She didn't exactly want to overtly attract attention toward them.

"It's still fresh news and the case is still ongoing, as you know, babe," Paul reasoned, taking Kaitlin's hand in his as they stopped in front of the grave they finally located. "They probably want to see who is visiting her... perhaps in case they see any potential suspects who look like they're visiting with a guilty conscience. Heck, maybe even..." Paul paused.

"What?" Kaitlin asked with curiosity.

"Well, maybe they have a remote guilty-conscience radar and they can come here and arrest me," Paul declared solemnly. "What would you do if I got arrested, Kaitlin?"

"Paulie?" Kaitlin let out an uncomfortable laugh as she tugged on his arm. "Don't be ridiculous and make me laugh disrespectfully at a cemetery, for goodness sake," she whispered. "Why would you get arrested, you nutty nut?"

Paul could not answer. He was gazing intensely now at the tombstone with the freshly-carved details of Linette's birthday: the date of death only displaying the year 2010.

"It's natural for a former colleague and friend to visit a late acquaintance," Kaitlin continued.

"You're right," Paul reluctantly agreed.

"I'm sorry, Linette, for whatever happened to you," Kaitlin said as she placed a bouquet of flowers in a myriad of colors, apologizing to this woman whom she'd never met, yet who's had such a tremendous influence, albeit indirectly so, on her own life. *I'm sorry for not yet being brave enough to release the identity of your killer. But I promise one day I will. Somehow, enough evidence will be discovered. The guilty will not be able to simply just roam free. Whatever I can do, I will... For you... for Bo... I will.*

She looked at Paul, and smiled.

He smiled back and nodded to her. She'd decided that in the new year she was no longer going to allow any awkward silences to drive a wedge between them. Where else would she be able to turn to? Who else could ever understand? Consciously, she would always fight to make herself feel like they were on the same boat.

Comrades-in-arms, she thought.

Perhaps they had both unknowingly waved their white flags, and surrendered together to the passage of time and life as it simply flowed.

Chapter 22

"Meredith," Tan started to say as calmly as he could muster, despite his increasingly rapid heartbeat. "Are you *finally* going to tell me why we've come to the middle of the woods alone?"

"Just keep going toward those rocks over there," Meredith insisted, repositioning the large backpack on her shoulders to ease the heavy pain on her shoulders.

"I mean, come on," Tan whispered now, stopping in his tracks and leaning closer to her ear. "If this is some sort of new fantasy, you should tell me and maybe I could cook up some creative twists as well before we start, baby." *I hope that damn dog Finn let out here doesn't suddenly appear before us as we're going at it, though,* he thought with a smirk.

"Tan…" Meredith insisted in a stern voice. "The rocks, come on… we're almost there. You need to sit down…"

Damn, I kind of like this new assertive side of Meredith, Tan thought. *I don't know if it's some new year resolution she's made, or that abortion changed something in her, but, I like it. Strangely, she reminds me now even more of… No more thoughts of Linette. Ever. The past two months have been close. Too close.*

"Alright, baby, I'm sitting, I'm sitting, lay it on me," Tan said suggestively. "As a matter of fact, why don't you lay *yourself* on me right here…"

"Is that how you did it?" Meredith asked, still in a serious tone of voice, much to Tan's surprise.

"Did… what?" He asked.

"Did you lure Linette to her death in the middle of the woods?" Meredith asked. She took off the backpack and placed it in front of her feet. "Or did you kill her elsewhere and bury the body later? I'm not exactly sure, but, then again, I guess the details don't even really matter…"

Oh, shit. "Baby, Mer, what in the *world* are you talking about?" Tan asked nervously, standing back up. "You *know* she committed suicide… Even the police discovered…"

"Cut the crap, Tan," Meredith bellowed, giving the backpack a kick. "This is your most crucial stuff: underwear, socks, necessities, toiletries, and, of course, your passport and some cash. Get out of Norway, Tan. Leave, and I promise I won't say anything to Lar or the *Politi*."

"Mer…" Tan said softly, placing his hands on her shoulders. "Baby, I don't know what that crazy Kaitlin woman told you… or what you think you… I don't know… *sensed*, with those powers you mentioned. But, it's all wrong. I only *thought* my suspicions may have led to her death, yes, but indirectly so, you know, as in pushing her to commit suicide. Not… come on, now!"

"You know, it's crazy," Meredith said sternly, removing Tan's hands from her shoulders softly. "I've been doing a lot of thinking lately. And, yes, you guessed it: especially after the abortion. I mean, I'd always thought that Finn, Bjorn and I had some sort of leverage over you and Anja. With us being jinns and all. As if we were somehow the cleverer ones… And you guys were duped somehow into The Group. I mean, as much as Lar is human, we all know he's living his lavish lifestyle. And we know how Anja is just in it for the fun and the riches as well. And, as for you, you just felt a sense of belonging, I suppose. Yes. We know. But…"

"Mer…" Tan interrupted with pleading eyes.

"But, silly me…" Meredith went on persistently. "Naively, I suppose some part of me also wanted to believe that you had truly fallen in love with me. And that this was why you've remained with us. I then realized over time, of course, that you were more turned on by getting your 'revenge' somehow on Paul through his wife than you were by me. But it took reading the diary you stole from her, and seeing her photos on television and her resemblance to me, and just putting two and two together to realize what an absolute *fool* I had been. To finally really focus on your thoughts and on the truth, rather than consciously ignoring every negative sense I had about you…"

"Baby…" Tan pleaded. "You're not a fool. Please, don't do this. This is my second chance at love. We can make it through this. The case is closed as far as the world is concerned. I can concentrate better on our job and life together. We can even reconsider a child, if you just…"

"Forgive you?" Meredith asked, meeting his eyes with tears in her own. "Can you? Can *you* ever forgive *yourself* for what you did to Linette? For what you had me do to our unborn *baby*?"

"Mer…" Tan whispered, closing his eyes as he placed his palm on Meredith's stomach. "Another chance. I'm begging you. Even Finn doesn't know…"

"Oh, Finn knows, you idiot!" Meredith exclaimed. "He knows I'm here talking to you, too. So if you try anything with me, you're over with either way. He knows. And he's kept quiet about you for this long only since he foolishly fell in love with Kaitlin. As did I, being foolishly in love with *you*. But, I can't anymore. So, go! Just leave and never hurt anyone else, please! It's the only way we decided we won't go to the cops or to Lar with the truth…"

"Lar will be so mad if I just run away," Tan said, staring at the ground. "He will be so disappointed in me if I leave, just like that. And my parents, how I can ever face them again…"

That's what you're mainly concerned with, Meredith thought with melancholy. *Not with losing me. Liar. 'Let's give our relationship and a new baby another chance.' You're still lying through your teeth!* "It's the least you deserve for the evil you've done," Meredith continued with a serious tone, wiping away her tears. "You have a flight leaving from Sola Airport this evening. We will know if you don't get on this plane, so don't try anything funny. The documents are in the front pocket."

"Baby, Please…" Tan pleaded, staring into her fierce eyes. They were no longer the eyes of a victim. They were no longer even the eyes that reminded him of Linette. Right when he felt himself being able to truly admire this strong woman now standing before him to confront him, he realized *her* love for *him* had already started to fade. How ironic life was.

"Goodbye, Tan," Meredith said, trembling as she fought the habitual instinct to give him a final soft kiss on his lips. "There is no other choice, no matter what my heart feels. My mind is *my* only weapon. My determination to set things right wins. Love can't. This is our reality. There cannot be any other alternative. Not when the tragic truths are too strong."

Chapter 23

Flipping through the applications on her phone, Kaitlin instinctively felt a pull toward the 'Calendar' section. She looked at the date. February 23rd. She'd been so busy with their moving away to their new apartment in Sandnes—slightly closer to Paul's office but worlds farther, or at least that's how she was hoping to feel, from the wooden area close to the city center. They'd decided to give the 'two-bedroom apartment going at the rate of a one-bedroom' place a try. In the midst of all of the packing and moving, Kaitlin realized she hadn't previously noticed what should have arrived the week prior.

A thought rose instantly in her mind. She dismissed it just as quickly, though slower than she would have just a couple of months ago. She again went back to that thought: the now exciting possibility that she actually relished in considering. A once-feared novelty in her life was one which she realized she would actually welcome now.

She ran quickly toward her dresser and put on her dark green cable-knit sweater. The local *Rimi* market was close enough. The breeze coming from the open window was surprisingly warm for the season, so she decided she didn't need anything bulkier. Putting on her pink and white Nike's, she grabbed her purse from on top of the shoe drawer right next to the door and ran out —coming back to the door to double-check that she'd locked it. Yes. She had. *Good*, she thought. *I haven't gone that crazy yet.*

As she made her way down the stairs and past the small artificial pond where two kids walked dogs bigger than themselves, Kaitlin entered the market and headed straight toward the back. Sibel had told her about the time when she'd first discovered she was pregnant with her first child. "I was only a couple of days later than usual. I mean, I'd had much later period arrivals as a virginal girl before my husband, but still—it felt different. I just *knew*, Kaitlin!"

Kaitlin realized that this was exactly what she was feeling in her heart. She paid for the tests. She'd grabbed two boxes just to be on the safe side. She ran home just as quickly as she had come to the market, heading straight to the bathroom.

Looking at her disheveled bun and smeared blue eyeliner in the mirror, she took a deep breath and smiled at how chubby her cheeks had gotten in doing so—like a blowfish. She had to admit she was kind of loving this new side of herself. Despite the test results, she told herself, she would aim to keep up this level of excitement for such things. Whether it was the possibility of a child, a new sweater, guests coming over for a special occasion or even just a weekly random friendly dinner: she would consciously make the effort to maximize whatever source of excitement she would be faced with.

She had to give it to Finn. *At least the bastard has been keeping his end of the deal in his note,* she thought. He had not called her, and she had not seen or felt him watching her ever since Bo was dog-napped.

Well, unless, that one night… Kaitlin forced the thought off her mind as soon as it popped in her head.

She'd decided to make the conscious effort to allow herself to be 'okay' for feeling nervous, and then just let it pass, focusing on her mundane but relatively safer daily chores, instead.

The good, she thought.

The routine and expected parts of life that everyone talked about. The occasional thought that she *was missing out* somehow on something 'bigger' would certainly come to her mind. She didn't have to fool herself that much. She was raised with wild expectations of success, after all, and she couldn't solely blame her mother for that, as she had developed them for herself ever since she began achieving academic success. Yet, she knew she had to try. After all, most recently, with The Group, she'd seen firsthand the repercussions of her fantasies, hadn't she?

She and Paul hadn't been using protection over the past month and as far as she was concerned that was all the proof she needed that she was about to get good news for the two of them.

The thought of *that* particularly passionate night (which Kaitlin lived through when Paul returned home from a rare night out at a club for Tim's birthday) still made Kaitlin blush.

She'd already fallen asleep after midnight, but she remembered how surprised she'd felt when he woke her up in the dark, with an uncharacteristically strong hard-on.

"Babe ... welcome back," she'd cooed with prodigious pleasure. What's gotten into you...? Mmm... And what time is it? I can barely keep my eyes open..."

"I just need your legs open..." he had whispered to her neck, thrusting deeper and harder.

He may have had a particularly sweaty workout session after work at the gym or, heck, he could have even become turned on by some young Norwegian hottie dancing seductively, she'd thought jealously right before falling back asleep, after he'd rolled over to the other side of the bed.

She had missed the playful and mischievously sexual side of her husband so much since their dating days, that she'd decided she didn't really care at that point.

But what happened later was something she swore she'd never mention to anyone: not even Sibel or Sandy.

What the... she recalled thinking at the time: as she woke up to the sound of... keys opening the door! Kaitlin had turned her head to see that their bed was empty. And then she heard Paul creep in slowly into their bedroom.

"Shh, go back to sleep, baby," Paul had whispered, taking off his clothes to put on his pajamas. "I'm sorry the party ran a little later than usual. Tim threw up two times and Jeanette made me drive him home. She still didn't get her driver's license. Those two are nuts..."

"You're... just coming in, *now*...?" Kaitlin had asked, sitting straight up in the bed with undisguised alarm. "Paul... what's going on?"

"Kaitlin... I just told you... I'm sorry..." Paul said and gave her a kiss. "You're right, I should have messaged you, but I had no chance, with Tim..."

Kaitlin drowned out the remainder of his explanation.

Oh my God, she thought tearfully.

"I... I think I just had a bad dream. I'm sorry, Paulie... I'm so sorry. It's Ok... Goodnight".

Oh, my God.

Chapter 24

Lar Iktar hated waiting, yet here he was: waiting for the only person he'd decided would be worth waiting for.

He hadn't seen him in a while, and was surprised that the thought of his arrival soon in his office suite excited him like a teenager.

Smiling, he took a big puff of the Cuban cigar in his hand, glancing out of the window at his view of downtown Oslo. *I hope this city will be a new start for both of us,* he thought.

A knock on the door had him straighten up in his swivel chair and run his fingers through his thick raven mane. "Come in."

"Master, you have a visitor," Nora said from the door, entering the office in all her statuesque and curvy glory—her seductiveness accentuated by her tight skirt and blouse, as well as a baby face ripened by full makeup. *It's lucky for these gals I am the way I am,* Lar thought with a smirk. *I'm able to give them an amazing life opportunity without any of the advances they'd surely face from bosses elsewhere.*

"He says his name is…" Nora continued, before Lar interrupted.

"It's Ok, dear… I've been waiting for him… tell him to come in."

"Yes, Master," Nora smiled, turning around to usher the visitor to come inside.

"Oh, Master…." Tan rushed in, walking hurriedly to Lar and taking his hand to give it a kiss.

"Welcome back, lad," Lar said, patting Tan's cheek. "Please, sit down… Nora, would you bring us two cappuccinos, please?"

"Yes, Master," Nora replied, closing the door behind her.

"You still like cappuccinos, right lad?" Lar asked Tan.

"Your memory always serves you correct, Master," Tan responded. "Thank you so much for this chance, you're…"

"How could I ever forget, lad?" Lar interrupted. "I told you I saw something extra special in you. We only met in person twice or so, but I saw something in you… that I hadn't seen or felt in a very long time…" *His dark eyes are just as mesmerizing as I remember them,* he thought. *He smiles nervously like a little boy caught raiding his mother's closet… Just like…*

"I know, Master," Tan went on. "I'm the luckiest person alive on this planet, to be honored by your presence and forgiveness and understanding and support and opportunity again now to be here…"

"Whoa… you're rambling… take it easy," Lar chuckled, leaning closer toward Tan in his chair. "I'm not doing you a favor. You *deserve* this… Stavanger wasn't as good to you, apparently, as I'd hoped, lad. But, in all fairness… I *did* warn you. *Don't* allow any of those ladies to fall in love with you…"

"I know, Master," Tan nodded sheepishly. "Meredith… she reminded me too much of, *her*… I guess it felt nice for a while… to pretend like all was Okay again. I mean, I got her to get rid of the baby, just like you said, but she was still so attached… *too* attached…"

"The thin line between love and hate is real, lad," Lar continued. "Jinn or human, doesn't matter. All creatures will try to get some sort of revenge when they feel they have been scorned. After all of the heartbreak and emotions dwindle down, anyway. It was only a matter of time before Meredith woke up from her enamored state and came to terms with who you were…"

"A murderer…" Tan whispered with a melancholy voice.

"No, lad," Lar stated firmly, reaching out with a firm grip on Tan's shoulders. "I told you: I'm not to hear that word again. You are *not* a murderer. You *had* to do what you did. You're a missionary, for a bigger purpose… Meredith simply discovered who you are: a man who did not love her back like she wanted to believe, that's all. You're meant for bigger and better things… You always were…"

"Thank you for the reminder, Master," Tan smiled now. "She still doesn't know that you know, right?"

"And she never will! No one will!" Lar exclaimed angrily.

"I'm sorry, Master," Tan stammered. "Of course not…"

"They would never understand!"

"I know, Master," Tan said reassuringly. "I didn't mean anything by it. I'm just happy… so happy…"

"Good…" Lar went on, more relaxed. "And you will be even happier, you'll see… How was your trip?"

"Well, it was strange to be forced to fly back to Turkey, Master," Tan said. "Only to catch a subsequent flight back to Oslo, to see you… If it hadn't been for your encouragement when I called you from the airport… I… I don't know what I would have done…"

"I couldn't let you face your family," Lar said softly. "I encouraged your transformation… into the higher being you now are, in control of your destiny. They would never understand… I couldn't do that to you."

"You're very merciful and understanding, Master," Tan replied gratefully. "I've made such a mess of things in Stavanger. I wonder if I can be any better here in Oslo?"

We'll both be better closer to each other, Lar thought. *I'm certain of it.*

His mind reflected on his 19-year-old self. In another part of the world. Born into a family and culture that could never understand unconventional love. A society that could never accept someone like him, where he'd have to lead a repressed, secret life, if he wanted to even survive. How he'd risked everything by coming to Norway after completing his education, and climbed up the professional ladder on his own, scratching the walls with his own nails. How he later swore he'd try his best to create an environment for others like him: unaccepted, lost, vulnerable to society's expectations and entrapments into only particular categorizations of 'normal', to live and work together and feel free to be their true selves. Regardless of who, or how many, they chose to embrace.

"Master…?" Tan asked, halting Lar's thoughts. "Is everything alright?"

"Sorry, lad, yes, everything's alright," Lar said with a smile. *I wonder how Abdul is doing back home. It's a pity he must have changed his name, for I could never locate him online, nor could I ever return back there. I wonder if he's been forced to marry some poor woman to appease his family, reproducing children for others rather than out of his own will. I wonder if he's ever been caught and reprimanded, or, worse. I wonder if he's alive, and if he thinks of me, too.* "I believe Oslo will be much better for you, as long as you no longer break the rules…"

"No more romantic love encouraged, I promise, Master," Tan stated firmly. "Although Nora *did* give me the look coming in here... I'm just joking!" He smiled.

"Don't even joke, lad," Lar exclaimed. *First that Linette girl. Don't make me encourage something similar to be done to Nora in order to ultimately save you for myself... when you finally realize we're meant to be together.* "Nora is merely a recruiter, just like you. You will be like family here in Oslo... but don't ever forget who your real family is here..."

He'd initially attempted to keep his distance. Placing Tan in another town. Testing to see whether his own emotions (which he'd always discouraged among the others) were real. But here Tan was. Fate had caused him to be ostracized by his housemates in Stavanger. It was all obviously meant to be so that he could be closer to him. Lar would never allow the others to find him here. He'd do his best to protect their destiny together.

"You are, Master," Tan said, nodding. "I know. Believe me. You are all I have now. You have nothing to worry about."

***

Sipping from his glass of wine at the local seaside outdoor café, Finn watched with disgust as Paul opened the door for Kaitlin to enter the passenger side of their car. *You fool,* he thought with a smirk.

He'd been doing his best to conceal himself from Kaitlin, as he watched them whenever possible. If she could hold her end of the deal and not go to the cops, he'd decided that he would, too. *I can keep my promises too, for love. I can also love her from afar—if that's what's necessary for the time being,* he thought.

It was painful watching them together. More painful than he cared to admit. He'd often tell Bjorn he was heading town to check out the new pretty exchange student in town and doing his research on her, but the truth was he could care less about their new target.

Kaitlin seemed to have grown even more beautiful than he remembered, along with her growing belly. It'd been so hard for him to resist the urge to face her again, and rub her stomach himself.

Lar advocates against all of this, but he isn't exactly one to preach, Finn thought. He'd seen him and Tan walking together when he visited Oslo recently, choosing to remain invisible to them, as well as quiet. *What good would it do to confront him about how he could still allow a murderer amongst another branch of The Group? Could it really be that he doesn't know? And Tan has him fooled? Or is it really Lar who has us all fooled?*

Either way, he knew he didn't have any other choice but to suck it in and move on with his work. All the while secretly pursuing his love from afar too, of course. *If I go to the police now, surely they'd get me in trouble of some sort for being an accomplice to a cover-up,* he thought with a sigh. *Where else am I going to turn to exactly if not The Group. My family? They don't give a shit about me.*

I wish she did, he thought. *I wish she'd been brave.* But he couldn't stay angry at Kaitlin for too long. She couldn't risk to lose everything, any more than he could. He really didn't want to believe that she was truly as naïve as she'd been playing off the whole thing. Her smarts was one of his favorite attributes about her. He liked to believe that their connection would always somehow be able to carry on… no matter what.

And it looks like it always will, he thought with a smile, petting Bo sitting beside him on the ground, chewing on his treat. *In more ways than one.*

Epilogue

Paul Maverick was in heaven.

"Who's my angel? Who's my angel?" He cooed, throwing baby Malin up in the air. She laughed with joy.

Their daughter had just turned five months old, and they'd spent the evening sharing a slice of cake from the local bakery, blowing out a candle.

Kaitlin can make a big deal of whatever she wants from now on, he'd decided. *If celebrating even our daughter's monthly milestones is to be one of them, so be it.*

"Whoa… my little birdie… is that a little tooth coming out already?" Paul asked his new favorite person in the whole world, now hanging on to his arms for dear life with a smile, with most of the full head of hair she'd been born with last autumn now shedding. He was secretly hoping she'd inherited her mother's looks, and that a full mane of auburn curls would now replace the minor bald spots on her hair.

Lowering her close to his face to kiss her on the cheek as she cooed, Paul noticed that Malin had begun to stare off into the distance. No. Scratch that, more like *fixated* on a certain spot behind him. As she did so, Paul noticed she was both smiling and giggling. He turned around to see what could be catching her attention so deeply, yet couldn't see a thing but the white wall.

Had it been some fly or bug?

For some reason he thought back to an article he'd read about animals who could see things their owners sometimes couldn't. Paul giggled.

Can little babies see things that aren't close-up yet? He wondered. *Oh, well.* He thought best not to mention this to Kaitlin. For all he knew, she actually would believe Malin was seeing ghosts or something. She'd even possibly try to convince him to move from their amazing new apartment —their amazing new beginning.

He looked at Malin once again. She was still staring at the blank wall and giggling. One more time, smiling now, he thought, *Oh well.*

241

CPSIA information can be obtained
at www.ICGtesting.com
Printed in the USA
LVHW091525190620
658098LV00009B/169/J